EDGE OF TRUTH

BY KIMBERLY ROSE JOHNSON

Edge of Truth
Published by Sweet Rose Press
U.S.A.

All Scripture quotations, unless otherwise indicated, are taken from the Holy Bible, New International Version®, NIV®. Copyright ©1973, 1978, 1984, 2011 by Biblica, Inc.™ Used by permission of Zondervan. All rights reserved worldwide. www.zondervan.com The "NIV" and "New International Version" are trademarks registered in the United States Patent and Trademark Office by Biblica, Inc.™

© 2019 Kimberly R. Johnson
ISBN 978-0-9984315-6-7
Cover Design: Jackie Castle
Editor: Fay Lamb

Printed in the United States of America

Acknowledgements

No book makes it publication without a lot of help. This book in particular has been years in the making with so many people helping me along the way I might have forgotten a couple. I'm leaving out last names on purpose since a couple of these people are or were in law enforcement. Special thanks to Tim, Mike, Dan, Teresa, Sherri, Miralee, Edward, Fay, Becky S., Becky D., and anyone else who helped me along the way. I could not have completed this book without each and every one of you. Thank you.

Dedication

To Miralee Ferrell. Thank you for always encouraging me, believing in me, and pushing me to be better. You played a big role in helping to not only make this book what it is but who I am as a writer. Thank you.

Let those who love the Lord hate evil, for He guards the lives of His faithful ones and delivers them from the hand of the wicked.

Psalms 97:10 NIV

1

The hair on Kara Nelson's neck prickled as she sat behind the wheel of her car parked near the Miami Beach Marina. Something wasn't right. If she'd been made…She flung the door open and ran.

A boom sounded, and heat stung her back. Running full speed, Kara tripped and flew through the air, hitting the pavement hard. Her hands smacked the ground first, and she flipped, her legs whipping over her head. She lay face up in the parking lot. Searing pain tore through her wrists, arms, shoulders, and neck.

A second explosion sent a ball of fire into the mid-morning air. Kara covered her head as debris smacked the ground around her. She lifted her head with effort, first looking at her dismantled undercover car then back at the marina. Drug lord, Luis Alvarado's yacht had moved out to sea and with it, her chances of wrapping up a year-long investigation. Where had the second blast come from? She struggled to sit up. Then the world went black.

Special Agent, Jeff Clark sprinted from his position on the dock to Kara as she lay still on the hot pavement. He knelt and felt for her pulse—faint, but steady. Thank God. Several sirens approached the popular marina. He grabbed his cell. "Gary, Jeff here. Kara's cover is blown. Someone just blew up her car. She's unconscious, but alive."

His boss, and head of the Miami DEA, let out a series of expletives. "Stay with her."

"Will do."

Jeff pocketed his phone and grasped Kara's hand. "Kara, wake up." Shaking her risked further injury. "Come on, Kara." He splashed a little water onto her face from the bottle attached to his belt. Her blue eyes fluttered open.

"Welcome back." He brushed blond hair from her face. "You had me worried for a minute."

"What happened?" Kara blinked up at him.

"Car bomb. You are one lucky lady. Feel up to talking?" He spoke softly and tried to ignore several citizens who looked on with sick fascination.

She nodded almost imperceptibly as pain washed over her face. "There was a woman aboard Alvarado's yacht. About five-foot-ten, one hundred thirty pounds, brunette. Only saw her from a distance as she entered the cabin, but she knew about tonight's bust."

It was worse than he'd expected. This sounded like an inside job. Who'd betrayed them?

The whine of sirens grew louder. A fire engine rolled to a stop. Firefighters quickly got the car blaze under control.

An ambulance parked nearby. Two paramedics, one male and one female, got out and grabbed their gear. The staccato of their shoes hit the pavement in regular beats. Couldn't they move any faster? He glanced over his shoulder—about time.

"Please move aside sir," the female medic said.

Tires squealed as a black sedan braked hard. Jeff glanced to his right where his boss stepped out of the car a few hundred feet away from where Kara lay. Jeff squeezed her hand once more. "I'll just be over there. Holler if you need me." He stepped back and walked over to Gary Rhine.

"How is she?" Gary peered toward the paramedics.

Jeff shook his head. "I don't know. She has cuts and bruises and was unconscious for a short time. There's more." He explained his theory about a traitor among them.

Gary's face darkened. "Not much to go on, and that's assuming the woman wasn't wearing a disguise." He raked his hand through his closely cropped hair. "Ride to the hospital with Kara, and don't let her out of your sight. Luis Alvarado has people everywhere, and I don't want them to get to her."

"Got it." Jeff turned back to Kara and the medics. His Glock sat snug against his side. The medics lifted Kara onto the gurney, raised it, then wheeled her to the ambulance. He flashed his badge. "I'm riding along."

"Fine, just stay out of my way." The female medic

pushed the gurney into the vehicle then stepped in.

Jeff peeked into the back of the ambulance—not much room, but he wouldn't risk leaving Kara alone with anyone. Not even a medic. He stepped in and sat, folding his six-foot-five frame until his legs scrunched up to his chest in the tight quarters.

Kara stared up at him, her face pale. He smoothed the hair draped along the sides of her cheeks away from her face. Awareness jolted him. He dismissed the sensation and let his eyes rest on her tanned skin that was already beginning to bruise. They weren't well acquainted—something he'd like to change. He'd admired her from a distance this past year. Anyone who could go under deep cover like she'd done had his respect. Due to the sensitivity of the operation, Jeff, along with several other agents, had been assigned to keep an eye on her from afar. This was the first time in nearly twelve months anything had gone wrong.

Thanks to Kara, they'd made several arrests and closed down more than a few drug cells. She took a deep breath and moaned. He looked to the medic. "Is she going to be okay?"

"Not my job to say."

He frowned at the woman—liking her less with each passing streetlight. Kara had to be okay. She was good at what she did, and the DEA needed her.

Kara stared out the window at the breaking waves along

4

Vero Beach. Much like the shells being pummeled ashore, her body had taken a beating when the bomb exploded. She glanced at Jeff who sat nearby—her constant companion since last week. He said it was a miracle she was alive—according to her doctor, he was right. But if God cared whether she lived or died, why had He let this happen?

An entire year undercover wasted. She'd been up for the challenge because the payoff would have been huge. They were within hours of taking down the biggest drug lord in Florida. How had her cover been blown? She'd racked her brain for the past week and a half, trying to figure it out. Luis Alvarado had welcomed her into his organization. After months of grooming, she'd worked her way up the ranks—a whole year wasted! She slammed her fist on the cushion beside her.

"Easy there. This place is a rental." Jeff walked into the room from the kitchen. He carried two glasses.

She reined in her thoughts. "Sorry."

"No harm done." He quirked a brow. "At least to me. Now that cushion…" Jeff handed her a glass of sweet tea, brushed her feet off the ottoman, and sat where they had been. "You're looking better."

Kara took a long draw from the glass then set it on a coaster. "Thanks. I'm feeling more myself too." She'd been confined to that miserable room for too many days. "Any word on Alvarado?"

"Negative. He vanished."

She focused on a lone seagull. "He's out there."

"We'll find him, but he's gone deep."

"When can we leave this place? Don't get me

wrong. A cottage on the beach is a dream, but I'm bored."

"Admit it. You're a workaholic." He quirked a grin.

"Guilty as charged. I've been working non-stop for too long. It's a little hard to turn that off." She reached for the new phone the DEA had supplied—still no messages. Sitting around here was almost worse than nearly getting blown to smithereens.

"We're halfway through your doctor-ordered recovery time. Relax and enjoy the quiet while you can."

"Easy for you to say. You're on the job." Jeff had been assigned to keep her safe in case Alvarado or one of his cronies came to finish what they'd started. Alvarado was as bad as they came. Kara had no doubt if the man learned she'd survived the blast he'd come after her. She'd be ready. Jeff wouldn't be assigned to her indefinitely.

2

Three Weeks Later

Kara slid beside Jeff into the backseat of Gary's sedan, parked at the Vero Beach Municipal Airport. The tinted windows allowed privacy from the outside world.

Gary turned and studied Kara's face.

She met his gaze.

"You're looking a lot better than the last time I saw you. I trust your accommodations were satisfactory."

"Yes, sir. Finding fault with a cottage along the beach would be difficult." Although torture at times, she'd needed to recuperate from the blast. Even after three full weeks, her body still hurt, but duty called. The DEA needed her, and she'd never been able to say no to the job.

Gary nodded and handed them each a file. "Once a doctor clears you, you'll be working on Operation Trail Ride in a joint taskforce of local and federal authorities assisting CODE, the Central Oregon Drug

Enforcement." He handed them each an intelligence file and opened his own.

Kara's heart lurched—*Oregon!* She worked out of Miami. What was her boss thinking, and what was Jeff doing here? She opened to the first page, skimmed through several pages, then looked up.

Jeff opened the file and looked down. "The field office in Bend can handle this. Why are they involving us?"

"CODE, in cooperation with the DEA, has an ongoing investigation that runs from Mexico's border through California and into Oregon, Washington State, and Canada. This is a huge operation. You'll be investigating a husband and wife team. We want to know the extent of the couple's involvement. The local authorities suspect they could be cell heads."

"I still don't see why you're sending us all the way to Oregon." Kara crossed her arms.

Jeff slumped into the back of his seat, the file open to a series of snapshots of a man and woman along with a teen girl. His brows furrowed.

"You okay, Jeff?" Kara placed a hand on his forearm.

Gary cut in. "This isn't just any husband and wife team."

"I'm not doing this. I recuse myself." Jeff closed the file, a steel glint in his gray-blue eyes.

"Hear me out before you say anything more." Gary's voice held a sharp edge.

Kara looked from Gary to Jeff and pursed her lips. The tension in the car was so thick it'd take a chainsaw to cut through it. Apparently, she wasn't the only one who didn't want this assignment.

"As I said, the smugglers have been crossing the border from Mexico into California and then up to Oregon on a regular basis. The only place they've been consistently tracked is to your stepbrother's ranch."

Whoa! She hadn't seen that coming. No wonder Jeff looked ready to crush Gary like an empty soda can.

"Eric and Veronica have been boarding horses that belong to known drug traffickers for approximately a year now. CODE has been trying to plant someone on the inside without success." He chuckled dryly. "It appears your stepbrother doesn't need any more employees. That's where you come in. You'll be on assignment at his ranch near Sunridge. We need someone who can infiltrate the operation and feed us information. Your job will be to keep your eyes and ears open and report all your findings."

Kara cleared her throat and never took her gaze off Jeff. "With all due respect, sir, you can't expect Jeff to investigate his own brother."

"Stepbrother," Gary corrected. "And they are only related by marriage. You have a problem with this?" He looked directly at Jeff.

"Yes. This is nuts." Jeff rubbed the back of his neck.

"Maybe, but you're CODE's last hope."

"What about Kara? Why's she involved?"

"You need a partner, and she needs to lay low until we find Alvarado and company. Who better than Kara? Besides, I believe she has a friend in Sunridge." He turned to Kara.

"That Sunridge?" Her voice squeaked.

Jeff looked at her with raised brows. "Problem?"

She shook her head. "No." Except Gail Foster lived there, and the last thing she wanted was to endanger a friend.

"The local contact is the taskforce leader, Sheriff Deputy Tad Baker," Gary continued.

"There's no one else who can do this?" Jeff's shoulders slumped slightly.

"They're out of options. You're a topnotch agent, and I have complete faith that you can remain objective and do your job."

Kara scowled. Of course, Jeff could do the job. But did he want to? She certainly didn't. Then again, what choice did they have? Jeff was perfect for the job, and she needed to lay low. No one would ever think to look for her in Oregon even if she had spent several years living there as a teen.

Jeff closed the file. "Fine. I'll do my job, but I don't like it."

"I understand," Gary faced forward and looked at them through his rearview mirror. "I know this is unusual, but you'll have the perfect cover. You mentioned once that your family believes you work for a bank. Is that still your story?"

Jeff closed the file in his lap. "As far as Eric is concerned, yes. My parents know what I do, but I never shared my change in careers with Eric. We aren't exactly close."

"Perfect. If Eric checks up on you, we'll make sure

he thinks you work at a bank. If any of the suspects start digging, they'll be led to believe you have connections in high places. I'll add a few extracurricular activities as well. We want the smugglers to think you're not the clean-cut guy you appear to be."

Jeff scrubbed his hand over his face. "I haven't seen Eric in almost seven years."

"Then I guess it's about time you two get reacquainted. Everything you need to know is in that file."

"What if Eric's involved?" he mumbled more to himself than to them.

Gary's brown eyes hardened. "You'll do your job." His words were short and clipped. "This goes without saying—follow protocol. We don't want anything to come back and bite us when it goes to trial. I find out that you compromised this operation in any way, your career is over. Am I clear?"

Jeff moved to open the door. "Yes, sir."

"Good. Since you've both been lying low, I took the liberty of having some of your stuff packed. Figured you'd need some of your belongings."

"Thanks." Jaw clenched, Jeff took the packet of information, grabbed his bag from the trunk, and walked toward the waiting Beechcraft.

"Do you have any questions, Kara?" Gary asked.

"When will I see a doctor for medical clearance?"

"I've arranged to have a doctor meet you at the DEA field office in Bend. There will be a vehicle for each of you at the Redmond Airport. You'll go on to Sunridge after you see the doctor in Bend, and Jeff will head to the ranch just outside Sunridge."

"You must have confidence I'm going to pass inspection if you're sending me all the way to Oregon," Kara said.

Gary pursed his lips.

She cleared her throat at his silence. "What's my specific role in this operation?"

"It's all in there. We're reprising your nail technician role since you're still licensed in the state of Oregon." He nodded at the file she held. "Use Jeff to access his family. You'll also find that there's another suspect. His name is Jake. Get close to him and see what you can learn."

She nodded. "And what about Gail? You mentioned she's the reason I was chosen for this job." She didn't like the sound of this assignment, but what choice did she have? Stay hiding in Florida indefinitely or work in Oregon. Neither choice appealed. Good thing Gary had managed to keep her and Jeff's name out of the media coverage of the car bomb. Alvarado might have discovered her true identity, but others had not. Otherwise, her undercover days would be over, even in Oregon. It was a miracle none of the onlookers had posted video or pictures to the Internet of them in the aftermath.

"She's your cover. Sunridge is small, and an outsider might be noticed. Use Gail however you see fit."

"She's a civilian, and I'm not an outsider. I lived there when I was in high school."

"That was a long time ago."

True and her parents moved away shortly after she left for beauty school. Somehow, she'd manage to keep Gail safe and do her job.

"You mentioned a bag?"

"There's a box already on board the plane. A female agent went to your apartment under the guise of investigating your death. While there, she gathered some of your belongings."

"My death?"

"Yes. I put the word out that you died while at the hospital."

Her stomach sank. She'd been afraid something like that would happen. It made sense to make it look like Alvarado succeeded and thereby get him off her tail, but it would devastate her family should word get to them. Maybe since they were on an extended trip to Europe, they'd never have to know. Hopefully, all this would be cleared up by the time they returned to the states.

"You're authorized to get necessities. Save your receipts." He handed her a metal briefcase. "Everything you should need is in here. Oh, and since you're known in Sunridge, I didn't prepare an alias for you."

She nodded. "Do I need to stay invisible in Oregon?" A few people there would more than likely remember her from her teen years, so she wasn't sure how that would be possible, especially if she was doing nails.

"Don't make the evening news, and you should be fine. I think you're relatively safe there. Luis Alvarado smuggles out of Peru, and you'll be dealing with Mexican traffickers in Oregon."

"I want to know the second you plug the leak and get Alvarado in custody." Kara stepped from the vehicle and looked around.

A dark car parked about a hundred feet from Gary caught her attention, and her pulse accelerated. She ducked her chin and quickened her pace. The fewer people who saw her face the better. She strode across the tarmac. Jeff must've already boarded.

The roar of the engines prompted Kara to take longer strides. Jeff stood in the doorway to the plane waving his arms. *What's he doing?*

She glanced over her shoulder. A man wearing a ski mask raised a semi-automatic and pointed it at her. She turned, crouched, and bolted toward the plane. A bullet whizzed by her head, narrowly missing her ear. Seconds later a searing pain tore across her right shoulder. *Lord, help me!*

The plane rolled away from her. Partially concealed by the plane, Jeff fired at her unknown assailant. Rapid gunfire punctuated the air. She dug in and pumped her legs as fast as they would move, running in a zig-zag pattern as bullets pierced the tarmac. A sharp sting pierced her right calf.

Her leg burned with every step. Intense pain continued to stab her right shoulder. She blocked the misery from her mind and pushed forward. Another twenty feet…ten…five. Kara reached her hand toward the moving door.

Jeff grasped her forearm and yanked her inside. Her shoulder screamed in protest. The door closed, and the plane shot down the runway.

3

Kara collapsed into the nearest seat and fumbled with the belt. Her arm burned like fire. She met Jeff's scowl. "Did you get the shooter?"

"No, he was using the Buick as cover. Gary may have had a better angle." His eyes widened. "You were hit." Jeff looked around the cabin and grabbed a towel from the tiny galley. "Here. Hold this against your shoulder." He squatted and wrapped another towel around her leg.

"You'd better buckle up." The force of the plane jetting down the runway pushed her back into the seat.

Jeff applied pressure to her calf. "I'm fine right here."

Kara nodded, in too much pain to respond, and closed her eyes. Her heart pounded as she tried to slow her rapid breathing. She gripped the armrest tight until they reached flying altitude then looked down at her stinging leg. Blood had seeped through the towel covering her calf. She closed her eyes and willed her stomach to settle. Dizziness overwhelmed her.

"Oh no!" She grabbed a sick bag and let loose. Jeff leaned across the aisle and pulled her hair away from her face. Finally, her stomach relaxed.

"Better?"

She nodded.

Jeff took the bag. "Be right back."

I can't believe I puked. She never had a problem with the sight of blood. What had come over her? Kara turned and watched Jeff walk to the rear of the Beechcraft King Air 350.

He sat back down and held out a can of Ginger Ale. "This should help settle your stomach."

Kara took the can and drank some. Then she leaned into the seat back and closed her eyes. "Thanks. I don't suppose there's a first aid kit on board?"

"Got it right here."

With one eye cracked open, she spied the box. "How are you with blood?"

"Apparently better than you." Jeff had her attention as he slipped on latex gloves and started to roll up her pant leg, bumping her wound in the process.

She caught her breath. "Just cut it off."

Jeff took scissors from the kit and cut away her pant leg. He sat back on his haunches. "It's not that bad really, only a graze."

"Sure bled a lot."

"Yeah, but you were pumping those legs hard." He ripped open an alcohol swab. "This is gonna sting." He motioned with his other hand and mumbled, "It would be easier if you could lie on your stomach."

Kara craned her neck and took in the cabin, which

consisted of single seats running the length of the space. "Watch out."

Jeff moved aside as she stood up halfway then lay down on her stomach in the aisle, resting her head on her good arm.

"That works."

A stinging sensation burned her right calf, but at least her shoulder had stopped hurting. She squeezed her eyes closed and held her breath, willing Jeff to hurry up.

"You have evasive maneuvers down to a science. I'm surprised the shooter was able to get you at all," Jeff teased.

"Yeah, well, lucky, I guess." She felt him put something cold and wet on her leg and pushed the pain out of her mind. Who had been firing at her? Definitely not the work of a sniper, or she'd be dead. Would Alvarado send an incompetent after her, or was this unrelated?

"How's that feel?"

"Not good."

"Figured as much. At least it's only a graze." He wrapped a bandage around her lower leg and secured it in place. "That ought to do until we can land and get you to the hospital."

"I'm not going to the hospital. Gary scheduled a doctor to meet me at the field office in Bend. I'm sure he can fix me up there."

"We'll see. I'd like to look at your shoulder. Can you get up, or do you need help?"

Kara rolled over and held up her good arm. Jeff

grabbed her wrist and pulled. Pain shot from head to toe. She winced. "Thanks."

"You're welcome. Now for your shoulder."

She held tighter to the towel covering her wound. "I think the bleeding stopped."

He gently plied her fingers off her shoulder.

She turned her head away.

"Yes. The bleeding stopped. Looks like the bullet only grazed the outside of your shoulder. You're going to have a nice scar to show off."

She heard him dig through the kit.

"This is gonna hurt."

She gritted her teeth to avoid screaming like a baby. Oh man, why did it have to hurt so much? Then again, she'd never had much of a pain threshold.

"Sorry about that. I'm going to tape the skin closed with some Band-Aids."

Kara nodded, and blinked back tears.

"Okay. That's the best I can do." Jeff closed the kit, tossed the wrappers into a receptacle, then sat down across the aisle. "Wish I had a video of your moves out on the tarmac. The guys would've loved it. I'd name it 'the flight of the crazy bird.'"

"I didn't want to give them an easy target. It worked too, for the most part." She touched her shoulder. "At least I'm alive."

"Yep. Maybe you could reenact the chicken run, and the DEA could record it to include in a training video."

Kara wanted to kick him with her good leg but grinned instead. He was razzing her like she was one of the guys. Couldn't complain about that.

Jeff watched Kara out of the corner of his eye. He hadn't stated the obvious, and sooner or later she'd come to the same conclusion. Luis Alvarado knew Kara Nelson was alive and well. Gary had his hands full on the ground. Hopefully, he caught the shooter. "Any ideas on who shot at you?"

"Don't know. But Alvarado isn't the only person who'd like me dead. You don't work in this business for long without making enemies along the way."

"True."

"You think Gary caught the shooter?" Kara asked.

"Don't know, but we can find out." Jeff pulled his phone from his pocket. Gary's voicemail picked up. "Jeff here. Wanted to let you know all things considered, Kara's fine. Bullets grazed her calf and her right shoulder. You catch the shooter? Call me." He pocketed the phone. "Guess he's busy."

Kara frowned and turned her attention to the file. Jeff stared at his own intel with unseeing eyes. Giving up, he laid the file aside and studied Kara's profile.

She shifted and glanced in his direction. He looked forward. But her image burned in his mind. Silky blond hair and a small face complemented her petite body. Guys probably hit on her all the time. Of course, that worked to her advantage when she was undercover. Too bad they were under the same chain of command, or he might ask her out.

It'd been a long time since his last date—seven years. "Hmm." Had it really been that long? Talk about being married to the job. There had to have been someone since Beth. But no, she dumped him when he announced he wanted to be a cop. Come to think of it, he'd signed on just after his last visit to see Eric and his family. It seemed the DEA had consumed all his time since.

"What?" Kara said.

"Huh?"

"You said hmm. Why are you hmming?"

"Nothing. Just thinking about the past." He cleared his throat. "You have a plan for when we land?"

Kara nodded and resumed studying the papers in front of her.

She wasn't going to make this easy. "Care to share?"

She closed the file and turned to face him. "I'll call my friend, go to the field office, and then to Sunridge. I figure we'll meet up there. You have my cell number?"

Jeff nodded. Hopefully, they wouldn't have any more surprises waiting for them on the ground in Oregon, and if Kara thought she was driving to the field office alone, she was nuts.

Kara sat in the Redmond Oregon Airport parking lot

behind the wheel of a white Honda Civic. She reached up to start the ignition and moaned as pain shot through her shoulder.

Jeff crouched at the driver's window of the sedan. "You sure I can't drive you? My SUV would be more comfortable." He pointed to the black Ford Escape he'd been assigned.

"That's nice of you, but as much as I love your SUV, I think this car better suits my cover." Jeff would be on a ranch, and an SUV could come in handy.

"Yeah. I guess you're right," Jeff said. "Okay. I'll give Eric a call before I show up at his front door."

"Why? You have the element of surprise. It's better if he doesn't know you're coming."

"Maybe." Jeff clenched his jaw, nodded, and walked away.

Kara started the engine and headed out. The sooner she saw this doctor the better. Her leg still throbbed. She pulled out and frowned. Jeff was riding her bumper. "I don't need a nursemaid." Any other day, she'd lose him, but her shoulder hurt too much to even think about evading him. She settled in and tried to ignore the SUV tailing her and the man behind the wheel.

Forty minutes later, Kara pulled into the DEA's parking lot and did her best not to limp as she walked into the building. The doctor Gary promised was waiting for her in a tiny vacated office. Kara filled him in on her injuries.

A deep frown creased the doctor's forehead. He sat in a nearby chair. "Your body's been through a lot of trauma in a short amount of time." He sighed and removed the bandage from her leg and then her shoulder. "Looks like your partner did a decent job of cleaning the wounds, but you need a few stitches." He applied a fresh wrap. "Too bad you didn't call ahead and warn me of your new injuries. I could've met you at my office or the hospital instead." He stood. "Let's go. I'll stitch you up at Saint Charles."

"No hospitals."

His brows raised high on his balding forehead. "The hospital is closer, but if you insist, I'll stitch you up at my office."

"Fine. Then will you clear me for active duty?"

"Not today. You were shot. Let's give it a couple of days at least."

Kara bit down on her lower lip to keep her mouth shut. No sense in angering the doctor. Besides, what he didn't know wouldn't hurt him. "If you'll give me your office address, I'll meet you there shortly. I have some equipment I need to requisition, and I need to give them some information about my cover while in Sunridge."

4

With Kara safely inside the DEA field office, Jeff pulled out of the parking lot. "Here goes nothing." The whole flight, all he could think about was how his family would react to seeing him. Would they send him packing or welcome him? Considering their past, either option was viable.

Thirty-five minutes later, he paused alongside the road and stared at the entrance to the ranch positioned to his left before crossing the single-lane country road. Then he drove under a sizable wooden sign mounted on upright logs, which read New Haven Ranch.

Jeff drove along the gravel road taking in his surroundings. Sturdy wood fencing enclosed the pasture and bordered the drive all the way to the house. After one-quarter mile, the road ended in a huge yard with a circular gravel drive. He whistled long and slow—Eric had done well for himself.

Several structures stood along the edge of the yard as well as a large barn. The barn door looked as if it were hand-carved, a grand star at its center. He'd passed houses along the road that didn't have as much curb appeal. The two-story log house had a covered wraparound porch, furnished with a swing, a few chairs, and a small wicker table. A modest cabin sat off to the left. Must've cost some serious money to build a place like this. Could Eric really be involved in drug smuggling? He didn't want to believe it, but where would the money have come from to support a place like this? He shook his head at the direction of his thoughts. He was here because it was his job, but Eric was innocent until proven guilty as far as Jeff was concerned.

He parked in the driveway and stepped out of his vehicle into the scorching heat. Grabbing his duffel bag, he sauntered up the porch steps. An old-fashioned bell hung next to the entrance. He swung the rope attached to the bell a couple of times and a loud dinging sounded.

A few seconds later, the door opened. Veronica, Eric's wife, stood before him. "May I help—?"

Jeff grinned. "Hi, Veronica. It's been a long time."

Her eyes widened. "Jeff? Is that really you?"

"In the flesh. I thought it was about time I come for a visit."

He studied her face for a second. Veronica hadn't changed much in seven years, except for a few lines around her hazel eyes. She looked the same as the day they'd met.

She opened the door wider. "We weren't expecting you. Where're you staying?" She laughed. "My goodness, that didn't sound very inviting, did it?"

Jeff chuckled. "Don't worry about it, and no, I don't have accommodations yet. I was hoping you wouldn't mind if I stayed here." He rubbed his chin wishing he were back in Miami.

Veronica's face paled. "Here? Of course, you're welcome to stay. We have plenty of room."

"Thanks. Is Eric around?"

"He's in the horse barn. Why don't you head out there? I'm surprised he didn't hear you drive up."

Jeff hesitated a moment in the entryway and took in the open layout. Dollar signs leapt out everywhere he looked, from the art hanging on the log walls to the expensive rugs covering the hard wood floors.

A door squeaked, and the sound of steady footsteps filled the quiet house. Eric came into view.

The strain on Veronica's face relaxed. "Eric, look who's here." She turned toward Jeff. "Excuse me while I go and prepare your room."

Eric stuffed his hands in his denim pockets. "It's been a long time, little brother. The banking business must be keeping you busy."

"Too long." A little gray showed around Eric's temples. "Veronica said I could crash here. I hope you don't mind. I have some time off and thought it was about time I came for a visit." Jeff studied his brother for any sign of their old issues. He seemed a little tense, but maybe it was the surprise of having an unexpected guest.

Pride mixed with uncertainty shone in Eric's eyes. "You're welcome to stay as long as you like."

"Thanks, but I insist I earn my keep." Jeff held his

breath. Open access to the ranch was essential to the operation.

"That's not necessary."

"Come on. This city slicker could use a dose of country life. It's been a long time since I worked the ranch at home."

Eric frowned, and his eyes took on a distant look. "You always did want more out of life than ranching. You find it yet?"

"I think so. But ranching is in my blood." Jeff loved working beside his stepdad as a boy.

"Since you insist on having a working vacation, there's more than enough to keep you busy. I'm shorthanded this summer. Two of my regular summer staff moved on, and I haven't found anyone acceptable to replace them."

"Bummer, I guess what they say is true. Good help is hard to find." If he needed help, why hadn't the DEA been able to get someone on the inside?

Eric nodded. "You thirsty? We have juice, soda, and water." Eric reached up and grabbed two glasses from the hickory cupboard. "What can I get you?"

"Water, please." Jeff looked around the kitchen. "This is quite a place you have. Even bigger than Mom and Dad's. When do I get the grand tour?" He grasped the glass Eric offered and took a long drink.

Eric placed his half-empty glass in the sink. "Come on. I'll show you around."

Jeff followed him through various rooms. The house must be seven thousand square feet or more. The five bedrooms were on the second level along with an office and three bathrooms.

The tour ended in the basement. "The great room is my favorite in the house. As you can see, over in that corner is our home theater, complete with raised seating and a large-screen TV that rises out of the console in the front."

Jeff paused in awe. This room was a guy's dream. To the side of the home theater sat a kitchenette with what appeared to be white quartz countertops and white cabinetry. A pool table and a Ping-Pong table stood in the back half of the room. Then he saw it—an old-fashioned pinball arcade game. "You've got to be kidding me." Jeff cruised over to the machine. "Nice!"

Eric shuffled his feet. "Come on. Let's go outside. Maybe later you can talk Lauren into playing with you. She's pretty good."

Jeff hadn't seen his niece since he'd arrived. "Where are you hiding the munchkin?"

"You better not let her hear you call her that. Lauren's fifteen now. She's probably up in her room reading or practicing the violin."

"Fifteen? I think the last time I saw her she was eight."

"Sounds right. So how about you—any wedding plans or children in your future?"

"Please—not you too. Every time I call home, I get the same question."

Eric grinned. "Just asking. Come on. There's more to see."

Jeff's shoulders relaxed. He didn't like the implications of what he was seeing, but it seemed that

Eric was beginning to loosen up. Maybe there was a logical explanation for the appearance of wealth. "How long have you had the pinball machine?"

"It's a new addition to the family."

"Cool." As they walked through the house, strains of violin music floated through the air. "Is that Lauren playing?"

"She's pretty good, huh?" Eric put a finger to his lips and motioned him to follow.

They headed up the stairs. At the third door on the right, Eric slowly turned the doorknob then opened it into a room painted light purple.

Lauren gasped and glared at her dad.

Eric stepped into the room. "Lauren, look who's here. It's your Uncle Jeff."

His niece set the violin on her bed, stood, and cast an impatient look at her father. Jeff couldn't blame her. They'd invaded her private space without even knocking, and she probably didn't remember him at all—his fault. He should have made more of an effort. Maybe then he wouldn't be here now investigating Eric.

"Hey, kiddo. I was admiring your music, so your dad brought me up to see you." He couldn't believe this was the little girl he'd once known. She'd sprouted to a couple inches shy of six foot and wore her almond-colored hair long and straight.

She stepped toward them. "Thanks, Uncle Jeff. I'm going to a music camp at Sunridge High, and I have three songs to learn."

"Sounds to me like you already know them." Jeff nodded toward her violin. "What're you working on?"

She handed him a few pages of sheet music. "It's a pretty challenging piece. I hope to get it down before camp starts. Do you play any instruments?"

Eric chuckled. "Sorry, honey. Your uncle and I weren't blessed with music lessons when we were kids." He turned toward the door. "We'll let you continue practicing."

Jeff handed the music back to Lauren. "Keep up the hard work. See you later."

Jeff walked shoulder to shoulder with his stepbrother across the ranch yard. "Lauren's a nice girl. You've done a good job."

"Thanks, but I'm sure Veronica had more to do with it than me." He guided Jeff into the horse barn.

Jeff paused in wonder at the size and design of the barn. It looked kind of like something from an old storybook. All the stalls were made with furniture grade wood and sanded to perfection. Carvings of horses and saddles decorated the posts on the sides of each stall. Quality craftsmanship greeted him at every turn. The sweet smell of grain, straw, and hay mingled. Jeff inhaled deeply. He loved being on a ranch again—even under these circumstances. Wood stalls lined two side walls with a small office and a well-stocked tack room along the entrance wall. A loft covered the office side of the barn.

Jeff's stomach knotted as he came back to reality. "How do you afford all this?"

A startled look crossed Eric's face then disappeared. "We board horses, give riding lessons, and conduct trail rides. Central Oregon tourism is big, and horseback riding is popular. We also have a website that helps draw business in."

"Tourists? Didn't you tell me once that Sunridge doesn't have any hotels?"

"There are several bed and breakfasts, but we're not that far from Bend and Redmond, so there's really no need for a hotel." He frowned. "Although I heard a rumor that some developer is looking at building a hotel on the edge of town. I suppose it's bound to happen sooner or later. Probably will be good for business too."

"From the look of things, business must be good already. Seems like you're raking in the money."

"Relax little brother. You're not on the bank's clock today. Stop worrying about money and enjoy your vacation."

Jeff chuckled. Good thing Eric thought he worked in a bank. "Sorry about that. It's hard to leave work behind sometimes." He'd find out soon enough how busy this ranch was. Maybe they *did* keep active with tourists. He really wanted that to be true.

Eric's cell phone rang. He pulled it from his pocket and frowned at the caller ID. "Sorry I need to take this. I'll be back in a few."

"No problem. I'll just wander around."

Eric nodded, waved, then quickly left the barn.

If drugs were passing through here, they were doing an exceptional job of hiding them. He saw no signs of anything unusual. The barn door opened wide and sunlight streaked in outlining the silhouette of a cowboy.

"Can I help you?"

Jeff rose to his full height. "I'm Eric's brother, Jeff."

"Uh-huh, and I'm the Lone Ranger. Eric ain't got no brother."

Although the man's claim should have surprised him, it didn't. He and Eric weren't close, so there was no reason anyone here would know about him. Jeff squinted. "I didn't catch your name."

"I didn't throw it." He turned and stalked out.

Odd dude. He'd seen that guy's photo in his intel—Jake Jones. Stats filled his mind—single, liked the ladies, wrangler, only employed at the ranch for the past year. Jeff moved to follow the cowboy but came to a halt when the barn door re-opened and Eric sauntered in, a tight smile on his face.

"Sorry to keep you waiting. Did I see Jake come in here a minute ago?" Eric spoke fast, and he looked everywhere except at Jeff.

"Could have been him. He didn't share his name."

Eric shrugged. "I have to meet someone on another ranch. Feel free to take one of the horses out for a ride." He paused before he pushed out the door. "I never have figured out why you went into the banking business. You always loved living and working on the ranch when we were kids."

"People change." He followed Eric to the door.

Eric glanced at his watch. "I gotta go. Dinner's at six. Don't be late, or Veronica will have a foal." Eric chuckled at his pathetic joke.

"Got it." Jeff watched him rush to his pickup and speed away. He scowled at the mixed signals Eric broadcast. There was too much going on here to figure out everything in one afternoon, but he'd get a start. At least Eric had begun to relax a bit. That is until he'd taken the phone call. Jeff wandered into the office in the barn and sat in the chair behind the desk. He couldn't see anything incriminating lying around.

"What are you doing in here?" Jake asked.

Jeff sprang up from the seat. "I was just taking a load off. I didn't think anyone would mind."

"Well, I mind. That's my desk, and I'd appreciate a little respect for my space."

"Sure thing. Sorry. I thought this was Eric's desk." He brushed past Jake and noticed a bulge on the right side of his waist. Looked like Jake was armed, but why?

5

Kara left the doctor's office with a prescription for painkiller and orders to rest for the next twenty-four hours—right, like that was going to happen. She tossed the script for the painkiller onto the passenger seat, threw the Civic into gear, and peeled out of the driveway. The doctor refused to listen to reason. She tried to explain her need to resume active duty after having so much time off already, but he'd have none of it. She felt fine. Her leg and shoulder didn't hurt at all. Granted the numbness hadn't worn off yet, but she could take the pain once it did.

The doc had put in a few stitches, and as far as Kara was concerned, she was good to go. She frowned. Gail would freak if she saw the bandages.

Gail had been a volunteer with the Big Sister program and had been assigned to her when she was a young teen. They had maintained a warm friendship through the years. Thankfully, Gail didn't know what she did for a living. She'd kept her employment with the DEA as quiet as possible to avoid the inevitable questions. It helped that her parents had moved from the area, and couldn't slip and tell anyone in Sunridge what she did for a living now.

She pulled into the mall's parking lot, slid into the nearest spot to the door, then pulled out her phone and called her friend.

"Hey there."

"Kara! It's so good to hear your voice. I was just telling Kurt how much I've missed hearing from you. It's about time you called."

"I'm sorry. Life's been crazy. But I have good news. I'm relocating to Sunridge."

She pulled the phone away from her ear as Gail squealed. Kara chuckled. Gail never squealed.

"When will you be here?"

"Actually, I'm in Bend right now. I have a little shopping to do, and then I'll head your direction."

"I can't believe this. You have to stay at our house until you get settled."

"Are you sure? I don't want to impose." She half-hoped Gail wouldn't have room. Endangering her friend was the last thing she wanted to do. Then again, it's not like she was followed to Sunridge.

"Nonsense. We want you here with us."

Gary's idea to send her along with Jeff was genius. No one would suspect an old friend of Gail's of being a DEA agent. To anyone who might remember her, she was simply a girl who enjoyed doing nails.

"Kara, are you still there?"

"Yes—sorry. I'd love to visit with you for a few days until I find my own place." She went inside JC

Penney. A cool blast of air settled over her as she entered.

"Perfect. I'll see you soon—the guestroom is ready. Um," Gail's voice faltered. "I feel funny asking this, but is everything okay? I've felt the need to pray for you lately."

"Everything's fine. See you soon." She closed her phone with a smack. Gail had been praying for her? Kara had been a little angry with God lately, but how could He ignore *Gail's* prayers? Gail was the most spiritual person she'd ever known. The woman went to church every week, attended Bible study and was on the prayer chain. Kara was doing well to even make a couple services a month, much less read her Bible.

Several miles outside of Sunridge, Kara turned on a radio station that played oldies. She tapped her fingers to the beat. Shopping had gone well. She'd scored a loose pair of khakis, along with a short-sleeved, button-up white top, which she'd changed into while in the store's dressing room. Her cell rang. She clicked the Bluetooth button. "Hello."

"I just got the call from the doctor," Gary said. "By the sound of it, Jeff played down your injuries."

"I was only grazed. No big deal."

"Either way, you're still on medical leave. Take a couple days off. Then check in with your CODE contact. Let him know you're in town, but on leave. Until the doc clears you, there's not much else you can do."

Kara looked down at the speedometer and eased off the gas pedal. Her jaw hurt from clenching it, and her calf had begun to sting again. She was in no mood to hear what Gary had to say, but good training trumped the attitude. "You catch the shooter?"

"Yep, but he's not talking."

"Anyone I know?"

"Denver."

She'd worked with him on and off over the past few years. She'd considered him a good cop, but apparently, he'd fooled them.

Kara expelled her breath in a whoosh. "Who's he working for?"

"Unknown. But he'll talk sooner or later. He also killed Logan."

"Why?"

"Again. Unknown."

Kara opened her mouth, but no sound came out. This was too much. Logan was a great cop and a friend.

"You still there?"

"Yes," she said barely above a whisper. "I need to go." Her heart constricted. Maybe a couple days off would be prudent, because right now she had murder on her mind, and if she ran into anyone involved with Luis Alvarado or his organization, there'd be a shortage of body bags.

Lord, I'm angry. I'm angry with You, Gary, the doctor, Denver. I'm downright ticked off. She ground her teeth together. *Never mind. You don't care anyway, or You would've stopped this mess before it happened. It wasn't enough to take Tony and Dee from me?*

She missed Dee. Her cousin had been her best friend. She couldn't think about Tony. Losing her partner when she was a rookie still hurt. From now on, she trusted no one. Heaviness settled on her shoulders. Anger consumed her, and revenge fueled the hate growing in her heart.

A short time later, a sign that warned drivers to reduce their speed flashed. Kara lifted her foot off the gas pedal then eased down on the brake. A banner hung across Main Street in Sunridge announcing the Fourth of July picnic in the park. She used to beg her parents to take her to that picnic but they never wanted to go. The town sported red, white, and blue flowers on every lamppost. It looked exactly the way she remembered.

Kara continued down Main and turned right at the first intersection. She parked in front of a modest two-story house, took several deep breaths, checked her reflection in the vanity mirror, and froze. Storm-filled eyes stared back at her. She blinked several times. *Get it together, girl.* Kara closed her eyes and forced herself to think happy thoughts. Gail would know everything wasn't fine if she didn't get her emotions under control.

Her friend ran outside and down the driveway.

Kara plastered on a smile as she slid out of the car.

Gail stepped up to the driver's door. "It's so good to see you!" She flung her arms around Kara.

Yeow! That hurts. She shifted to avoid the pressure on her shoulder

"I can't believe you're here," Gail said.

"Me neither." Kara held her friend at arms' length, avoiding eye contact. "You look good."

"Thanks. Get your stuff and come inside."

Kara hooked the new duffel bag stuffed with her

purchases over her good shoulder and linked arms with her friend as they moved indoors. A round table near the bay window of the kitchen was set with a white linen tablecloth along with a vase in the center filled with blue hydrangeas beside a plate of fruit, cheese, and crackers. Tall glasses of lemonade beckoned.

Gail talked non-stop as she attempted to cram months of sharing into the space of a few minutes.

Kara chuckled.

"What?"

"Do you realize you haven't even paused for a breath, much less a bite of food?"

Gail clamped her lips shut and touched her palms to her flushed cheeks, causing Kara to laugh even harder. Gail tittered then laughed.

Kara wiped tears from her eyes as she caught her breath. She needed this more than anything right now. There was nothing like a laugh session with a friend to release pent up tension.

"I'm glad you're here, Kara." Gail stood. "Come. I'll show you where you'll sleep."

Kara followed Gail up the carpeted stairs. She winced with every step. At the top, she took a second to recover and admired the décor. The hallway walls were covered with family photos. She even spotted one of her.

Gail stopped at the second door on the right then walked into a room painted in a soft shade of blue. The bed and nightstand were white, and a wicker chair sat in one corner. Sunlight streamed through the lacy curtains. Kara grinned with satisfaction. "You've done a nice job with this room. It's cozy."

"Thanks. Please make yourself at home." Gail sat on the corner of the bed and watched as Kara hung her purchases in the closet.

"Is that all you have?"

"No. I have a box in the trunk, but I'll get it later." She still had no idea what had been packed for her, but Kara hoped the agent had included her underthings since she hadn't purchased any new ones at the mall.

"Only a box?"

Kara nodded.

Gail frowned.

"What gives?"

"Nothing really, but I'm wondering why you're relocating to Sunridge. It's not exactly a major metropolis like Miami. I'd think you'd prefer a city." She shrugged. "Isn't that why you left to begin with?"

"No. I left to go to beauty school and get my license in cosmetology. You know all I ever wanted to do was nails." Miami happened later.

Gail chuckled. "Now that you mention it, I do recall you being somewhat obsessed. But what brings you back to town? I didn't know you were even considering a move, and it seems so sudden." Her frowned deepened. "You're limping. Are you okay?

"I'm fine." She understood Gail's concern. She'd be worried too if a friend showed up like this at her doorstep with a single duffel bag and a lone box, but she couldn't tell her what was going on without endangering her in the process. The less Gail knew about her real reason for being here the better.

Gail rose from the bed. "You're not running from some boyfriend or anything like that are you?"

"Relax. I don't have a boyfriend. My apartment in Miami came furnished, so I don't have a bunch of furniture and stuff, and I'm not a clotheshorse. You know that."

Gail closed the door and lowered her voice. "Your parents mentioned some time ago you accepted a position with the DEA. Did you quit?"

Kara shook her head. She should have expected that. Her mom adored Gail and apparently kept in touch even all these years later. Kara opened her mouth to respond, but Gail cut her off with a wave of her hand.

"I don't know what you do there, and I don't need to know, but I find it strange that you would suddenly show up in town. And anyone with eyes can see that you're injured. If you're in some kind of trouble, I'd like to help."

Kara sighed. So much for keeping her occupation on the down low. "I can't tell you why I'm here. And yes, I'm injured. Nothing serious though." At least not serious to her way of thinking. If Gail knew they were bullet-related injuries, she'd probably pass out from the shock. "I'll be in Sunridge for the duration of my assignment. No one here can know I'm DEA. It's detrimental to my safety and those I'm working with."

"I understand. I won't tell anyone, and I'll warn Kurt not to say anything."

Kara groaned.

"What? I tell my husband everything. Don't worry.

No one else knows."

"Good. Now this is what you can tell people. I'm a nail technician, and I plan to open a shop in town soon."

Gail grinned wide. "At least you have a strong cover. Anyone who remembers you will have no trouble believing it. Do you ever regret going to beauty school?"

"No. I love doing nails, and it's come in handy on quite a few cases."

"Good. Let me know when you're up and running. I could use a manicure. And I'd never pass up a free one." She winked.

Kara tossed a small pillow at Gail, which she dodged.

"What? You need customers to make your business look legit right? I'm just trying to help."

"Thanks, Gail. I appreciate it, and I'm happy to do your nails. It's the least I can do since you're letting me crash here. What can you tell me about this town that I don't already know? Anything exciting?"

"About the most exciting thing happening this summer is a music camp over at the high school."

"Sounds like fun." The event was already on her radar. DEA intel provided information about the immediate family members of their suspects. Lauren, the daughter of Eric and Veronica Waters, would be attending.

"It should be. One of the employees from the school where I'm the principal is running the camp."

"Really—are you involved?" She already had the 4-1-1 on Jessica Swift, the event coordinator, but Gail didn't need to know that.

"A little bit." Gail glanced at her watch. "I have to shove off soon to get some last-minute work done for the camp."

"I didn't realize you were musical."

"I'm not, but there's lots of stuff to do that's not directly related to music. Why don't you relax here for a while? Then maybe later, if you're feeling up to it, and if you're interested, you could go over to the high school. Aren't you into music?"

Kara couldn't contain her smile. "Yes, I think it's safe to say twelve years of piano lessons qualify me as being into music."

Gail moved toward the door. "That's right. I forgot. I need to get over to the school now."

"Maybe I'll stop by later today and see if the person in charge needs more volunteers." Right now, she needed some acetaminophen. Her leg and shoulder were screaming.

"Okay. But don't overdo. You look wiped out." Gail closed the bedroom door behind her.

Kara pulled Tylenol from her purse then washed them down with a gulp from her water bottle. The bed was irresistible. There'd be time later for recon. She rested her head on the pillow and closed her eyes. The doctor may be able to keep her off active duty, but he couldn't shut down her swirling thoughts. And Gail's comment about the music camp intrigued her.

6

Kara startled awake to the ringing of her cell phone. "Hello."

"You in town?" Jeff asked.

"Yes. I'm at my friend's place."

"How'd it go with the doctor?"

"Fine." No way would she elaborate. She didn't need him riding her to take it easy. "How are things on your end?"

"Okay."

Seemed they were both less than talkative.

"Can you get away?" Jeff asked. "I have some news."

Kara checked her watch and nearly dropped her phone. She'd been sleeping for two hours. "There's a small park in the center of town. You can't miss it. I'll meet you there in thirty minutes."

Kara sat on a wood bench along a paved walking path

and breathed in the scent of pine needles. Lush green grass flanked the pathway and tall pine trees dotted the otherwise dry landscape. Screams of delight filled the air as children played tag on the playground—it looked like the monkey bars were the base. She'd preferred playing cops and robbers as a child, and she always played the cop. Life had been much simpler back then. The bad guys didn't try to kill her when she got too close.

Jeff and his long stride grabbed her attention. She chuckled. A few moms admired Jeff as he walked by. His tall, lean build clothed in jeans and white polo shirt fit right in with the country town. She couldn't blame the women. Jeff was very good looking.

He casually walked past her. She raised her voice. "Excuse me, sir."

Jeff looked over his shoulder. "Me?"

Kara nodded. "I think you dropped this." She held out a twenty.

He stuffed his hands in his pockets and pulled them right side out, revealing nothing but fabric and lint. "Thanks." He sent her a crooked smile, eyes twinkling. "I wonder how that happened. Can I buy you a soda as a thank you?" He pocketed the twenty.

"Sure." She spoke under her breath as she walked alongside him, careful not to limp. "I want that back by the way."

He chuckled. "I thought you might." A flying disc landed at his feet. Jeff reached down, picked it up, and flicked it back to the kids. "The park was a great idea. Lots of people saw us," he spoke softly.

"So where do we go from here?"

"I've been thinking about that. We need to strike up a friendship."

"No problem there. I think we're on the right track." She followed him into the ice cream shop to complete the ruse. Several people turned to stare as they walked into the bustling business. She flicked a grin to the teen behind the counter. "Hi there. My friend and I would like two large sodas."

Jeff carried their cups to the soda fountain and filled them then sat at the only vacant table. "This place smells like waffle cones."

"Mmm. My favorite," Kara said. "Let's head back to the park. At least there I won't be tempted to expand my waistline."

Jeff grabbed his soda and led the way. "I'm settled at Eric's. The ranch is topnotch."

"You suspicious?"

"Of course. Anyone would be, but there's nothing obviously illegal going on there. I'll let you know what I find out. By the way, Gary called."

"And?"

"He said to make sure you were okay. Any idea why?"

"That's all he said?"

"No."

Kara's mouth felt dry in spite of the soda. Anger at Denver's betrayal and Logan's murder weighed heavy.

Jeff sat on a nearby bench and pulled her down beside him. "You want to talk about it?"

"Nope. A couple days of down time, and I'll be good as new."

"The offer stands if you change your mind."

Kara saw the look of sympathy in his eyes and squirmed. She didn't want his pity. "Got it. Now let's talk strategy. What's the situation at the ranch?"

"Jake Jones is the head wrangler. He's abrasive and doesn't like me, so I'll let you work on him. Tourists come out for trail rides and locals board horses."

"Okay. I'll check out Jake." He was already on her radar since Gary had mentioned him. "We need to plan another meeting. Any ideas?"

"Not right now. Lay low for a couple days, wait for your medical clearance, and then we'll get to business."

She was tempted to salute him. Instead she forced a smile. "Fine. I'll be in touch." She made a point of thanking him for the soda then took a pen from her purse and cradled his wrist before writing her number on his hand. "Call me," she said loud enough for those nearby to hear.

A woman smirked and looked like she wished she'd found his twenty—nothing like making an impression on the locals. She sipped her soda and observed the moms watching their children at play. A lone, overdressed brunette caught her attention. The tall woman had separated herself and her son from the other moms who were visiting in small groups—odd. She walked along the path that led toward the woman who wore dark trousers, heels, and a short-sleeved teal blouse. There was something familiar about her. Maybe they'd gone to high school together.

A ball rolled toward Kara and stopped at her feet. She reached down and handed it to the tow-headed little boy, who looked to be about three years old.

His mother trotted up beside him and glared at Kara. "Leave my son alone!"

Kara took a step back and raised her hands. "I was only handing him the ball. I didn't mean any harm."

The woman's glare softened to a wary look. She nodded, took a step back, and pointed to the grass several yards away. "Timmy, go take your ball over there and play." She watched her son bounce the ball then glanced back at Kara. "I'm Marci. I'm sorry for snapping at you."

"It's fine. You can't be too careful."

"Thanks for understanding." She shot a pensive smile toward Kara. "I haven't seen you around. Are you new in town?"

"Sort of. I'm Kara. It's funny you ask. I thought you looked familiar, but I guess we never knew one another. I lived here when I was in high school." Maybe a little name-dropping would help ease the woman's mind. "My friend, Gail Foster, is letting me stay at her house until I find a place of my own."

Marci grinned. "She's the principal at the elementary school, right? I hear she's a nice lady." She held out her hand. "Sorry about earlier. Most of these women," she motioned toward the other moms, "don't like me. Guess I'm not used to people being nice."

Kara shook her head. "Why? You steal one of their husbands or something?"

Marci's eyes narrowed. "Guess I was wrong about you." She turned her back on Kara.

Talk about touching a nerve. "Marci, wait. I'm

sorry. It was only a joke—a stupid one. I didn't mean any harm."

Marci spun back to Kara, arms crossed. Skepticism and something else she couldn't read stared back from Marci's azure eyes.

"I should go." Kara ignored the knot of warning in the pit of her stomach and headed toward Gail's house. She wasn't sure what, but something significant took place at the park just now, but was it good or bad?

7

Sunday morning, Kara sat with Gail and Kurt in a pew about four rows from the back. The pianist played softly, accompanied by a keyboard that sounded like an organ. Kara studied the church bulletin, noting they had a lot of activities. A man stepped out from the front row and walked up onto the platform then asked everyone to stand and join him in worship.

Kara's alto harmony blended with the voices around her. She closed her eyes and focused on the words to the familiar tune flowing from her lips. The tension in her shoulders melted, leaving her at ease until she opened her eyes. Jeff sat a few rows up, and reality hit Kara hard.

She was here on an assignment because God had allowed her cover to be blown. Kara thought when she became a Christian several years ago that He'd watch out for her. Didn't the Bible say He'd never leave or forsake her? She stopped singing, and the tension returned. How could Jeff stand there and worship? How could he sing songs of praise to a God that allowed the bad guys to destroy lives, hers included?

Gail nudged her shoulder and whispered. "Everything okay?"

Kara forced a smile and nodded. She had to keep up this charade for her friends, so she resumed singing, but her heart wasn't in it. God had turned His back on her when she needed Him the most. Kara knew the risks when she'd signed on with the DEA but always believed that God would take care of her. She'd trusted Him completely, only to be abandoned in the scariest moment of her life. Fine. If He was going to abandon her, then she'd make it on her own. Things couldn't get much worse.

After church, Kara sat in the backseat of Gail and Kurt's sedan as they headed home.

Gail turned and cast a quizzical glance her way. "What'd you think of the service?"

Kara's thoughts whirled. She'd spent the time during the sermon working up a plan of action for Operation Trail Ride. "It was fine. I saw the announcement in the bulletin about the community picnic in the park this afternoon. Are you planning on going?"

Gail gazed at her husband. "We wouldn't miss it."

Kurt nodded. "After the picnic, we'll drive out to Lake Aimee. It'll remind you of Miami with its sandy shore." He made a sharp right. "But as you know, you won't find any palm trees, only pines.

"Do they still shoot off the fireworks over the lake?"

Kurt nodded. "It's quite a show. You up for a full day of fun?"

"Sounds like a must-see event. How did the lake get its name?" She'd been to the lake as a teen but always wondered about the origins of its name.

"Beats me," Gail said. "But I hear it means much loved."

"Hmm." Kara leaned against the headrest. *Much loved.* Life with the DEA had been non-stop for the past year and always busy even before that. At the rate she was going, she'd never find a special love.

A text message drew her attention. The DEA had been busy. They already secured a lease on a storefront property in downtown Sunridge. The back half of the property had been converted into a studio apartment. She was to drop by in the morning and spend a few hours putting her new nail salon in order. Playtime was over, and now the real work would begin.

Jeff strolled through Sunridge Central Park. He'd joined Eric's family for the Fourth of July picnic. Small groups of people spread throughout the park. Blankets and camp-style chairs littered the grass, and every picnic table appeared occupied. A rustic pavilion stood center stage where a montage of live music would be performed throughout the day. The scent of roasting hot dogs drifted through the air, causing Jeff's stomach to rumble.

Veronica turned toward him as they walked along the paved path. Her designer jeans and fancy top out of place in the casually dressed crowd. "I had Eric set up our canopy yesterday. It's that blue one with the white chairs underneath."

Jeff followed the direction of her finger and smirked. A huge banner that said WATERS FAMILY hung from one side of the canopy to the other.

Lauren grabbed her mom's hand. "Can I go see Jessica?" She pointed to a picnic table off to their right.

Veronica nodded. "That's fine—just check in every now and then." She shook her head at his niece's back as Lauren took off across the lawn.

Jeff chuckled. "She didn't waste any time ditching us old fogies."

"You know teenagers." Veronica turned to Eric. "Honey, after you drop off the cooler, will you take Jeff around and introduce him to our friends?"

Jeff missed Eric's reply. A familiar figure caught his attention a few feet away from the canopy. Kara's ponytail swung from side to side as she shook her head. Her cuts and bruises were no longer visible—she must have used some serious makeup to cover them. She looked cute in khaki pants and a loose-fitting T-shirt.

A grin spread across his face. The time off had served her well. He followed his family to their reserved area, all the time keeping an eye on Kara until she spotted him and waved.

"You're already making friends with the ladies, I see," Veronica said.

He scratched the back of his neck and squinted into the bright sunshine. "That's Kara. We met at the park the other day."

Veronica fussed with the picnic basket and cast furtive looks toward his co-worker. It seemed Veronica was more than a little curious.

"Do you want to meet her? I could introduce you."

"I don't know. There's still stuff that needs to be set up." She moved the cooler.

Eric nudged her forward. "Go ahead. I can take care of things here."

"No. I want to make sure everything's just right. You go."

Eric shrugged. "You heard the lady." The men walked side by side over to where Kara stood visiting with a tall woman.

"Hi, Gail," Eric said.

The auburn-haired woman turned at the sound of her name. Her face broke into a generous smile. "Eric, how are you?" She reached back and gently took Kara's arm. "You haven't met my friend Kara Nelson. She recently moved here from Miami."

Kara grinned. "Hi."

Eric nodded. "This is my brother Jeff. He's from Miami also. But I guess the two of you have met."

A gleam lit Kara's eyes, and she shook his hand. "Yes. I hope you're hanging onto your money."

Eric and Gail both gave her an odd look, but neither questioned her statement.

"I think so. I sure appreciated you giving back the twenty I dropped. A lot of people would have kept it."

"Anytime."

Eric chatted with the women for a few minutes. Kara seemed to be listening intently, but Jeff could see that her attention was divided.

Kara waved to someone near the playground. "Excuse me. I see someone I'd like to say hello to. It was nice meeting you, Eric." She looked at Jeff. "Maybe I'll see you around."

"I hope so." Jeff watched as she walked across the grass with no visible limp. Her leg must be healing fast.

The men said good-bye to Gail and walked toward their picnic area.

"Lady caught your eye, I see," Eric said. "She's cute. You should ask her out."

Hmm, maybe Eric was on to something. Jeff raised his brows. "I might."

Veronica waved the men back to their picnic area.

"Looks like the food's ready." Eric picked up the pace.

Jeff grabbed a soda and sat on the blanket. Veronica placed a plate piled high with fried chicken on a portable table. Jeff's stomach rumbled. "I haven't had homemade fried chicken since I was a boy." He leaned in close and inhaled deeply. "Smells tasty."

"Thank you. I see your friend is talking with Marci." Veronica grinned, but the smile didn't reach her eyes.

Jeff turned and spotted a tall brunette woman with Kara.

"She shouldn't associate with that woman," Veronica ground out between clenched teeth.

Jeff felt his eyebrows rise. "Really. Why?"

Eric held up a chicken leg and waved it at his wife. "Will you stop? I told you there's nothing going on between Marci and me. I barely know the woman." He turned to Jeff. "I'm pretty certain Veronica has managed to turn every married woman in this town against Marci. She does ads. I hired her a couple weeks ago to design a campaign for the ranch. We spent quite a bit of time together one evening going over the print ads, and Veronica has it in her head that Marci—"

Jeff hooked a thumb on his belt loop. "This is none of my business. No need to explain. And who Kara chooses to visit with is *her* business." Jeff glanced over at Veronica who was shooting missiles with her eyes at her husband.

Veronica's face tinged pink. "Excuse me." She stood and walked toward their truck.

"I'm sorry about that, Eric." He'd done it this time. Veronica would kick him out for sure.

"No need. Veronica isn't mad at you. She just can't stand Marci. Strange, too, because my wife usually gets along with everyone. I don't understand why she won't believe me about Marci. We seriously only had dinner together to go over the ads. That's it."

That did seem kind of extreme even for Veronica. But maybe Eric had given her reason to doubt him before. Jeff leaned back on his elbows and watched Kara. Why had she homed in on the one woman Veronica couldn't stand? He sighed. A text popped in on his cell. *Meet me tonight at Lake Aimee near the restrooms.*

Darkness closed in around the lake. Long shadows from the ponderosa pines danced across the sandy beach. Prickles of anticipation rippled through the crowd. Kara strolled toward Gail and Kurt who sat snuggled together on a quilted blanket along the shore. In spite of the large turnout, quiet had settled over the shoreline. Crickets chirped, oblivious to the impending fireworks. Gail patted the spot next to her. "Come join us. The fireworks will be soaring over the lake any minute. You don't want to be wandering around when all the lights go off."

Kara looked around and spotted the restrooms on the edge of the sandy beach. "I need to visit the ladies' room. Don't worry about me. I'll watch the show from wherever I'm standing."

"Okay. We'll pack up and leave when it's over, so if we're not here when you get back, meet us at the car."

Kara nodded and hustled across the grass toward the restrooms while at the same time keeping a look out for Jeff. Where was he? She stopped and pretended to get a rock out of her shoe.

A thunderous boom accompanied by bright red, white, and blue fireworks announced the beginning of the show. A live brass band added to the drama with patriotic music as the fireworks burst overhead. The sky glowed with the display.

Kara crossed her bare arms. She forgot how cool the air became in the evenings. Where was Jeff? About five minutes into the show, someone gripped her arm. She jumped then quickly turned and looked over her shoulder—Jeff. He motioned for her to follow him deeper into the trees.

Jeff stood close and spoke in hushed tones. "Who's Marci? Veronica told me to warn you to stay away from her. She related to the case?"

"I don't think so, but I'm not ruling anyone out just yet. She's familiar looking, but I can't place her. It's driving me nuts too—but Marci didn't seem to know me so maybe she has one of those faces."

"Hmm. I'm guessing she has one of those faces."

"You're probably right." She shrugged. "The other moms don't accept her. I'm not sure why. Which by itself isn't that big of a deal, but today, when I was visiting with her at the park, she acted strange. Her eyes were dilated and her hands shook. This might be a stretch, but I think she could be using drugs. If so, maybe we can flip her and find out who her supplier is at the very least."

"Maybe, but not yet," Jeff said. "As for the moms not liking her, I believe Marci is to blame for that. Is there anything else going on?"

"I have an office space with an attached apartment lined up, so I'll be out of Gail and Kurt's place soon. How about you? Find anything interesting?"

"Not yet, but things are going well with my family."

"Good. I need to get over to the ranch soon," Kara said.

"Agreed. I have the feeling my family would like it if you spent more time with me."

Kara couldn't help smiling. She wouldn't mind spending more time with him. She missed the camaraderie they'd had in Vero Beach when she was recovering from her car bomb injuries.

The loud boom of the fireworks' grand finale cut off Jeff's words. The crowd cheered and clapped. Applause rang out, and Jeff's warm breath brushed her neck. Tingles zipped through her.

"Stop by the ranch, and we'll talk more." Jeff's words tickled her ear.

Cool air assaulted the space Jeff had left when he moved, and she shivered. She'd never reacted to any of her partners like that before—not even Tony. Then again, Jeff wasn't just anyone. He'd been with her through one of the worst times of her life, and she'd come to depend on him as more than just a partner. He'd become a friend. They'd been thrust together under the worst of circumstances. His easy way had made the ordeal not only bearable, but enjoyable at times. She shut off her thoughts—no time for introspection.

Kara rubbed her hands up and down her arms. The park lights came on, and she picked her way through the crowd. A scream burst through the air. Kara stopped and listened. Someone plowed into her from behind, knocking her to the ground. Air whooshed from her lungs and searing pain stabbed her shoulder. She rolled over and looked up into angry eyes.

8

Kara stared back into the eyes of a livid young man—probably not more than twenty-three—who'd fallen on top of her. The guy wasn't budging. "You mind?" Kara pushed hard at his chest with her good arm. At this rate, her shoulder would never be the same.

He blinked and pushed up, fighting to gain his footing. "Whoa. Sorry, lady. My girlfriend and I just had a huge fight, and I wasn't watching where I was going."

"No harm done." Unless you count the headache and throbbing shoulder his jolt had caused. Too bad she couldn't snap his picture, just to be on the safe side. She took a mental picture instead. Coffee-colored short hair, clean-shaven, small eyes, medium-sized straight nose, and full mouth—nothing overly defining about the average-looking guy.

She watched as he strode away. Who was his girlfriend? Kara backtracked the guy's steps.

An older man stopped her. "You okay? I saw that hooligan barrel into you."

"I'm fine. Did you see the woman who screamed?"

"Afraid not." He looked around with a frown covering his face.

"That's okay." Kara searched the sea of faces. No woman stood around looking sad or angry. Concern edged into the back of her mind. Someone had screamed, but who? Had the guy knocked someone else down too? She tucked away the encounter and made her way to Gail and Kurt.

Kara sat in Gail's kitchen munching on a bagel, enjoying the quiet of the morning. Sunlight filtered through the window and cascaded onto the table, warming the room.

Gail walked into the kitchen. "Do you want a ride over to the high school?"

"No, thanks," Kara said. "I'm only sticking around for the first couple of hours to help with registration. When I'm finished, I have a few errands." She'd drawn a quick sketch of the guy she'd encountered last night and planned to show it to Jeff. "And then I'm heading over to my new place." She patted her duffel bag sitting on the chair beside her. "I'm all packed and want to get settled. I'm sure glad the apartment came furnished."

"So it's moving day?"

"Yes. The sooner I get moved in, the quicker I can start taking clients."

"I suppose that's true, but we'll miss having you

here. I'll call and schedule a manicure soon."

Kara stood, enveloped Gail in a hug, then pulled back. "Thanks. It'll be on the house. Then you can tell all your friends about me."

"You sure you want me to do that? I know that's not the real reason you're here."

Kara stiffened. That Gail knew she worked for the DEA was more than a little disconcerting. "As far as anyone else is concerned, I'm a nail technician, and that's exactly what they need to think for your safety and the safety of my partner."

"Partner?"

"Forget I said that."

"Said what?"

"Nothing. I've enjoyed staying with you, but we both know I can't live here indefinitely. Five days are long enough to entertain a house guest." Four days too long in her opinion. She loved her friend, but she valued her own space.

"Not according to Eric Waters. His brother, Jeff, is planning on staying a few weeks."

"That's a long visit." Kara poured a second cup of coffee and took a sip.

"Yes, but Eric says they haven't seen each other in years. He's looking forward to spending more time with Jeff, and his niece seems to adore her uncle."

Kara wrapped the bagel in a napkin and took a quick gulp of coffee. "Speaking of his niece, I need to go. I'm supposed to be at the music camp a half hour early."

"Okay, I'll see you later."

Kara was almost to her car when Gail called to her. "Kara, how did you know Lauren would be at the camp today?"

"Jeff must've mentioned it. I saw him at the lake last night."

Gail turned back to the house with a smile lighting her face.

Kara chuckled to herself. The idea of her and Jeff. Preposterous! Well, maybe not preposterous, but not possible. They were partners and friends, nothing more. She didn't have time to complicate her life with romance.

The perma-grin plastered to Kara's face hurt as she greeted yet another student while seated at the registration table in the high school hallway, but still no Lauren. A surge of musicians had arrived when the doors first opened for registration and now only a few stragglers remained to register. She wanted to make a connection with Jeff's family. Lauren seemed to be the perfect solution. Hopefully, she would show soon.

The door opened once again, and Lauren walked in accompanied by her Uncle Jeff. Kara's breath caught in her throat and her face warmed. Good grief, she was behaving like an insecure girl. She schooled her face and willed her pulse to slow but failed miserably when his eyes crinkled in her direction. Gail's suggestion was going to her head, and she needed to silence it.

Lauren beamed at her. "Hi! I'm Lauren Waters."

Kara found Lauren's name on the registration list. "Here you are. Glad you could make it. Everyone's gathering in the gym." She handed her a packet and sent her off in the right direction.

"Thanks!" Lauren turned toward Jeff. "See you later, Uncle Jeff."

Kara watched her bounce down the hall, violin case in hand.

Jeff didn't move.

Kara looked up. "How's it going?"

"Fine. I'm surprised to see you. I thought you were new in town."

"I am, but I figured volunteering would be a great way to meet people."

"Smart. Did you enjoy the fireworks last night?" Jeff asked.

"Very much." Except for how it ended. Kara reached for a stack of papers and began to clean up the registration table. She heard the door click shut. Jeff had left without saying good-bye—again.

Jeff strode to his SUV, started the engine, then took out his phone and called Gary on a secure number. "Gary, Jeff here. Do you have Eric's financial records for me yet?" He heard papers shuffling on the other end.

"Yes. Looks like the money trail's a dead end. His wife, Veronica, comes from money, and it appears her family fronted the finances for the ranch."

Jeff sat a little taller and didn't try to hold back the grin that spread across his face. A little good news on the home front was always welcome.

"I don't mind checking on this for you, but remember, you have the local DEA at your full disposal."

"Right. I haven't had time to get over there yet. Things here are busy."

"At least touch base with Tad Baker. He's a local deputy and the task force leader. He should be a big help."

"Got it." Maybe Tad would have some information on Jake.

9

A business sign that read Nails by Kara, snagged Jeff's attention. He hadn't spotted that place the last time he'd been in town. Jeff pulled into a parking spot on the side of the street. He opened his door, got out, and looked again.

This was not one of Kara's better ideas. If he wasn't mistaken, she had used that same cover prior to her time in Miami. Jeff walked over to the salon and tried the door. Locked. He peered through the large window. The place looked empty except for a small desk and a few chairs. A light came on in the back of the office.

He knocked on the door. Kara must have come into the room from the back and turned on the lights. He knocked again, and she entered the front room. She walked to the door and unlocked it.

Jeff stepped over the threshold, locking the door behind him. The stuffy room smelled stale. "What are you thinking posting a sign out in front like that? Whether you choose to accept it or not, you're still a target. Alvarado is out there somewhere, and advertising a business with your name on it is going to show up on any search they do."

Kara kept her voice level. "I'm doing my job the best way I know how. Yes, I've used this cover in the past, but it's a great way to meet the locals."

"So is working in an ice cream shop."

Kara crossed her arms. "You'd be surprised what people will tell you over a paraffin wax. I suppose putting my name on the sign might not have been wise, but the DEA set all of this up. If someone who wants me dead tracks me down because my name is in the title of this business then so be it. At least that way I can deal with them instead of constantly looking over my shoulder. I refuse to play the victim."

"I guess I'd feel the same way in your position, but be careful." It was her life, and she had to live it. But that wouldn't stop him from keeping an extra close eye on her.

"Any new developments on the case?" She perched on the edge of her well-used desk.

Jeff walked to the nearest chair and sat. "The money angle didn't fly. Veronica comes from money, and her parents helped out." He shrugged. "I'll keep digging. It's strange though. You'd think I'd know my own sister-in-law was rich."

"Not necessarily. There are lots of rich people out there who don't wave their money for the world to see."

"True. Thanks."

"No problem. How're you doing? It must stink investigating your own brother."

"Stepbrother. We're only related by marriage."

"Right. Stepbrother or not, I think it's awful that you have to investigate him."

"Me too, but I'm determined to do my job regardless of the outcome." He propped his ankle up on his knee. "It was convenient you have friends in town."

Kara crossed her arms. "I guess, but I hated putting their lives in danger. I'm glad this spot opened up, and I could get out of their place."

He nodded. "How did you end up as a nail person anyway?"

"I went to beauty school right out of high school. Worked in a shop for about a year after I graduated and decided it wasn't for me." She pried open a box. "As you can see, though, it follows me wherever I go." She pulled out a few bottles of nail polish and placed them on the desk. "The local DEA arranged for me to open up shop here and provided the supplies and permits." She dug through another box. "You want to give me a hand? I have to get this place set up for business ASAP."

"Sure. I can help for a couple hours. What needs to be done?"

"Everything. I'll start on the paint if you'll unpack the boxes. I'll take inventory later. Just keep the supplies in the center of the room so nothing gets ruined."

"Okay, but maybe I should paint. I have no idea what all this stuff is." He felt like a man in the lingerie department—lost.

Kara stuffed a roll of masking tape in his hand. "On second thought, have at it. I hate painting."

Jeff made quick work of taping off the moldings

then began to cover the walls in a light green paint while Kara sifted through the various boxes. "Aren't you supposed to have some special chairs and such for a place like this?"

Kara raised an eyebrow in his direction. "So the macho man has been inside a salon."

He sputtered. "No. I—"

Kara laughed and held out her hand. "It's okay. I'm only teasing. I know they have these places everywhere. A walk through any mall and you'd know what kind of equipment to expect. Other than an armoire that's coming later today, the chairs and stuff are being delivered tomorrow. I wanted to get the paint on the walls and sort through my supplies before it all arrives."

"Looks like you've emptied most of the boxes. I saw a paint brush in the corner," Jeff teased.

She checked her watch. "I'll be right back to help. I need to run across the street and place an ad in Wednesday's paper announcing my grand opening."

Jeff watched Kara go out the door, manila envelope in hand, then jog across the street. She had a great setup here. She was right. This was the perfect cover and might yield information about their case.

He moved the roller down the wall with even pressure. Before long, a second wall was covered in the soft green tone.

The front door opened, and Kara ambled back in.

"That was fast."

"I'd already talked with them over the phone. I just needed to drop off the ad copy and a check." She grabbed the paintbrush and worked on the edges Jeff's roller couldn't reach. "Speaking of fast, you accomplished a lot while I was gone."

"I spent one summer working as a house painter."

Kara nodded. "So how do you propose we make this work? You took off last night without answering me."

"I know. Sorry about that. I thought I saw someone in the bushes watching us."

"Why didn't you say something? I could've helped."

He shook his head. "No. You would've had too many questions to answer with your friend. She keeps a close eye on you."

Kara pulled a piece of paper from her back pocket, unfolded it, and handed it to Jeff. "This guy ran into me last night after the fireworks."

Jeff studied the face. "You're talented at this. Wish I could draw."

"Does he look familiar?"

"I don't know. Have you shown this to Tad?" Jeff asked.

"Thought I'd run it by you first."

"I haven't seen him." Jeff shook his head. "Does he concern you?"

She shrugged. "He said he had a fight with his girlfriend, but I couldn't find her when I went looking. It could've been an accident like he said, but I sketched him just in case."

"Mind if I make a copy of this?"

"Sure. But I want the original back."

Kara might not be concerned about this guy, but he sure was. It seemed to be too much of a coincidence that someone was listening to them in the bushes. Then some dude tramples Kara. "Tell me about Gail. Have you known her long?"

"Practically forever. She was a cool big sister when I was in high school."

"What're you talking about?"

"That's how we know each other. She was a volunteer in the Big Brother/Big Sister program."

He nodded. Even though it made things a bit more complicated to have her friend here, he was glad for her presence. Friends helped keep life in perspective.

"What in the world?" Kara dropped the brush. She ran to the door, flicked the lock, and flung it open.

Jeff followed close on her heels then looked up and down the street. No one appeared to be in a hurry. Only a few pedestrians were out. A mom and her three children entered the ice cream shop across the street. A guy in his mid to late twenties pushed his bike into the repair shop a few doors down, and an elderly gentleman shuffled along the sidewalk. Kara turned and frowned.

She walked back inside, pulling him in with her and gentled her voice. "I'm almost sure I saw someone at the front window watching us. But I only caught a flash of a body."

"First, I see someone last night. Then you get trampled and now this. What's going on?"

"Do you think it's Alvarado or someone related to this case?" Kara asked.

"Hard to say. But in the meantime, make sure you're extra careful." He watched Kara cringe and fought his desire to give her a shoulder to lean on. She'd been through so much these past weeks.

"There's no way he could have tracked me down

already."

"We're talking about Luis Alvarado. The man has eyes and ears on two continents. If he wants to find you, he will."

"Thanks for the pep talk. You really suck at this cheering up thing."

"Didn't realize that's what I was doing." He grinned. "Something Eric said gave me an idea. You might hate it, but hear me out."

"Shoot."

Jeff stepped closer. "We become a couple."

Kara backed up a step. Her heart rate increased. Could she pretend to have feelings and not actually fall for him? She already found herself attracted to him. He took another step toward her. Her right foot bumped the last unpainted wall, and she stopped.

Jeff stood directly in front of her, all six-feet-five inches of him, his arms perched on each side of her shoulders, palms flat on the wall. "Think about it, Kara. If we appear to be romantically involved, the chances of someone suspecting we're working together would be slim, even if you are being followed. We have to spend time together, and you need access to the ranch. They'd think we're a couple. End of story."

Kara licked her lips. He looked down at her, his gaze bored into her, waiting for her reply. She didn't want to do this, but their options were limited. She needed to spend time on the ranch, and Jeff's idea solved that problem. "Fine, but don't overdo it, okay? I have friends in Sunridge, and I don't want this getting back to my parents."

Jeff lowered his arms and backed away. "Don't worry. Your parents are in Europe. I'm the one with family nearby." He crossed his arms and drew a slow breath. "I wouldn't suggest this if I didn't think it would work."

"Your idea is good, and it'll give me the perfect cover. No one will wonder why your girlfriend is hanging out on the ranch."

Jeff smiled. "We should be seen together in public, but not too much. We don't want to look like we're trying to draw attention to ourselves." He paced the room a couple times and spun back around to face her. "Have dinner with me tonight at the diner."

"What time?"

"Six. I'll pick you up here."

"No, let's meet there. I never let a guy pick me up on a first date." Kara could see the surprise in his eyes. "If it's an awful date, I have my own transportation, and I can leave whenever I want. Gail knows that's how I roll, so I don't want to mix things up."

"Fine. See you at six."

Kara watched as he sauntered out the door. For the first time in five minutes, she breathed freely. This definitely complicated things, but then again, it made the case easier. If she and Jeff appeared to be dating, she wouldn't have to use Lauren, and no one would suspect the real reason for her presence on the ranch. Her job had just become easier—or maybe more difficult.

10

Jeff glanced out the window and spotted Kara from his seat against the back wall of the diner. She pushed open the door and waved when she spotted him. Her sleeveless white blouse skimmed her body in all the right places, and her light blue skirt stopped just above her knees. He ran his hand over his face and tried to focus on the reason he was there—to set up a sting.

She wasn't beautiful in the classic sense, but her petite frame and small heart-shaped face were as cute as they come. He pushed down feelings of attraction that were bubbling to the surface.

Kara slid into the booth across from him. Her eyes danced. "Isn't this place great? I came in earlier today to check it out."

Jeff looked around and shrugged. The fifties décor didn't fit with the rest of the town, but it did have a certain charm. "I like the menu."

"Do you know what you want to order?"

"Definitely the Cardiac Burger," Jeff said.

"No way. They really call it that?" Kara studied the

plastic covered sheet. "A half-pound of ground beef, smothered in secret sauce, cheddar cheese, bacon, jalapeño peppers, onions, lettuce and tomato. Unbelievable. That sounds like a lot of grease. You're a daring man." She pointed to the salad section. "I'm sticking with the grilled chicken Caesar salad. I've heard they're huge and delicious."

"Boring is more like it." Then again, boring could be nice. Life had been far from boring lately, and this case was as hot as a jalapeño pepper.

A tall brunette wearing a white apron around her ample waist approached the table. "Are you ready to order?"

After placing their orders, Jeff took a long drink of water and lowered his voice. "Any more mystery visitors show up at your window?"

"Not that I've noticed, and I've been watching," Kara whispered back. "We could be jumping to conclusions. Maybe the person in the woods was a kid messing around, and the guy in the window could've been curious about a new business in town."

"True, but I sense trouble."

Kara's shoulders sagged. Then she moved back into character with practiced ease and a smile firmly planted on her face. She glanced at Jeff. "Are you enjoying the time with your brother?"

"I've liked being on a ranch again. The location may be different, but ranching is pretty much the same everywhere."

"I forgot you grew up in the country. Montana, right?"

"Yes."

"I've heard it's pretty."

"It is."

"How'd Eric wind up in Central Oregon?"

"Veronica has family in the area. The only time I've ever seen them was at the wedding. Our families have never been close." He raised his eyebrow. "Food's here."

The waitress placed a huge jalapeño bacon cheeseburger in front of Jeff and a generous salad in front of Kara. She speared a forkful of lettuce.

Jeff's eyes bulged as he studied his cheeseburger, but he didn't take a bite. They weren't kidding when they named it the Cardiac Burger.

Kara grinned as she reloaded her fork. "Something wrong with your burger?"

"No, just bigger than I expected. I'm surprised they found a bun big enough." He picked it up, took a bite, then chewed slowly. The enthusiasm he normally felt when eating a juicy burger was absent. The mystery person wouldn't leave his mind. Why had someone been watching them, but more important who? He had to find out. A deep frown settled on his face, and he set the burger down. He couldn't eat with so much to think about.

"You better watch out. That look on your face might send people ducking for cover." She took a sip from her straw and coughed.

"You okay?"

She choked out, "swallowed wrong." Tears filled her eyes. She coughed a few more times then took another drink of water. "I'm fine."

"I hate it when that happens."

"Tell me about it." Kara looked down at what was left of her salad then at his half-eaten burger. "What do you say we get out of here and go back to my place. I have Rocky Road ice cream." She waggled her brows.

Jeff laughed as he held up his burger and continued to chew.

Kara shook her head. "Your mind is a million miles away, and I suspect you haven't even tasted one bite. How about you get a to-go box and bring it with you?"

"I'm good. This burger should come with a warning." He patted his stomach then stood.

Once outside the diner, Kara slid her hand into Jeff's. "Let's walk. It's cooled off some, and the temperature's perfect." They strolled in silence until they reached Kara's apartment. She unlocked the door and opened it wide, inviting him in, but he didn't enter. She placed her hand on his arm. "What's wrong?"

Jeff shook his head. "Nothing. I should head back to the ranch." He covered her hand with his own. "By the way, you look great tonight."

"Thanks. You look nice yourself. Once I get a feel for the situation at the ranch, we should meet to discuss strategy."

"Agreed." Jeff turned to leave, but Kara grabbed his arm.

"Are you sure you're okay? If there's something you want to talk about I—"

"I'll let you know." No way did he want to let on how concerned he was about the guy at the lake.

Neither he nor Kara had said anything critical to the operation, but not knowing who to look out for was unnerving. It'd be best to keep Kara nearby just in case they'd somehow been followed. "Come by the ranch tomorrow? We can go horseback riding to add some credibility to our cover."

She nodded. "Sounds like a plan. I'm serving lunch at the music camp, and then the delivery guys are supposed to bring my salon furniture between one and three. Maybe we could also talk about what's bugging you."

"Maybe." Jeff turned and walked to his SUV. He didn't want to upset her by suggesting Luis Alvarado had found her. Then again, if it were one of his cronies, she'd already be dead. No. This had to have something to do with their current assignment.

11

With the sun finally down, Kara dressed in all black and slipped out the back door into the alley. The town seemed to be asleep as she drove down Main Street and made a left toward the ranch. She turned off onto a forestry road and maneuvered her car behind some tall brush and between several tall Ponderosa Pines.

Satisfied her car was well concealed from the road; Kara shut off the engine and slid out. She pulled a blanket, thermos, collapsible chair, and night vision glasses from the backseat then found the perfect spot to sit and wait. From her concealed vantage point she had an adequate view of the ranch's main entrance. Anyone entering or leaving in a vehicle had to pass by here, including anyone who might try and spy on her. If anything unusual happened tonight, she'd be ready and waiting.

Silence surrounded her. Even the crickets seemed to be resting. She settled deeper into the seat and sipped the strong black coffee she'd hurriedly made. Guilt gripped her. She should've told Jeff what she was up to, but in all fairness, the decision had been split second. It's not like she planned a stakeout tonight. Surely, he'd understand why she didn't include him. Especially with the way he was acting during and after dinner. By his own admission, the case was getting to him. Maybe she'd discover something that would wrap things up quickly.

The intel suggested that drugs were being smuggled onto the ranch and from there delivered to a major distributor. Apparently, the Mexican drug cartel employed the suspects, Fernando and Andrea Gonzales, but every time they'd been detained, no drugs had been found. Yet in spite of this, large quantities of cocaine always flooded the market soon after the Gonzaleses' departure. The coincidence was too big to ignore.

Luis Alvarado, the king of corruptness and all things evil, flashed in her mind. She clenched her teeth. Someday, she'd come face to face with that man again, and this time she would take care of business. No way would he be allowed to terrorize another human being with his unscrupulous ways. More than one of his associates had disappeared in the past year as well as countless other people victimized by his drug-related crimes. As soon as he was arrested, she'd gladly testify against him. But Luis was trouble for another day.

Two hours later, a small beam of light moving from the direction of the house caught Kara's attention. The person carrying the flashlight stopped near the entrance to the ranch driveway. She leaned forward in her chair and spotted what looked to be a man, but she couldn't see his face. Wearing the night vision goggles she stood and slunk closer. The guy had his back to her and appeared to be waiting for someone. She stopped and knelt behind a large rock. From there, she would have a decent view of his face when he turned around.

The man's cell phone rang. He cursed and snatched it up. "Where are you?" He walked a little farther away.

Kara strained to hear but didn't dare get any closer.

"No. I'm on my way." Footsteps crunched on the gravel driveway. Then he darted across the road and faded into the woods. She'd check the dirt near the road for prints in the daylight tomorrow.

The risk of being caught was too great if she followed. If only he would've turned around and let her see his face. One thing she knew for certain—she'd never heard his voice before.

Later that morning, Kara squinted at herself in the bathroom mirror and tried to ignore her pounding headache. Puffy eyes hinted at her lack of sleep. A few strategically placed ice cubes ought to do the trick. She lay back on the bed as the ice cubes did their magic.

The phone jingled. Kara rolled over and snatched it from the bedside table. She checked the caller ID—eleven thirty. Yikes, no wonder Gail was calling. She stumbled from the bed. "Hi, Gail. I'm on my way." She ended the call, pulled her hair into a ponytail, then splashed water on her face. Glancing at her reflection in the mirror, she stopped. "Oh my goodness." The campers could wait. Makeup was a must today. Five minutes later, keys in hand, she hustled to her car.

Gail spotted her and made a direct line toward her.

"You said you'd be here at eleven. Is everything okay?"

Kara whispered. "I had a late night."

Gail's eyes widened. "Oh."

Kara scurried to the cafeteria and flung open the swinging door. Random smells of past lunches assaulted her nose, much like the lunchroom at school when she was a kid, but the distinct smell of marinara sauce wafted through the air. Soft voices filtered from the kitchen. She hustled to the back of the room and entered through a swinging door. Two women worked side by side at the center island.

"Kara. Glad you made it."

"Yeah. Sorry I'm late."

Jessica Swift, the camp director had filled in for her. Even in a hairnet, Jessica managed to look stunning with her perfect figure and creamy completion.

"Time got away from me." Kara snatched up a butter knife.

Jessica pulled the hairnet from her head and her long dark hair flowed freely over her shoulders. "Don't worry about it. The reprieve was nice. I never thought I could be tired of music, but even I need a break sometimes."

Kara slowed her breathing, trying to relax. "Thanks, Jessica. What can I do to help?"

"How about you take over for me and butter the bread?"

Kara washed her hands and got busy. "How's the camp going?"

Jessica unwound the apron from her tiny waist and loaded the napkin dispenser. "Better than I expected.

This is the first time I've organized a music camp, and it amazes me how supportive the community has been to an outsider like me."

Kara paused with her knife midair. "What do you mean an outsider?"

"I moved here from Seattle last fall to teach music at the elementary school, but I grew up in the Portland area."

Kara nodded. "The people here have been very kind to me too, especially the Waters family."

"That's Lauren's family, right?"

"Yes. Do you know them well?" Maybe Jessica would have observed something she'd missed.

"Not especially. They attend my church though. I'm really enjoying listening to their daughter play the violin here at camp. That girl has talent."

The cafeteria doors opened, and a small group of teens entered. Jessica excused herself and went over to the students. Kara chewed her bottom lip. It seemed the Waters hadn't made much of an impression in Jessica's mind. The family must keep to themselves in spite of being involved in the community. Why? Were they simply private people, or did they have something to hide like CODE believed?

12

Jeff felt in his pocket for the pin-sized cameras the DEA had approved. He climbed into the barn loft and hid one, placing it in a crack between the floorboards directly over Jake's office. Then he headed back down and tucked the other mini-cam inside a small hole in one of the stall posts. This position would capture anyone entering the front door of the barn.

Satisfied with the camera placements, he grabbed a pitchfork and made his way into a stall. Jeff swiped at a fly then pitched the soiled straw into a wheelbarrow. The smell and the heat were annoying, but tolerable. His thoughts drifted to Kara as they had many times since their "date" last night. Worry nibbled at his brain when he considered the feelings beginning to form toward his partner. He had to shut off that kind of thinking before he did or said something he'd regret. The razzing he'd take from the other agents and the unprofessionalism of falling for his partner were enough to get his mind refocused.

Eric stepped into view. "Jeff, when you're finished,

would you throw some fresh straw and grain into a clean stall. A new horse is coming in later."

"Sure thing." Jeff wanted to ask about the horse, but Eric disappeared as fast as he'd arrived. There were several clean stalls already. He'd pour grain into the closest one and bed it with straw. On the other hand, if the animal was skittish, maybe Eric would want it a little farther away from the other horses. He'd have to ask Eric. Pitchfork laid aside, he went in search of his stepbrother.

Eric stood hands on his hips near the fence facing Jake, his wrangler. What he'd give to be privy to that conversation.

Jake nodded toward Jeff as he approached but then walked away.

Eric looked over his shoulder and frowned. "What's up?"

"Sorry to bother you."

"No bother. What do you need?"

"Which stall do you want bedded?"

"I don't care."

Jeff turned and hesitated.

"What?" Eric asked.

"Nothing." He made his way toward the barn. Now wasn't the time to grill him about Jake. The crunch of gravel drew his attention to the driveway where a Honda Civic drove toward him—Kara.

She parked near the barn and moseyed toward him holding an impressive looking camera. He whistled softly. Except for the backpack she wore, Kara nailed the cowgirl look with jeans and a red tank top. Cowboy boots peeked out from under the hem of her jeans, and a brown cowboy hat sat atop her head.

"Hi there!" Kara waved.

"You've been shopping." Jeff noticed Jake standing near the house gawking at Kara but ignored him as he strode past Jake and greeted her with a quick peck on the cheek. He lowered his voice. "What's in the backpack?

"Telephoto lens and it's heavy. It's in a hard case stuffed inside my pack. Since last night, I decided to never leave home without it."

"Last night?"

"You'll see. Ready to ride?"

He took a step back and led her into the barn. "Almost. Take a seat. I have to finish this stall before we can go riding."

"No problem. Can I help?"

He smirked. "See that pitchfork over there? It's used to scoop out leftovers."

Kara backed away, hands raised, palms out. "I don't think so. Mind if I wander around a bit? It's been awhile since I've been on a ranch."

"Knock yourself out. If anyone asks, tell them you're with me."

Kara grinned. This had worked out perfectly. While Jeff finished, she could snoop. She still needed to check for footprints from last night's surveillance. She hadn't stopped on the way in because she didn't want to draw attention to her car parked on the side of the road, but maybe a quick walk would be a good idea. Hopefully, no one would think twice about someone exploring the ranch on foot.

Kara paused and watched a young girl, her long blond pigtails flying from beneath her helmet, bounce past on her horse in the exercise yard. She couldn't help remembering herself at that age doing the same thing. She had only ridden a handful of times with a friend, but she'd loved every minute in the saddle.

"Hi there. Can I help you?" a man called out behind her.

Kara turned. Looked like the footprints would have to wait. A guy wearing a black cowboy hat and chaps raised his hand as he approached from the direction of the main house—must be Jake. She waved back. Walnut-colored hair peeked out from under his Stetson. She'd seen his picture in her intel, but he was much more attractive in person.

"I'm waiting for Jeff."

Jake sauntered toward the exercise yard as Kara turned to watch the young girl ride past. "The kid comes out every day to exercise her horse. The mare's a beauty, don't you think?"

"Yes, but I don't know much about horses."

Jake gave her a sideways glance. "I imagine a pretty thing like you is a quick learner."

Kara smiled, but inwardly cringed at his suggestive tone.

He sidled up close. "I'd be happy to teach you a

thing or two about horses."

She rolled her eyes and moved a step away. "No, thanks." She raised her camera to her eye and shot a few pictures of the rider.

He cleared his throat and had the grace to look embarrassed. "Nice camera."

"Thanks. It's a hobby." She pointed to the fenced-off land. "What do you call that area?"

"That's the outdoor arena. Behind the barn we have the round pen for training the young horses. Wanna check it out?"

She glanced at her watch. Jeff would be looking for her soon. "I'd love a tour, but it has to be quick." Jake directed her toward the barn then guided her around the side toward the back.

Jeff watched from the barn door as Kara smiled at Jake. He knew that look—tolerant disgust. He'd witnessed it more than once this past year when she'd been undercover investigating Luis Alvarado. He stifled a grin and moved away from the door. The sooner he finished the quicker he and Kara could go riding and see the lay of the land.

He covered the stall with fresh straw and had two horses saddled in record time. With everything done, Jeff went in search of Kara and found her alone on the porch swing holding a sweating glass of lemonade. "You ready to ride?"

Kara patted the space next to her. "Come join me. There's some for you too." She pointed to a glass on the small table near the swing. "Your sister-in-law spotted me in the yard with Jake. I told her you'd be looking for me soon, so she invited me to wait here."

Jeff sat, wiped his forehead with a bandana, then leaned back and drank deeply. "Ahh. That's delicious. Where'd Veronica go?"

"She took off when you came out of the barn, something about needing to call a friend."

Jeff chuckled. This charade might be easier to pull off than he'd thought if Veronica already believed they were a couple or at least on their way to becoming one. "The horses are saddled. You ready?"

Kara set the glass on the table. "Absolutely." She stood and slipped on the backpack then wrapped the camera around her neck. "I haven't ridden in awhile, so I hope you chose a calm horse for me."

"Don't worry. You'll like Blaze. We're taking a trail that's supposed to be level and smooth."

Jeff walked toward the barn with Kara beside him and pointed at her horse. "What do you think?"

"He's big."

Jeff chuckled. "They usually are, but as horses go, he's not large. Blaze is gentle, and I think you'll like him. Just do what I do, and you'll be okay." He handed her the horse's lead and watched as she mounted the black Morgan with ease. Impressed with her agility, he smiled and mounted Lauren's white quarter horse, Lulu.

"Can we head to the road?"

Jeff waited for Kara to come alongside him.

"Why?"

A little ways from the barn, Kara explained in a hushed tone what she'd been up to the night before.

"Okay. We can swing out that way." His tone sounded strained to his own ears. "You know, since we're partners, you should've told me what you were doing last night."

"Sorry. I'm used to working alone." She led him down the driveway and across the main road to the spot in question and peered at the dusty earth. He dismounted and crouched next to some footprints. "Looks like a cowboy boot, size ten or eleven maybe."

Kara nodded, dismounted, and snapped several pictures. "I agree, and it's not mine. I wear an eight." She led her horse a little closer to the trees. "This is where I hid."

Her prints were clear along with some fresh deer tracks. Jeff grabbed a broken juniper branch and swept the ground, eliminating Kara's tracks. Thankfully, traffic was nil, and this area couldn't be seen from the house. "That ought to do it."

Kara nodded. "Who do you suppose was out here?"

"Not sure, but he's about average size and wears cowboy boots." He mounted. "Let's ride." His stomach knotted as they traveled further into the woods. Eric always wore cowboy boots, and if he remembered right, he was about a size eleven.

A rock chuck scampered across the path, but his horse ignored it. Jeff tried to relax and motioned for Kara to come alongside him. "Did you happen to hear him speak?"

"Yes, but I didn't recognize his voice. Of course, he was talking in a stage whisper. So it's hard to say for sure." Kara glanced over at him. "What are you thinking?"

"Do you think it might've been Eric?"

"I would've told you first thing."

Relief embraced him. He nodded.

"Any other new developments with the case?" Kara asked.

"There's a new horse coming in today. I placed two surveillance cameras in the barn. Hopefully, it will be the Gonzaleses. It'll be interesting to see what goes down when they arrive. I want to wrap up this assignment ASAP."

"I agree, but it's nice working with a friendly face instead of the bad guys."

"Can't imagine why. Alvarado and his crew were so friendly," Jeff teased.

She rolled her eyes. "Yeah. It was so much fun working for Miami's most notorious drug lord. Every girl should be so lucky to have a boss that tries to kill her." Sarcasm dripped from her voice.

As they came out of a heavily treed area, Jeff spotted a couple of riders off in the distance on the other side of the river just before they disappeared behind some brush. He reined in his horse. "Did you see that?" His pulse quickened. This could be the break they were waiting for. "Let's check it out." He pushed his horse into a faster gait.

Kara came alongside him. "Hold on. I don't want to get caught in an ambush."

"We're an innocent couple out for a ride. Why would they attack?"

Kara sighed and felt for her side arm. "For the record, I don't like this."

"Noted. Stay close." Their horses' hooves crunched dried grass and weeds on the hard earth, sounding loud in the quiet afternoon. Would the riders hear them coming and bolt? Maybe they should slow down.

Kara moved in as ordered. "You *do* realize we could be riding into a trap?"

Jeff pulled his horse to a stop and tried to keep his voice neutral. "What do you suggest?" He stomped down his frustration. Kara seemed to have forgotten he was the senior agent in this partnership. But she had good instincts, so he'd hear her out.

"I say we continue as if we never spotted them." She pointed off to the right. "That side trail over there seems to head up. We can find a lookout and check out the situation from there."

Her plan seemed reasonable, but they could lose sight of the men. He'd taken that route just the other day. It was a bit of a steep climb, but from what he'd seen of Kara's riding, she could handle it. "Fine. We'll do it your way this time, but I hope they don't disappear. There's a decent-sized boulder near the river. We should be high enough from there to see quite a distance." Jeff turned his mount and stayed on a deer trail. Kara's horse snorted as she followed close behind him on the narrow path flanked by junipers and low-lying shrubbery.

When they came out of the brush near the bank of

the river, Jeff turned and watched Kara pause, seemingly mesmerized by the view. The slow-moving river flowed as a red-winged black bird sang out from atop the boulder just ahead. Too bad they didn't have time to enjoy the sight. "No time for sightseeing. Come on."

Kara pursed her lips and nodded. "I know what's at stake, but if we're being watched, we need to look like we're out here to enjoy the scenery."

She had a point, however he was anxious to get up on that rock before the men disappeared, if they hadn't already.

After dismounting and tethering their horses to a large juniper, Jeff led her to a flat-topped boulder. He found a toe hold and climbed up. "Hand me your camera. We might be able to take a few surveillance shots."

Kara secured her foot in the same spot Jeff had and stretched her arms up pulling herself to the top.

"I'm impressed by how fast your body has healed."

"Ha. Not fast enough for me." She sat on the smooth rock and rolled her shoulders then stretched her arms. "You see them?"

Sitting tall, he held binoculars to his eyes. "Sure do. Check it out. Across the river."

Kara reached out her hand and put the lenses to her eyes. "Three of them. Here you go." She gave the binoculars back to Jeff. She slipped the pack off her back, pulled out the case, and removed a telephoto lens. "Maybe I can get a decent picture to circulate to the team." After connecting the lens to the camera, she rolled over onto her stomach and took shot after shot.

"Great idea." He studied the terrain and spotted a small arsenal propped against some rocks but didn't see any additional riders. "We're far enough away I don't think they noticed us. We could find a safe place to cross and get a closer look."

"Didn't you see those machine guns?" Kara pointed.

"Yes. But," he turned to Kara and lowered his voice, "we have to find where they're stashing the drugs. No one carries that kind of fire power unless there's a reason."

"If we move in close and get caught, we blow the entire operation. We'd do better to stay and watch from here."

"Agreed." Jeff didn't like it, but Kara was right. He watched the men closely while Kara snapped several more pictures. "I'm glad you thought to bring that camera along."

"Me too. I'd requested some equipment when I first stopped in upon our arrival, and I picked it up the other day from the DEA in Bend when I was getting my medical clearance."

The men grabbed the weapons and rode off in the opposite direction from them. "Show's over." Jeff followed their progress until they disappeared among the tall pine trees.

Kara put the camera away. "Want to go check the area now?"

"Not yet. Let's monitor it for a while, see if they come back, especially after the Gonzaleses show up."

She shifted and stared off into the horizon. "I've

been so busy. This is the first time I've really noticed the mountains since I've been back. I can't get over how close they look. Then again, I guess they really are close. It's been too long since I've been in Central Oregon."

"Maybe if we ever get a free day, we could go up to Mount Bachelor or hike one of the Three Sisters." He kept his focus on the land in case anyone else showed up.

"I'd like that. I'm surprised they have snow this time of year."

"I believe the Sisters always have snow along the peaks." Jeff stretched out his legs and leaned back on his palms, keeping his gaze on the landscape. The gritty rock dug into his hands. "I noticed you met Jake."

Kara looked over at him, eyebrows raised. "I'm surprised you were paying attention."

"He seemed a bit too interested in you."

"Watch out, Jeff. You sound jealous." She grinned. "You're right, though. He did seem interested. I set him straight and told him I'm with you."

"Very funny. What'd he say?" He'd have no problem putting Jake in his place where Kara was concerned. She may be a DEA agent and able to take care of herself, but she was also his partner and fast becoming a good friend, and no one messed with his friends.

"Relax," she teased. "Let's talk about something else."

"How's the leg doing?"

"Fine. The stitches are gone, and it healed up well."

"Any headaches?"

"Nothing related to the concussion if that's what you're asking. Why the sudden concern?" She glanced his way.

"Just making conversation."

"I don't like to think about that week."

"Sorry. So, how do you like pretending to be my girlfriend?" He grinned wide.

Kara's jaw opened, but she snapped it closed fast and chuckled.

"What?" He shrugged. "That's a good question."

Her eyes twinkled with laughter. "I'll have to get back to you on that. It's too soon to tell." She stood. "Hold this?" She handed him the camera then climbed down from the boulder.

After lowering the camera to her, he followed.

"I don't think anyone's coming. It's been over an hour."

Jeff agreed. But the men could be watching, and he didn't want to tip them off. "Let's just walk. We can check out the location later. I don't want anyone surprising us." He picked up a smooth rock and flung it at the river. The rock skipped three times.

"Not bad. Maybe we should mount up." She fingered a rock and flipped it into the river with a plop.

Jeff nodded, untied the reins from a low branch, and swung into the saddle. "I used to skip rocks with my dad and Eric when we were kids. Never was all that skilled at it though."

"Looked good to me."

"Thanks. Did your equipment arrive for the nail salon?" He watched as Kara slipped her foot into the stirrup and mounted Blaze. She moved like a pro, and only a few hours ago, she'd been concerned the horse was too big. Guess she'd underestimated herself. One thing he knew for certain though—she'd be sore tomorrow. They headed back side by side.

"Yes. I'm all set up and ready to open in the morning. Gail's my first customer. I have an opening if you're interested." She wiggled her eyebrows.

"Ha. You're not getting your hands on me. Those places are for women."

"Not true. Lots of men get their nails done. In the past about a quarter of my clients were men."

"I doubt that had anything to do with them wanting their nails done. They probably just wanted to be up close and personal with a cute woman."

Kara chuckled. "You think I'm cute?"

He swallowed hard. "I didn't mean—"

Kara giggled. "Relax. I won't hold it against you."

He felt his face warm even though he knew she wasn't offended. "Any of your clients ever ask you out?"

"I don't date clients."

"How about cops?"

She shook her head and rolled her eyes. "Don't even get me started."

A small part of him ached at the cynicism he heard in her tone as his own memories of a long-lost love surfaced. Beth had refused to date cops too. She'd broken off their engagement the same day he announced he was leaving the bank to go into law enforcement. At thirty-three, it seemed he'd been single forever. But it was for the best. He and Beth would never have lasted. She wouldn't have understood assignments like this one. Didn't matter now anyway. Beth had married a loan officer, and he'd moved on.

"Any news on the sketch I gave you of that guy from the park?" Kara asked.

"Not yet. This case gets more complicated at every turn." The ranch came into view and a truck with a horse trailer sat near the barn. "Looks like company."

13

Jeff paused in the doorway of the barn with his and Kara's horses in tow and allowed his eyes to adjust to the dim light. He tied off both animals, removed their gear, then gave them each a rub down and brush. Kara had offered to help, but he knew she needed to get back to town. The nail salon was her cover, and she needed to spend at least *some* time there.

After leading Blaze and Lulu to their stalls, he approached the new arrival. The horse whinnied when Jeff reached out his hand. He spoke softly, "Hey there, boy." He glanced around for something to identify the stud and his efforts were rewarded. Someone had hung a sign over the stall entrance. "Lightning. Does that mean you're fast?"

"Nah, he has a lightning bolt mark on his side."

Jeff turned to find Jake coming out of the tack room. "Kara and I noticed a trailer in the driveway earlier, but by the time we got back here, it was gone. Did the owners leave?"

Jake nodded. "They don't stick around much when

they come to the area. Lightning is a temporary boarder from out of the country. He'll only be here 'til they find a permanent place for him."

Radar activated, Jeff asked, "Where are they from?"

"Mexico."

Just as he suspected, the Gonzaleses had arrived. Jeff grasped the handles of a wheelbarrow full of waste and moved it toward the door. "Mexico? That's quite a drive. I hear they quarantine the horses that come in from other countries. That true?"

"Yep."

He stopped and turned back to Jake. "Why'd they bring Lightning here?"

Jake glared at him. "You ask a lot of questions."

"I've been accused of that more times that I can count." He chuckled and gripped the wheelbarrow. "I'll take Lightning out for some exercise if you want."

"Do it myself." Jake moved alongside him. "Let me. I'll dump it on my way to open the arena gate for Lightning."

"Sure. Thanks." With Jake out of sight, Jeff walked through an open door into the closet-sized ranch office, which sat in a corner of the barn. Jeff fingered through loose papers on Jake's desk, but nothing of interest caught his attention. The sound of whistling, and a sweet scent drifted in from an open window. Veronica. He sighed and hurried from the room.

"There you are. I've been looking all over for you." Veronica's eyes sparkled. "Did Kara tell you I invited her over for dinner tonight?"

"No. I don't think she mentioned it."

"Surprise." She turned to leave then called over her shoulder. "Feel free to quit a little early today and take a shower before dinner."

Jeff sniffed his shirt and decided to knock off now. Kara would be back in an hour, and he definitely needed a shower. Maybe he'd get in a game of pinball too.

Jake strolled into the barn, nodded at him, and went directly to the office. Jeff frowned. If only Veronica hadn't come looking for him

Jeff took a long drink of water from his glass and listened to the conversation that flowed around him at the large dining room table. Kara sat across from Eric, who wrapped up a story from his and Jeff's childhood.

Laughing hard, Kara crossed an arm over her belly and then held up her other hand. "Please no more stories. My stomach can't take it. I'm afraid I ate too much." She turned to Veronica. "You're a fabulous cook."

"Thanks. It's something I enjoy." Veronica reached out and grasped Lauren's hand. "Maybe next time Lauren will cook her famous mac and cheese for you."

Lauren's face flushed deep red. "It's *your* recipe."

"True, but you add your own special touch."

Jeff winked at his niece. "Sounds like a winner to me. I can't wait to try it sometime." He turned to Veronica. "Do you mind if I show Kara around?"

"Not at all. Eric told me you're rather taken with our great room."

"You could say that." Jeff turned to Kara. "You've got to see this room." He stood and held out his hand. Veronica and Eric exchanged a look and remained seated at the table. With only a second's hesitation, Kara slipped her hand into his and whispered as he guided her from the room. "What's the rush? We should visit with your family."

"We did visit. Besides they don't mind. Did you see the look on their faces? They're tickled that we're spending time alone together." He led her down the stairs to the pinball machine. "Isn't it great? It's just like the one at the arcade when I was a kid." Jeff released Kara's hand without waiting for a reply and pulled back the plunger. He could do this all day. The bells sounded as the ball hit various objects. His mind slowed down to the rhythm of the game, and the stress of the past few weeks seemed to melt. The machine lit up with a wave of lights in a crescent shape and played a ditty.

"Does your family like to play matchmaker? I know mine does," Kara said. "My poor mother is convinced I'll never marry and have children. Whenever I'm home for a visit she tries to set me up with any available bachelor." She chuckled. "I'll never forget the time she invited this guy over from church to have dinner with us. Halfway into the meal, he mentioned his fiancée. Honestly, I'm not sure why he even came. You'd think he would've figured out what my mother was up to. Anyway, when he announced he was to be married in a month, my mom choked on a piece of chicken, and I had to give her the Heimlich. I felt so awful for her. All that hard work cooking for hours, and he was taken."

Jeff glanced at her with a grin. "My family isn't that bad—at least I don't think they are. I don't go home much. In fact, this is the first I've seen Eric in seven years. We've never been close."

"Really?"

Jeff couldn't help but notice the surprise in her tone. "My parents and I talk on the phone, but it's hard to get away for a visit, especially since they live in Montana. If they didn't live so far away, I'm sure we'd see each other more. Besides that, when do I have time to go home?"

"Point taken."

Jeff missed the ball. He pulled back the plunger and the next ball soared into play. "Maybe I'll swing over to Montana before I head back to Miami."

"Good idea." Kara stood at his side and bumped his arm. "Are you going to hog the game all night, or do I get a turn?"

"Okay, hold on. As soon as I hit the ball, jump in front of me and take over." Kara moved smoothly into place and didn't miss a beat. Between the two of them, they scored an all-time record high. Jeff placed his hand on her back. "Let's go for a walk."

Kara shot him a look filled with questions. "Sure, but we should see if they need help washing the dishes first."

As they passed by the kitchen, the dishwasher whirred and clean pots and pans sat drying on the counter. "Looks like the dishes are done." He guided her out the door and down the driveway.

Kara grasped Jeff's arm and tucked her hand around his bicep, her touch gentle, yet firm. He took a deep breath and let it out trying not to focus on the kaleidoscope of feelings her touch evoked.

"I love this time of year. Whoever invented daylight savings time is my hero." A rare, sincere smile lit her face.

"You're in a happy mood tonight."

Kara kicked at a stone and watched it bounce a few feet. "Your family is a lot of fun." She paused. "And so are you."

Slow down, Kara. You're taking us to a place we can't go. Then again, it felt nice to be with her like this—friends and confidants, just so long as it didn't go further.

Kara stopped and looked around. "This place is so picturesque and perfect."

"What do you mean by perfect?" he gently prodded.

"For starters, I love Central Oregon. The mountains are incredible, and my friend Gail lives here. And then there's you."

Panic gripped his stomach, and alarms went off in his mind. "You're not getting mushy on me, are you?"

"No, I'm serious. You've been a good friend to me since the explosion, and I'm grateful. In fact, I'd venture to say you're one of my best friends."

Jeff squeezed her shoulder. "Tonight was fun, but you must have a better friend than me. We've really only known each other a few weeks." Okay, more like four but who was counting? It's not like he and Kara hadn't known each other before this case. They'd been acquaintances at best. This conversation was getting way too touchy feely for him.

"You okay?" Kara asked. "You're awfully quiet."

"Well, actually—"

Kara pulled away from him as though burned. "Oh no. I'm sorry. I just realized how you must have taken what I said. You must think I'm a complete moron." She touched her hands to her face. "I'm so embarrassed. My mouth leaped ahead of my brain."

"Relax. You didn't say anything wrong." He rubbed the back of his neck and squinted up at the setting sun. "But you did kind of freak me out. I thought maybe you forgot we were only pretending to be a couple."

"No. I didn't. Believe me." She turned and headed back in the direction of the house.

He followed.

Ahead of him, she mumbled something about being embarrassed.

"Look, Kara. It's fine. Don't worry."

She let out a sigh. "Can we please talk about something else?"

He took a deep breath. "Fine. Consider it dropped. Any success with the pictures you took?"

"No. Face recognition came up empty."

Jeff sighed. "Too bad." The idea of arresting his brother or sister-in-law became less and less appealing with every minute he spent with them. He and Eric had a rocky past, but things seemed to be going well between them now. He didn't want to lose the ground they'd gained since his arrival.

"I'd like to go back out tomorrow and investigate where we saw the men," Jeff said.

"Okay. I need to open my salon for a couple hours in the morning, but I'll be able to get away in the afternoon." The sun had set and dusk created shadows across their path as they walked back along the driveway. Kara tripped over a rise in the uneven surface.

Jeff reached out and steadied her before she fell. "Careful."

"Thanks." Light shone from the windows as the house came into full view. They walked up the steps and inside. Kara found Eric and Veronica watching television. "Hi, there. I need to head home now. Thanks for dinner."

Veronica stood then walked them to the door. "Are you sure you won't stay for dessert?"

"Sounds wonderful, but I really need to head home."

"I understand, but please take some with you." She hustled into the kitchen and came back holding a small covered plastic dish. "Let me know what you think of the pie. I'm considering entering it in the Deschutes County Fair."

Kara smiled. "I will. Thanks for everything."

Jeff walked Kara out to her car. He encircled her in his arms, and she caught her breath. He whispered in her ear. "Relax, we have an audience. I'll meet you at your place later tonight. Wait up for me."

"Okay. I'll see you soon."

14

Kara opened her apartment door and allowed Jeff to enter. "Nice performance at the ranch tonight. I have to say you caught me by surprise after our conversation."

Jeff grinned sheepishly. "Sorry about that."

She closed the door, walked toward the only two chairs in the room, and sat down on one of the overstuffed easy chairs. "What's up?"

Jeff remained standing, shook his head, then mimed squishing a bug with his hands.

"It's clean."

He sank into the other chair.

Kara leaned forward. "You want something to drink?"

Jeff shook his head. "No, thanks."

She cleared her throat. "Why'd you come over?"

"A horse came in today from Mexico while we were out riding. I suspect it's the Gonzaleses' horse, but I couldn't locate any paperwork to confirm." He leaned forward. "I wish I'd been there, but I'm certain it was them. I'll check the pictures on the cameras when I get back. I couldn't do much with everyone around this afternoon." Jeff sank against the back of the chair and let a sigh escape.

Kara's voice softened. "Don't feel bad that you missed them. It might even help you in the long run. They may have become suspicious if it appeared you were waiting for them. Besides, if you had stayed near the barn, we wouldn't have seen the intruders out on the range or gotten those photos. I have a strong feeling one is related to the other."

"I talked with Eric before dinner, and he said he allows a couple of the teen boys from church to come out and target practice."

"Reasonable explanation, except no shots were fired. And I don't know any teens with machine guns." She looked directly into his eyes. "Sure makes him look guilty."

"Not necessarily." Jeff frowned. "Maybe he does allow some teens out there, and this was unrelated. He might have no idea what's going on."

Kara raised a brow. "Maybe." Clearly, Jeff didn't want to believe his stepbrother was involved, but she had a hard time accepting Eric was an innocent in all of this.

Jeff rested his ankle on his knee. "Any more mystery people peering through your window?"

"No," Kara said. "But I'd like to know who's been keeping an eye on us."

"Whoever it is, if they're related in any way to our case, we'll get them."

"I hope you're right, because I don't like being

stalked." This job was complicated enough without the addition of some unknown factor. "Probably some kid and nothing to worry about."

"Probably." He stood and walked to the door. "I'll see you tomorrow."

Kara followed and watched as he drove away. It was strange working with a partner. She never dreamt they'd experience so much awkwardness. For her part, she'd keep her emotions in check. No way would she allow herself to fall for her partner, but what about him? He seemed to be holding her at arms' length, but when she looked into his eyes, she saw something else. Something neither of them would admit. And when he held her...no she couldn't go there. "Be professional, girl." She turned from the door and locked up.

Jeff drove back to the ranch with a purpose. Time to check the pictures on the hidden cameras.

He parked his car and sauntered toward the barn. The door squeaked as it opened— he'd oil it later. He walked past Lightning's stall—empty.

He'd been gone for forty minutes tops. He clenched his teeth. Now he'd have to wait until the next time the Gonzaleses showed up to establish contact. He retrieved his cameras and hustled from the barn to his room. He'd download the pictures onto his computer and see for himself what had happened in the barn today.

15

Kara placed the open sign in the window of her salon and sat behind the desk. The clock ticked ever so slow. Gail would be here soon, but not soon enough. She tapped her fingers on the desktop. Stakeouts were more exciting than waiting for clients.

Twenty minutes later, the door opened, and Gail walked in. "Good morning, Kara." She stopped and looked around the space. "This is nice. Simple, but you've done a superior job."

"Thanks. Come have a seat." Kara tried to envision the room through Gail's eyes. The desk sat to the right of the entrance with her schedule book and phone on top. A nail table was situated straight ahead as the customers entered. The pedicure station was in the front corner of the store. A small display of polish hung by each station. She had a perfect view of the entrance no matter what her task. Gauzy white curtains covered the window to give a little privacy.

"I haven't had my nails done since forever. What a treat."

"You deserve it after taking me in on such short notice. Just tell all your friends about me."

"I already have. I expect you should have a full schedule soon."

"Thanks." The front door opened and Kara looked up. "Marci!"

"Hello again," Marci walked over to the manicure table.

"How have you been? I haven't seen you since the Fourth of July picnic. Would you like to schedule an appointment?" Kara continued to work on Gail's nails.

"I'm fine. I was hoping you take walk-ins."

"I do today. Can you give me thirty minutes?"

"Perfect. I'll be back."

Interesting that Marci would be her first real client. Kara finished Gail's nails and promised to see her later at the music camp where, once again, she was on kitchen duty.

Marci slipped back into the nail shop about two minutes after Gail's departure. "I'm so glad there's finally a nail technician in town. I always have to drive to Bend to get my nails done. You do a good job, and this place will be hopping."

"I'll do my best." Kara soaked Marci's fingers in warm, sudsy water then got to work. "What do you do for a living? Your hands are so soft."

"Thank you. I'm in advertising. I write print advertisements and sometimes commercials."

"No dishpan hands here—lucky girl."

"I wear gloves."

"Not luck then, brains. Guess you have to be smart

to write ads."

"I like to think so."

Conversation flowed between the women, and Marci's fingers were perfectly polished with a French manicure in no time. "What do you think?"

Marci held her fingers out in front of her. "As nice as any fancy spa. Thanks."

"You're welcome. Be sure to spread the word."

"Sure thing, but I don't think the women in this town put much stock into what I say." Marci paid and walked to the door. "Thanks again."

Kara frowned at her retreating form. What was up with Marci? Single mom who held a good job. She seemed like an intelligent person, but many of the women in town shunned her. Why? They couldn't *all* think that Marci was out to steal their husbands.

She'd have to do more digging into Marci's life. Something wasn't right.

Kara slipped on plastic gloves then served ham and cheese sandwiches as the students passed by with their lunch trays. She spotted Lauren in line as she scooted her tray along the counter. "Hi, Lauren, how's it going?" Kara placed a sandwich on the teen's plate.

"Fine. Are you coming out to the ranch again tonight for dinner?"

"I don't think so, but I'll be out later to ride with your uncle."

A hungry camper nudged Lauren forward.

Kara placed sandwich after sandwich on plates until a familiar voice caused her to look up. Her eyes widened. "Jessica! I'm surprised to see you in the lunch line."

Jessica laughed. "Even I have to eat sometime. Are you coming to the recital tomorrow night?"

"I don't know. I'll have to check my calendar."

"I hope you can make it. The students sound great."

Kara promised to try. Jessica nodded and moved on down the counter. The lunch line filtered through quickly. After lunch, Kara wiped down the tables, folded them up, then found a broom and cleaned the floor. Anything to get out of washing dishes sounded good. Those industrial-sized sinks held way too many pots and pans.

"Kara."

She turned to see Jessica striding toward her.

"I forgot to mention earlier that I noticed you in church with Gail last Sunday and thought you might enjoy the singles' group. We meet this Friday night." Jessica handed her a small piece of paper with directions.

"Thanks." Kara folded the paper and stuffed it into her pocket.

"You're welcome. And if you want to bring that cute guy you had dinner with the other night, feel free."

"You were at the diner?"

Jessica nodded. "I was sitting by the door when you walked in. I'm not surprised you didn't notice me. You were looking for your date, who, by the way, couldn't keep his eyes off you." Jessica giggled and waved as she walked away.

Why would Jeff be staring at her? It's not like he hadn't seen her a thousand times. She tucked her thoughts away and focused on the students' conversations.

It was a stretch to think someone at this camp might be involved with drugs, but you couldn't predict users or dealers based on their interests. Maybe she'd get lucky and hear a name or place involved in the local drug scene.

Kara found a place to park near the barn and next to a car she didn't recognize. There were a few extra vehicles today. Could something be going down? Her heart rate increased a little in anticipation. The sooner she finished this assignment the quicker she could be on Luis Alvarado's case. Before she slid out of her car, she secured her Glock in her belt holster and made sure the oversized T-shirt she had on concealed it. Kara entered the barn unsure of what she'd find. As her eyes adjusted to the dimness, she spotted Jake grooming one of the horses. He appeared to be alone.

"Back again? You're not sore from your ride yesterday?"

"Not too bad. Is Jeff around?" In truth, her rear felt like it did the day after she rode her bike for the first time in months, but she'd never admit it to anyone. She reminded herself to walk without altering her gait.

"He's out on a trail ride with a small group of tourists. He'll be back soon. I'd be happy to keep you company." He winked.

Kara forced a smile. "Thanks." Why'd she always get roped into investigating the creeps? She plopped down on a nearby bench and crossed her legs. "How'd you get into ranching?"

Jake slid a brush down the shiny coat of a well-groomed horse. "Kind of fell into it, and it stuck. Served me well too. The horses don't complain or drive me nuts, and I make enough to live on."

"This ranch must be doing well for Eric to hire full-time help."

"We do all right between boarding, lessons, and trail rides. Veronica is a highly sought-after trainer, which keeps things busy too."

"Really?" This had been in her intel, but she'd seen no evidence to date. "I usually see you out here with the riders."

"Stick around and you'll see. Veronica is quite the accomplished horse woman."

"Is she working today?"

"No. Things are quiet this week, but her regular classes will resume next week."

Hmm. Why would a busy trainer take a week off?

"We're lucky too. We couldn't be in a better location. I suppose there are parts of the country that wouldn't be able to support this business, but Sunridge is ideal. Of course, Eric has his side job, which I'm sure

114

helps."

Kara tried not to appear overly interested. "Side job?"

The barn door opened. "There you are," Jeff said. "I need to rub these horses down. You okay with waiting?"

"Sure. Take your time." She watched as Jeff handled a horse as though he'd been doing it his whole life. Too bad he couldn't have waited a few more minutes. She was within seconds of learning what she suspected was valuable information about Eric. From the closed look on Jake's face, she could tell their conversation was over. A sigh escaped her lips.

Jeff quirked an eyebrow. "Everything okay?"

"Fine."

Kara leaned back against the barn wall and shut her eyes. What could Eric's side job be? A gentle hand rested on her shoulder.

"Ready?" A brown cowboy hat covered Jeff's head as he looked down into her face.

"Sure. Do you mind if we walk today? I don't feel like riding."

"Saddle sore?"

She shrugged. "Just busy. Your sister-in-law wants her nails done at four o'clock."

Jeff addressed Jake, "I'm going for a walk. I'll be back soon."

Jake waved him off. "The horses aren't going anywhere."

Kara and Jeff walked down the driveway toward the main road. "Did you learn anything last night?"

"Yes. I captured several shots of Andrea and Fernando Gonzales. Jake was also in the pictures, but no drugs were evident, which leaves us where we started. On top of that, they packed up and left while I was at your place."

Kara pursed her lips. "You think they're onto you?"

"Impossible. They've never met me. They'll come back, and when they do, I'll make my move."

"How long can you stay here without making your family suspicious?"

"Things are going well. The house is so large, they hardly know I'm here." He took his hat off and smacked it against his thigh. A puff of dust flew off. Then he settled the hat back on his head. "I guess I could tell Eric I got laid off. Maybe make something up about the bank being bought out."

"Might work. Are you positive he doesn't know you're DEA?"

"Yes." He nodded. "A long time ago, I worked for a bank. Eric was furious when I left the ranch to pursue my own interests. He thought I should stay and help run our parents' spread in Montana." He chuckled dryly then sobered. "Eric had nothing to do with me for a long time after that. I guess he got over it after he met and married Veronica, because several years ago, he invited me to come and visit. He's done some serious upgrades to the place since then. Anyway, I never told him I quit my job at the bank to pursue a career in law enforcement."

A tabby cat rubbed up against his leg. Jeff picked up the creature. "This is Marmalade. She's one of the ranch's many felines." He stroked the cat's back. "I imagine Eric's happy to have the extra hands—especially since he's hardly ever here."

The animal, apparently not accustomed to being held, squirmed and jumped from his arms. "Not a very friendly cat." Kara chuckled. "I'm curious about one thing."

"What's that?"

"Why on earth were you working in a bank? That seems so far removed from anything I can picture you doing. Of course, I never imagined you on a ranch either."

"A buddy of mine landed a job at a bank and convinced me it was my way out of Montana. He put in a good word with the manager. I interviewed, and the bank hired me. I attended college at the same time. It was tough taking a full load of classes and working almost full time, but I was determined. I'm good at math and graduated near the top of my class." He shrugged. "It seemed like a smart decision at the time."

"Wow. You ever miss it?"

"The bank?"

"Yes."

"Never. I was miserable there. I may have gone back home after graduation if Eric hadn't given me such a hard time about moving and taking the bank job." He sighed. "Anyway, it's all come full circle, and now I can use that time in my life to my advantage."

"True. Changing subjects—Jake mentioned that Eric has a side job."

"News to me. Like I said, he's gone a lot. I'll check

it out."

They moved closer to the edge of the road as a car neared. "I have some other news," Kara said. "Our escapade at the diner the other night was a success. Jessica, the camp director, spotted us and assumed we're an item. We've been invited to her church's singles' group meeting Friday night. Apparently, she attends the same church as Gail and your brother."

Jeff shook his head. "I don't know, Kara. Maybe pretending to be a couple isn't such a great idea after all."

"The fresh air getting to your brain?" She frowned at him. "Let's remember whose idea this was in the first place, and it's perfect. Now that we're into this, there's no way we aren't finishing it. We have a perfect cover. When the Gonzaleses return, we'll make friends with them and earn their trust." She snapped her fingers. "Then we'll swoop down so hard and fast they won't know which way to turn. Jeff, you're a genius. I just wish I had thought of it first."

Jeff reached for her hand. "Okay, Miss Sunshine. I'm a genius. We'll continue to establish ourselves as a couple so when they come back, they won't suspect our comings and goings. I don't know about the singles' group though. One of us should be at the ranch if they return."

Kara took a deep breath and let it out slowly. "Good point. But if a horse is being delivered, we simply won't go."

Jeff nodded. "How're you holding up?"

"What do you mean?" They retraced their steps

back to the ranch.

"I know that whole thing in Miami with Alvarado had you pretty angry."

"Oh. That. Let's just say I'm looking forward to finishing this assignment so that I can kick some butt in Miami. I want him behind bars, and if I have to put him there myself, then fine."

"Hold on." He stopped walking. "If you get anywhere near Alvarado, he'll kill you. Let the team do their job. They'll get him. And when it's safe, you can go back."

Kara glared at him. "Shows what you know. Do you realize they don't have a clue where he went? He could be in South America or staying at some local dive. I'm sick of trusting people to do their job."

Jeff stopped, took her by the shoulders, and stared into her eyes. "Don't do anything stupid, Kara. Besides ruining your career, you could wind up dead. Gary knows what he's doing. I trust him with my life, and so should you."

"Right." She heard the sarcasm in her voice, but couldn't help it. How could Jeff be so naïve?

All conversation ended as they entered the ranch yard. Jeff walked Kara to her car. "Promise me you'll behave."

Distracted by Jake's image in her peripheral vision, Kara ignored his plea. Instead, she turned around, stood on tiptoes, and lightly kissed Jeff's lips. After only a brief hesitation, he wrapped his arms around her and returned the kiss. She pulled away and smiled up at him. *That felt a little too real.*

Eyebrows raised, Jeff whispered. "Where's our audience?"

Ignoring her racing heart Kara winked. "Look over my shoulder. I have to go."

Jeff watched her drive away and saw Jake watching as well. He lifted his hand to wave and couldn't help the smug smile that crossed his face. This pretending to be a couple could be harder than he realized. He'd have to learn to expect the unexpected and keep his focus on the job he came to do. His feelings for Kara were growing every time they were together. He rubbed the back of his neck. Somehow, he would have to pretend to fall for her and not actually do it—but was it already too late?

16

Kara rolled a bottle of fiery red nail polish between her palms. "I think this color is going to look great on you."

Veronica smiled and splayed out her fingers.

Kara applied the polish with care, the whole time wishing the woman would say something, anything, but Veronica was positively mute. Talk about a long appointment. "Jake tells me that Eric has a side job."

"Oh that." Veronica waved her free hand in the air.

"Careful. You don't want to ruin your nails. I have a drying light you can use as soon as I'm finished."

Veronica laid her hand back on the table. "He delivers feed, hay, and straw to farms and ranches. That, along with picking up the slack at the ranch, keeps him pretty busy most of the time. I'm just glad Jake's around to run our ranch. Of course, now that Jeff's here, things are running even smoother. I've actually been able to take a little time off."

"I didn't realize you were so hands-on?"

"There's no way you would. Since Jeff's arrival, I've

taken advantage of the extra help and stayed out of the barn. Mucking stalls used to be my job when I wasn't training."

"Eww. Not my favorite thing to do." *Explains the calluses.* "So what did you do before Jake?" Kara tightened the lid on the polish and turned on the drying light.

"Eric and I worked the ranch ourselves for the most part. We had a couple kids that helped out after school and in the summer, but they left after Jake arrived. Just as well. I don't know how we would've paid all of them." She placed her fingers under the light.

"So Eric started doing deliveries after Jake came on?"

"Yes."

"Does he miss working the ranch full time?"

Veronica looked down at her hands then fixed her gaze on a fake plant in the corner of the room. "I imagine so."

"Then why not get rid of Jake and do the work himself?"

Veronica whipped her head toward Kara, her eyes wide. "Funny, I've wondered the same thing and every time I ask, he changes the subject. I guess he enjoys getting out."

"Don't we all. I'd go crazy if I sat around here all day."

"Yes, well." She pulled her hands away from the light. "You think they're dry enough?"

"I suppose. But be careful. Today's on me. A little thank you for dinner the other night."

Veronica stood. "Thanks."

"You're welcome." Kara watched as Veronica bolted from the salon. She stood and flipped the open sign to closed. The mention of Eric's side job had Veronica jumpier than a Mexican jumping bean. Time for a little more investigating. She grabbed her keys and headed out the back.

Kara's tires crunched along the gravel driveway. She parked in what had become her usual spot and walked over to the arena where Jake was exercising a horse. "She's beautiful," she called out.

Jake waved and kept on working. "Back so soon?"

"Here goes nothing," she said under her breath then raised her voice. "Yeah. I only had one client today. Can I try that?"

Jake stood in the middle of the arena. He held a rope attached to the halter. The beast trotted in circles around him. He shrugged and slowed the mare to a stop.

"Climb over the fence and walk slowly toward me. Daisy's a bit skittish."

Kara did as he instructed.

"Okay. Now put your right hand here and your left there."

She placed her hands on the rope. Jake hiked himself onto the fence. He made an odd clucking sound, and Daisy began to move in circles around her.

"Don't the horses get dizzy?"

"Never asked one."

"Do you do this with all of them?"

Jake shook his head. "Only when their owners request it. Have you had enough yet?"

Kara nodded, and Jake moved in to take over. He definitely knew his way around these animals. She admired the ease with which he handled the mare as she made her way to the perimeter of the arena.

"You and Jeff going to ride this evening?"

"No, not tonight." She sat on the railing the way he'd done earlier.

"Then why are you here?"

"I came to see you."

His eyebrows rose. "Me? I thought you and Jeff had something going on."

Kara crossed her arms. "Just because I'm seeing Jeff doesn't mean I can't talk to you. I was hoping you would teach me how to saddle a horse. I want to surprise him."

Disappointment flickered in his eyes. "Sure. When I'm done here, I'll teach you."

"Thanks. Do you mind if I sit and watch?"

"Suit yourself."

Jeff studied Kara from the kitchen window. When she'd driven up, he'd expected her to come to the house. Instead she sat on the fence, visiting with Jake. His mouth stretched down into a firm frown. He didn't like the way Jake looked at Kara. The hungry-for-fresh-meat look on Jake's face made him want to feed him his fist. But she could handle herself and Jake too, if necessary.

"What'cha looking at, little brother?"

Jeff jerked away from the window and joined Eric at the table. "Nothing. Kara's out there talking to Jake."

Eric looked out the window for a second. "Doesn't look like anything to be worried about to me. She's probably just saying hi before she comes in to see you. No need to be jealous."

"I'm not jealous." He yanked a chair out from the kitchen table and sat.

"Careful. Veronica will have a fit if you break one of her chairs in a jealous rage."

"You don't know what you're talking about."

"Maybe you should enlighten me then," Eric said.

Jeff met Eric's eyes and held his stare. Oh, how he'd like to, but not yet. Instead, he cleared his throat. "You remember when I said I'd be here for a few weeks? The thing is, I got laid off, and I'm between jobs right now. I was wondering if maybe—"

"The bank laid you off? I didn't realize." Eric frowned and patted Jeff on the shoulder. "Don't worry about it. We have plenty of room, and you've been a great help. Fact is, I'm too busy to do much at home, and it's been nice knowing you were here to make sure everything runs smoothly."

"You don't trust Jake?"

"I didn't say that. He's done a good job. But I trust you. So consider yourself home."

Eric sure knew how to make this job harder. "Thanks. This means a lot to me."

Eric wiggled his brows. "I didn't do it just for you. I know Mom and Dad would like to have a few more grandchildren. The way I see it, if you stick around for awhile you and Kara—"

Jeff held up his hand. "Slow down. You're moving a bit fast, don't you think?"

"Me. You're the one who's jealous because she's talking to another man. Seems to me your feelings run deeper than you're willing to admit."

Jeff clamped his mouth shut.

Eric rose from his chair and left the room chuckling.

17

Kara sat with Jeff and his family at the music camp recital. The orchestra played a song she didn't recognize. It seemed the whole town had turned out, including Jake, who sat a few rows behind them. Kara took shallow breaths and fanned herself with a program in the stuffy hot room. She glanced at her watch. They'd been sitting for about forty minutes now. Jeff sat to her right with his arm draped across the back of her metal chair.

He leaned over and whispered in her ear. "How much longer do you think this thing is going to last?"

Kara poked him with her elbow. "I don't know. Shush."

Lauren lifted her violin to her chin and prepared to play with the group. Smooth, clear tones projected from the instruments and were surprisingly good, considering they'd only had four days of practice together. Applause rang out in the auditorium as the trio stood to bow. Kara glanced at her program—one more song to go. Thank goodness, since her legs had fallen asleep. She took a deep breath of warm air and shifted in her seat.

Jessica glided to the microphone at the front of the stage. "We have a special surprise song for you this evening. The violin students competed for a chance to play a duet with me. I have yet to tell them who won, so this will be a surprise for everyone." Her face glowed with excitement. She turned toward the violin section. "You all have worked hard this week, and I'm proud of each and every one of you, but one student stood out. Lauren, I'm very pleased with your accomplished performance and would be honored if you would join me."

Lauren beamed with pride and carried her instrument under her arm with the bow in her opposite hand. She sat in the chair indicated.

Jessica joined her with her own violin. "Lauren Waters and I will be playing *Air in D Minor* by J.S. Bach." Seconds later, the hushed auditorium filled with strains of the haunting melody.

As the duet concluded, applause erupted, and the audience stood to their feet. Kara glanced past Jeff, where Veronica stood, dabbing at her eyes with a tissue. Kara felt sorry for the rest of the musicians. She wouldn't want to follow that performance.

After the finale, Kara and Jeff joined the rest of the audience in another standing ovation then shuffled toward the exit along with half the town. Kara whirled around when someone grabbed her arm. Jessica pulled her aside as she stepped out of the auditorium into the adjoining hall.

"I'm glad you made it! What did you think?"

"Everyone did a great job, but that duet was

fantastic."

"Lauren is a talented musician, and the rest of the students did wonderful as well. I'm already looking forward to next year, but that's not why I stopped you. Are you going to make it tomorrow night to the singles' group?"

"I'm not sure yet. You'll have to wait and be surprised." The singles get together had Kara's mind.

Jessica's smile sagged a little. "Okay, I understand." She reached out and gave her a quick hug. "I'll see you when I see you."

A camper approached with her parents and captured Jessica's attention, so Kara used the opportunity to head toward the exit. She liked Jessica, but the whole singles' group thing made her uncomfortable.

Kara spotted Jake nearby talking to a few teenagers in the corner of the hall near the water fountain. Adjusting her course, she bent over the fountain and strained to hear what they were saying. She caught a few snippets but nothing that made any sense. The teens moved away and Kara straightened. Jake made eye contact and winked. *Ugh*. She waved and turned away.

Maybe it was time to step things up a notch or two with Jake. She needed to get into his inner circle. Her gut told her he knew something, and she intended to find out what.

As Kara left the school, she spotted Jeff leaning on the hood of her car. The sound of cowboy boots clicked on the pavement behind her. She glanced over her shoulder. Jake followed a few feet behind but then veered toward his own vehicle when she looked at him.

What was he up to?

Jeff stepped toward her.

"Sorry for the wait. Jessica grabbed me, and before I realized it, you were gone." She moved to open her car door and slid behind the wheel.

Jeff shrugged. "No problem. What'd she want?"

"To know if I planned to attend the singles' group." She pulled her door closed and lowered the window.

Jeff squatted and rested his forearm on the sill. "Oh. Will I see you at the ranch tomorrow?"

"Yes."

Jeff walked away.

Kara's jaw dropped. Would that man ever learn to say good-bye? She'd wanted to talk to him. Oh well. It'd keep 'til morning.

Thirty minutes later, Kara lay sprawled on top of her bed. She wasn't looking forward to pursuing her plan with Jake. If he turned out to be innocent, she'd feel bad for toying with his emotions. Maybe there was a better way to get close to him.

Kara sighed and rolled over. Her first order of business tomorrow would be to make friends with Jake. She'd bake cookies in the morning and bring a dozen to him—of course, Jeff would expect cookies too. She drifted off to sleep with visions of oatmeal cookies dancing in her head.

Kara found Jake in the barn office. "Morning. I hope I'm not interrupting. I brought you a little thank-you gift for teaching me how to saddle a horse." She held out a paper plate piled high with warm oatmeal cookies.

Jake reached for the plate. "For me?" He closed his eyes, put his nose to the plate, and breathed in deeply. "If these taste as good as they smell…" He took a bite from the top cookie. "You need me to teach you anything else?"

Kara laughed. "I'll let you know. What are you up to? I didn't realize you did paperwork too. I thought your job was more hands-on." She sat in the folding metal chair next to the file cabinet.

Jake had devoured three cookies and was working on a fourth as he poured coffee into his mug. "Most of my work is hands-on, but there's a little bit of office work."

"Like?"

"Oh, you know, the usual. Ordering feed, scheduling lessons and trail rides, dealing with the public. There's more, but I don't want to bore you."

"You're not," Kara assured. "As a business owner, I find this side of your job easier to relate to. What else do you have to do?"

"I have to muck out the stalls. Want to help?" Jake stuffed another cookie in his mouth and stood.

Kara laughed. "That's the second offer I've had this week. Maybe I should learn after all."

He nearly choked on his cookie. "Well, all right! Watch me. You'll get the hang of it."

Kara followed Jake to a stall. When he finished, fresh straw lay on the ground, and the sweet smell of grain filled the air.

"You're a master stall cleaner."

Jake made a deep bow and passed a pitchfork to her. "Your turn."

She stifled a moan and got to work. As she'd hoped, the cookies had put Jake at ease. He chatted about the ranch and told her a few things about the various clients who had horses boarded with them.

"Jeff mentioned you have clients from out of the country. International customers must make you feel proud of all your hard work."

"I just do my job," Jake spat.

She waited for him to offer more information, but his loose tongue seemed to have tightened. She glanced his way as he heaved a fork full of soiled straw from the adjoining stall into the wheelbarrow. His sudden silence made her wonder. If he knew anything about the Gonzaleses, he wasn't talking. This conversation wasn't over by a long shot, but for now, she'd let it go. Pushing too hard could backfire.

Kara tossed the last of the straw into the stall then looked up. Jake stood with his arms crossed. He looked quite pleased with himself. She attempted a smile, which felt more like a grimace.

Jake burst out laughing. "You're quite a sight. That pretty blond hair of yours is growing straw."

Kara reached her hand up to her head. Sure enough, several pieces poked out. She ran her fingers through her hair then brushed the dust off her jeans and handed back the pitchfork. With a smirk, she left the barn. "Thanks for the stall-mucking lesson," she called over her shoulder.

"You better run on home and take a shower before that boyfriend of yours sees you," he hollered after her.

Oh no, Jeff!

He walked down the front steps of the house and headed straight toward her. There was no way to avoid him, and he looked incredible. He had the cowboy look down. Jeans and a form-fitting white T-shirt. Cowboy boots and a brown hat completed the look. She squared her shoulders.

"Hey, Kara! What brings you out here so early?"

"I baked you some cookies." She walked to her car then turned with the plate and stopped short. He stood mere inches from her, practically pinning her against the car. "Here." She thrust the plate into his hand and slid a little to the side, creating more space between them. Talk about invading a person's space. If she really did smell like a horse, she didn't want him that close, especially when he looked and smelled so good.

His eyes twinkled. "Looks like you've been busy." He raised a cookie to his mouth and took a bite. "Thanks. It's not every day I get fresh baked cookies."

"You're welcome. We need to talk. Do you have a few minutes?" She gently nudged past him.

"Sure. What's up?" He started to guide her toward the house.

"I'd rather talk where we can't be overheard. Think you can slip away? Maybe meet me in the park or at my apartment?"

"I'm not busy now. Let's go for a drive. We can take my rig."

"Fine." Kara followed him to the SUV and climbed

in.

Jeff drove down the driveway and made a right onto the main road.

"I have an idea I want to run by you. But hear me out before you cut in."

He glanced her way. "Okay. Sounds serious. You're not breaking up with me, are you?"

She glanced his way. Big mistake. He flashed a drop-dead gorgeous smile. Staring straight ahead she cleared her throat. "One of the adults on the ranch has to be dirty. I have no problem getting close to Veronica, and you've got Eric covered, but you and Jake aren't connecting, so that leaves me. I've been thinking about how I can get close to him and earn his trust. I need him to confide in me, so I can learn something to help close this operation—"

"I don't like where this is going."

"You said you wouldn't interrupt." She took a deep breath and let it out slowly. "I could encourage his advances and get him to trust me."

"My turn now?" he snapped.

"Yes."

"Thank you. In theory you have a great idea, but how would you pull it off? He won't buy it since we've already established ourselves as a couple."

"I'll tell him we're not serious, but I don't want you to know about him and me."

"Yeah right. He's such a peacock. He wouldn't be able to keep his mouth shut. You'd be forced to choose between the two of us. That would leave you farther from him than you are now, assuming you'd choose me.

I suppose we could covertly communicate, but posing as a couple sure makes working together a lot more convenient."

"Good point. I hadn't thought all of that through, but I still think it could work."

"No. I'm lead on this case, and I say we stick to the plan. I appreciate your willingness to put yourself on the line so to speak with Jake, but there has to be another way."

Irritation flared. This was why she liked to work alone. She took a calming breath willing her pulse to slow and her response to be professional rather than argumentative. After all, he made a valid point, but she didn't have to like it. "I made progress with him this morning, so maybe just being willing to help out will be enough." She gripped her hands in her lap and felt her face warm. If they ever worked together again, she'd demand to take point—it was only fair.

"I think it will. Jake responds well to being treated with respect. By showing an interest in what he does and being willing to pitch in, you scored major points. What do you say I turn around, and we check out where we spotted those men when we were riding? I want to see if they left any evidence laying around."

"Works for me. I'm assuming we have the place wired."

"As of yesterday. When I presented the photos of the Gonzaleses, video surveillance was approved. But the Gonzaleses' contact is smart. I'm not sure we'll pick up anything. They must conduct their business off the ranch."

"About that. I found out from Veronica that Eric's side job is delivering hay, straw, and grain. What if he's delivering more than just feed?" She shut her mouth and waited for her news to sink in. By the way Jeff's jaw flexed, she'd say he was more than a little bothered by the information.

"I'll look into it," Jeff said. "Did Veronica say anything else?"

"No." Kara shifted in her seat. "Wait, she told me that there were two kids who helped Eric out before Jake was hired. Apparently doing deliveries didn't start until Jake showed up."

"Nice work, Kara."

"Thanks." She pursed her lips and studied Jeff's profile. "You're sure calm about this."

"Just doing my job." He found a pullout and swung the car around. "You ready to go exploring?"

"I'm always ready, but could we stop by my place real quick so I can get cleaned up?"

"Why? You'd end up smelling more like horse anyway."

She frowned. "Do I stink?" Looking bad she could deal with, sort of, but smelling bad, no way.

"Relax. I didn't mean that you smell. I just figured you'd want to take a shower after you went riding, and there's no sense in taking two and dirtying more clothes."

"Oh, okay."

Back at the ranch, they went into the barn, and she glanced around for Jake. He must be outside somewhere working. Kara felt Jeff's gaze resting on her as she saddled Blaze.

"When did you learn to saddle a horse?"

Kara focused on the task of cinching the straps. "Yesterday. How'd I do?"

He checked the cinch straps. "Looks like you did well. The straps are nice and tight. Who taught you?"

"Jake."

Jeff's brows rose, but he didn't comment. Kara knew what he was thinking, but it didn't matter. She hadn't been flirting with Jake. She mounted. Time to investigate the scene where the mystery men had been.

18

Kara followed Jeff's lead and guided her mount past sagebrush and juniper trees along the high desert trail to the river. A warm breeze kicked up dirt around them.

She blinked rapidly to clear the dust from her eyes. "How do we get across the river?" She'd heard stories of people drowning in river crossings, and she didn't want to become a statistic.

Jeff flicked a glance her way. "We'll find a slow moving, shallow spot. It's more of a slow-moving stream than a river this time of year."

Didn't look like a stream to her. "How do you suppose those men got there the other day?" She looked around the terrain, hoping to spot an easier way to get to the other side.

"There're several options. They could've come in from the road or from the other side of Eric's property or rafted in on the river. This ranch is huge. I'm sure there are plenty of ways to get onto the property unnoticed."

"We can take a road in?" Why didn't he say so from the start?

"Sure, but this is the more direct route. See how shallow the water is through here, only a foot at the most. Follow me."

Kara swallowed the lump in her throat and guided Blaze into the meandering river. To her amazement, he didn't mind the water at all and crossed without mishap.

"Let's walk the horses from here. Look for footprints, litter, and drug paraphernalia. With this wind and the dry ground, I doubt there'd still be any footprints, but you never know."

An hour later, Kara sank onto a large porous rock and wiped sweat from her forehead with the back of her hand before taking a drink from her water bottle. "Nothing but deer tracks. Whoever was here didn't leave anything behind."

Jeff sat beside her. "I agree. And it appears we're no closer to knowing who was out here that day." He put binoculars to his eyes, looked to the north, then panned right. "I see nothing unusual." He frowned. "I wish we could do some serious exploring without raising suspicion, but we'd almost need to camp to cover this amount of territory. Bureau of Land Management property butts up to Eric's, so there's a lot of ground to cover."

"I noticed the BLM property on the map. There's no reason to assume the traffickers aren't using that land. We need to plan an overnight trip. Maybe we could pull together a small group of agents to pose as tourists and set up some kind of campout trail ride."

Jeff grinned. "That's a great idea. No one would suspect a thing. From what I understand Eric caters to the tourists, so I don't see why we couldn't pull it off. I'll contact Tad with CODE, and see what we can work out."

Kara rose and untied Blaze from a large juniper tree. "Come on. There's nothing more we can do right now. She swung up onto Blaze. "Before I forget, have you given any thought to coming to the singles' group meeting tonight?" She really didn't want to go alone.

"That's not my kind of thing. I don't like those social gatherings. I'll pass. How about you?"

"I might. Jessica seems nice. I'd like to get to know her, and it would be fun to have a friend close to my age to hang out with while I'm here. Gail is great, but she's more like a mom." She guided Blaze back through the shallow water and up the slight embankment.

Jeff held his hand to his heart. "You wound me. I thought I was your friend. Am I not good enough for you anymore?"

Kara laughed. She enjoyed this lighter side of him. "You're plenty good enough, but you're not a girl. We ladies need to stick together."

"Then by all means, don't let me keep you from your bonding."

Kara chuckled. Jeff's playful side didn't come out often enough. As they rode into the yard Kara spotted Veronica entering the barn. She glanced at Jeff. "I wonder what she's doing. You mind taking care of Blaze for me? I want to talk with Veronica." Kara dismounted then patted Blaze's neck.

Jeff turned to her, his eyes questioning. "Sure. Care to share what you're up to?"

"Later." Kara strode ahead and entered the barn. She spotted Veronica sitting behind Jake's desk in the office and knocked on the doorjamb. "Hi. Mind some company?"

Veronica's attempt at a welcome smile failed miserably. "Of course not. Have a seat." She motioned toward the folding metal chair across from the desk.

"Thanks. I've never seen you out here. Don't you and Eric keep an office in the house?"

"Yes." She shrugged. "I'm a snoop. I can't help myself. I need to know everything that's going on, and Eric's been keeping to himself. I'm usually out here more since I'm a trainer, but things have been a little slow of late." A horse whinnied loudly. Veronica startled.

Kara puzzled over Veronica's admission and jumpiness. Why not talk to Eric about her concerns? Unless she was afraid of the answer. Kara could hear Jeff tending to the horses and tried to ignore him. "I'm sorry for prying. If there's anything I can do to help, or if you just want to talk, I'm a good listener." She motioned toward Veronica's hands. "Your manicure is holding up well."

She held out her hands and looked at them. "They are. You do good work. I'll be sure to let my friends know about you. Speaking of that. How is it you're here and not working?"

Kara shrugged. "I set my own hours. Most people work this time of day, so I adjust my hours for when they're free."

"Oh. I hadn't thought of that." She rose to leave, and Kara stood.

Veronica placed her hand on Kara's arm and spoke softly. "Please don't tell Jeff I was snooping in Jake's office. He might tell Eric."

"Don't worry, Veronica. I know how to keep my mouth shut." Kara turned to leave the office and tripped over a loose board. "Looks like that board needs to be fixed."

"I'll let Jake know."

"Or I could tell him. I'm going to be out here a while with Jeff."

Veronica's expression relaxed a little. "Thanks. I'll be in the house if anyone needs me."

Kara waited nearby and watched Jeff groom Blaze.

He looked over his shoulder. "You and Veronica have a nice chat?"

"Uh-huh." She sidled up to Jeff and lowered her voice. "I found a loose board in the office. Think there could be anything under it?"

"Could be. Give me a second, and I'll take a look."

Jeff let Blaze out to the pasture then followed Kara. "Hmm. The board is warped so I doubt it's some kind of hiding place. I'll check with Eric and see if he wants the board replaced."

Kara's cell phone rang. She checked the caller ID and mouthed "Gary" to Jeff. "Kara here."

"How're things going?" Gary answered on the other end.

"Fine." Kara's gut clenched. Something about the

tone of Gary's voice set off all kinds of alarms. "What's up?" She motioned to Jeff that she was going to take the call outside and left the barn.

"Luis Alvarado has people in your area. There's a hit out on you."

She lowered her voice. "Is my location compromised?" She leaned against a fence post for support. How had everything gone wrong so fast? Where was God anyway? Didn't He want her to put away the bad guys and help stop drug trafficking?

"Unknown. We're putting out feelers, but we both know it's only a matter of time before your location is compromised." He cleared his throat. "I know I don't have to tell you, but be careful."

"Don't worry. I'll will."

"Word on the street is that Luis would kill you himself if given the opportunity."

Kara's heart skipped a beat. That only meant one thing. This was personal for him—not good. He had a reputation for exacting revenge in the cruelest of ways. A shudder snaked through her. "I'm sure the fact that I deceived him tops his list of reasons to want me dead. Plus, I know things he wouldn't want his mother to know, much less the US government. It's amazing what you learn simply by dusting a room at the right time."

"Yeah. I saw the deposition you gave. Hang in there. We're working overtime trying to find Alvarado, and when we do, we'll let you know."

"Thanks." She slid the phone back into her pocket. Even if they found and arrested Alvarado, the hit would still be in play. *Lord, I know we don't seem to be on the same page of late, but if You could keep me alive, I'd sure appreciate it.*

Jeff sauntered up to her. Concern etched on his face. "What's wrong?" He took her hand and guided her to a private bench nestled in the shade of a huge juniper.

Kara eased down beside him and leaned forward resting her forehead in her hands. "Alvarado has people here."

"Already?"

She nodded.

"How much time do we have?"

"I don't know." She heard the edge in her voice. "Sorry. I didn't mean to snap."

He grasped her hand and gently squeezed it. "I think we should pray."

"Already did. Though I doubt it will do any good. God doesn't listen to me."

Jeff blinked. "Wow. What's up with the attitude?"

"Nothing." She stood. "I need to get out of here. Are you going to take care of the camping trip?"

"You still think it's a good idea?"

"Yes, and the sooner the better. I doubt anyone will be able to find me in the middle of nowhere. And even if they did, I'd be surrounded by trained professionals."

"Okay. I'll set it up. Be careful."

"Always."

19

A glance in the mirror displayed pale lips. Kara applied a fresh coat of burgundy lipstick and swished a little powder over her face before hopping into her car. The singles' group would begin in fifteen minutes, and she didn't want to be late. The directions looked simple enough, and it should only take a few minutes to get to the address Jessica provided. She should've asked whose house they were meeting at.

Regardless of Alvarado's people being in town, she had a job to do and would not stop living.

Kara took a left out of the alley and drove down Main Street. A glance in her rearview mirror showed a yellow pickup truck several car lengths behind. Hadn't that same vehicle been parked across the street from her apartment? At the next corner, she made a quick right, sped up, and made another right. Punching the gas, she slid to a stop back on Main Street in time to see the pickup turn around the corner and follow the same route she'd taken.

Kara pulled back out onto Main to follow the

pickup. "Bingo." The truck sat parked along the side of the road. She memorized the plate and continued on by. The vehicle didn't follow this time. Kara pulled out her cell and called the local sheriff's office. "Tad Baker, please." The voice on the other end informed her he was out for the evening. Now what? She called the DEA field office, and a guy she'd met her first day in town answered.

"Kara Nelson here. Someone was following me, and I need their plate run." She gave the number and was told to hang on.

A glance in her rearview mirror revealed an empty road. She continued on toward the address of the singles' get-together.

"The vehicle is registered to Sean Wilkins. There's a security code attached also. He must be law enforcement of some kind." He rattled off a Bend address. "Does that name mean anything to you?"

"Nothing. Thanks for checking."

"No problem. Everything okay?"

"Fine. I owe you, Max."

He chuckled. "I'll be sure to collect. Saw you in here a few weeks ago. That was messed up—you doing better?"

"Yes, no more bandages. I gotta go. Thanks, again." She turned onto a long gravel driveway flanked by ponderosa pines. Why would someone in law enforcement be tailing her? Something felt wrong, but for now, other matters were more important—like who frequented these singles' meetings. Kara went up a slight hill and passed a small cabin on the right as she continued to the top. The directions indicated the place sat at the end of the long driveway. Several cars were parked along the edge of the gravel lane. She pulled up behind the last vehicle and took a deep breath. Then she climbed out of her car and headed for the door.

Laughter and the smell of Italian food floated through an open window. Sounded like they were having fun. She knocked on the deep red door of the white clapboard house, and a tall man with dark hair greeted her. She'd seen him someplace before. The DEA intel file—Tad. No wonder why he had the night off. Tad held out his hand. "You must be, Kara. Jessica mentioned she'd invited you. I'm Tad Baker."

Kara shook his hand. "It's nice to meet you."

"You too." He opened the door wider and stepped aside for her to enter. She walked by an open door to the right leading to a bedroom and spotted his sheriff's deputy uniform on the bed.

Jessica sat in a brown leather chair near the couch, visiting with a dark-haired woman in her mid-to-late twenties. The couch seemed to swallow up the petite stranger. Kara set her course directly for the two women.

"Kara!" Jessica stood and greeted her. "I'm glad you found Tad's place okay. This is my friend Becky Graham. We teach at the same school."

Becky rose and hugged Kara. "It's so nice to finally meet you. Jessica's mentioned you several times."

Kara's arms hung at her side for a moment, but she quickly recovered from the surprise of such a friendly greeting and gave Becky a quick squeeze. "Thanks."

Jessica motioned toward the couch. "Take a seat. How's business? I saw your sign the other day when I was in town."

Kara sank into the soft cushion and sighed. "It's fine."

"That good, huh? Don't worry, it's bound to pick up as soon as word gets out that we have a nail salon in town." Jessica held her hands out in front of her. "Come to think of it, I could use a manicure myself."

Kara handed Jessica her business card. "Give me a call or text. I work weird hours, but I try to make myself available when it works best for my clients."

Jessica stuffed the card in her purse. "Thanks." She motioned toward a guy with curly hair who had to be at least six foot two. He was talking to a young woman in the corner. "That's Greg and his wife, Kelly. He's been leading our Bible studies for years. He'll start by reading scripture. Then he'll open the floor for questions and comments."

Kara swallowed the lump in her throat. If she'd known this was a Bible study, she may not have come. For some reason, she'd had the impression this would be a social gathering. Oh well, she'd have to make the best of it.

Everyone in the room bowed their heads to pray, and Kara followed their lead. She opened her eyes when Greg said amen. He then turned to a passage in his Bible and read from the book of Hebrews.

Why was someone following her, and did it have anything to do with the hit? Or had someone been assigned to protect her without her knowledge? There was nothing she could do about any of that right now. She had enough mysteries to solve without adding to the load. Were drugs stashed beneath the loose board in Jake's office, or was it really only a warped board? But if there was a cache beneath, who had put it there? What bothered her the most, though, were the guys out on the range. Who were they, and why hadn't they seen them again?

Kara came out of her musings when she heard the flow of conversation around her. People were beginning to stand and move toward the food table.

Jessica sat down beside Kara on the couch then leaned in and spoke quietly. "How'd you like the Bible study?"

"It was interesting." Not a complete lie as she'd had time to think about the case.

"I'm glad. We meet every other week. I hope you'll come to our next meeting. The bulletin at church usually has an announcement with the details."

"Thanks."

Kara made a point of introducing herself to several members of the group as they stood around feasting on lasagna and French bread. One never knew when it would pay to know someone.

Jeff sat in the darkness of Kara's apartment, his knee bouncing up and down. He pressed the button on his watch to illuminate the time—nine thirty. Keys rattled in the door. *Finally!*

Kara flipped on the light switch. He noticed she didn't so much as flinch when her eyes rested on him. "Making yourself at home?" She kicked the door shut with her foot and sat in the cushy chair next to him.

"Yeah, thanks. I had an interesting phone call about an hour ago."

"Really?"

He nodded. "The field office called."

Kara frowned. "Why?"

"We're partners, and apparently, you turned your phone off."

She pulled her cell out and took the ringer off vibrate. "No. I just didn't notice it vibrating. What's going on?"

"Your tail was Sean Wilkins. FBI."

"Interesting. Why would the FBI be following me?"

"Good question. Think I'll go find out in the morning."

"I want to come."

He shook his head. "Not a great idea. I'd rather deal with this without the object of our discussion hovering."

"I don't hover," Kara said.

Jeff rolled his eyes. "Fine. You don't hover, but I would appreciate if you'd let me do this on my own."

"Why do you care so much?"

"We're partners. That's what partners do." Besides she had already almost been killed on his watch once, and he didn't plan to let that happen again. He needed to know if this Wilkins dude was friend or foe.

Her lips pursed, and she looked at him with doubt in her eyes. Hadn't she ever had a partner that cared whether she lived or died? Kara definitely needed to get away from deep cover work if she couldn't remember something as basic as that.

He cleared his throat. "How was your meeting?"

"Good. Turned out to be a Bible study led by a guy named Greg."

"Tell me about it."

"There were about ten or so in attendance including Tad Baker."

"I didn't mean tell me about the people. I was hoping to find out about the topic and what kind of speaker this Greg guy is."

Kara stood and went to the refrigerator. "Oh. Sorry I can't help with that. As soon as Greg started talking, my mind wandered to the case." She held up a pitcher of lemonade. "Would you like some?"

He shook his head and stood. "No. I should be going." Sadness for Kara gripped him. Running from God and blaming Him for all her recent problems only made things worse for her. Life was too complicated to deal with it alone. He wanted to help, but the only thing he could think to do was pray. "Come by the ranch tomorrow? I have a floorboard to replace."

Kara turned from pouring her drink. "I'll be there. See you tomorrow."

Jeff let himself out. The lock on the door clicked into place before he moved toward his SUV. His skin prickled. He paused and looked around, listening for anything out of place. Just to be certain, he walked several feet down the alley and then back. Nothing seemed out of place, but he couldn't shake the feeling that something wasn't right.

He reached for his sidearm at the screech of an alley cat. Rapid footsteps faded into the night. He ran to the end of the alley—whoever had been there was gone now. First thing tomorrow, he'd pay a visit to Wilkins.

20

Kara looked up from a magazine when the salon door opened and Tad Baker entered. "Good morning, Tad. You don't strike me as the manicure type," she teased.

He chuckled. "Nope. Working on Saturday, huh?"

"Afraid so." She motioned for him to have a seat in one of the overstuffed chairs.

He sat with his ankle propped on his knee.

"What brings you by?"

"I received your note to come and see you. What's up?"

Kara frowned. "Do you have it with you?"

Tad reached into his shirt pocket and held out a piece of paper.

She scanned the handwritten note. "Do you mind if I hang onto this?" Maybe she could have it analyzed.

"Not at all. Is there a problem?"

"I didn't leave this for you. Are you aware of who I am?"

He shot her a confused look. "Of course, I know

who you are. The DEA sent you to assist with Operation Trail Ride, and you're Jessica's friend."

Kara spoke in a low tone. "Yes, but my presence here has been kept quiet."

She saw awareness in his eyes.

"Have you been compromised?"

"It's possible. I've come to Sunridge with baggage of my own. I received an unsettling call yesterday."

Tad frowned. "Tell me more."

"The most powerful drug lord in Miami wants me dead and his people are said to be in the area. There have been a couple incidents, but nothing substantive. I spotted someone looking through my salon window, and when I went to investigate, they disappeared. That reminds me. Do you know a Sean Wilkins?"

"I do. He's with the FBI. Why?"

"He involved in this operation?"

"Yes. What's going on?" He sat forward.

"Hang with me a minute. Does he know I'm on the case?"

"I don't know."

She raised her brows.

"Normally he'd know, but my superiors made it clear that your involvement in this case was need to know only." He sat in the chair across from her and leaned back. "Sean doesn't need to know about you."

Kara chuckled softly. "I caught him following me last night on my way to the Bible study. When it was clear he'd been made, he backed off."

"I'll talk to him and see why he was following you."

"Thanks, but my partner is convinced that's his job.

Since he doesn't know who I am, I think he followed me because I spend so much time at the ranch." She shook her head. "To him, I'm a suspect."

Tad ran his hand over his face. "There's something I hadn't anticipated. How do you want to handle this?"

If everyone knew she was on the case, they'd stop wasting valuable man-hours following her, but if even one of them was dirty, she could be asking for trouble. She took a deep breath and let it out slowly. "For the sake of the case, I think you should let them know about me."

"Are you sure?"

"Yes."

He rose. "Okay." He turned to leave.

"Wait a second, Tad." She stood and walked up to him. "Why do you think you were used to deliver the note? Any ideas?"

"No, but I'll give it some thought. In the meantime, I'll keep my eyes open."

"Okay, and if I find anything new, I'll let you know."

He pulled out a business card and handed it to her after writing on the back. "My cell and home numbers are on the back if you can't reach me at work."

She added the numbers to her phone then stuffed the card in her jeans pocket. She locked up the shop after Tad left then flipped the open sign to closed.

After tossing toiletries, extra ammo, and a change of clothes into a duffle bag, Kara went out the back door. She wouldn't run, but she refused to sit around and wait for trouble.

21

Jeff forced himself to take one stair at a time as he came down the porch. He'd had a busy morning, thanks to Sean. The guy had been more than a little miffed at him for waking him up at eight thirty on a Saturday, demanding to know why he'd been following Kara. For some reason, Sean believed he should be allowed to sleep in on his day off. Jeff smirked. Sean had thought Kara was involved with the drug smugglers. He'd set the guy straight in short order. Boy, was he angry when he found out Kara was DEA, and he hadn't been notified.

Jeff spotted Kara's parked car. His pace quickened as he strode to the barn, her typical first stop. He wasn't disappointed. He found her in the tack room snooping around. "Find what you're looking for?"

Kara sucked in a breath. "You scared me."

"Sorry." He walked further into the room. "So, did you?"

"Did I what?" She placed her hands on her hips.

"Find what you're looking for." Jeff held back a

chuckle that threatened to escape his lips. Mud streaked across her nose. He sauntered over to her, invading her space. Her eyes opened wider. Jeff touched her nose. The tingle zinged up his arm. He saw the confusion in Kara's eyes, which mirrored his own. "You have mud on your nose."

Kara's face reddened. "I wonder how that got there." She moved past him toward the door.

He'd made her blush. Had she felt the same connection he had? Is that why she moved away so fast? He understood the instinct to flee. They couldn't get involved. A little voice in the back of his mind pointed out they wouldn't always be partners. Jeff followed Kara into the tack room.

She had her back to him as she removed the bridle from the wall. "You want to go riding?"

"Sure. But before we go, you can help me with that loose board. Eric wants it replaced."

Kara whirled around to face him. "Oh yeah, I almost forgot." She put back the bridle.

He grabbed a hammer on the way to the office.

"Where's Jake?" Kara walked beside him.

"Out on a trail ride. I figured now would be a good time to take care of this. Even with Eric's go ahead, I don't want to irritate Jake."

"I hear you."

He glanced up at Kara as he pried the nails from the board. Her eyes danced, he assumed, in anticipation of what they might find.

With the last nail removed, he lifted the board. Jeff sat back on his haunches and stared into the empty space.

He grinned wide and replaced the board, pounding down the threaded nails with a little more zest than necessary. He and Eric may not have been close as kids, but he didn't embrace the thought of someone in his family being involved in drug smuggling. He'd do his job and do it well, but he had a right to feel happy about not finding any incriminating evidence.

Kara slipped from the room without a word.

Jeff stood and went to find Kara. He didn't have to go far. She was in the process of saddling Blaze. He chose Lulu, Lauren's quarter horse. They saddled the horses in silence then mounted.

"You want to ride to the river?" Jeff asked.

"Sure. I think we should try a different route though. I'd like to get a better feel for the land, and I don't want to be predictable."

Made sense. With Alvarado's people here it likely meant one thing—a hit man or multiple hit men would be studying Kara's habits. Jeff rode beside her, alert for anything unusual.

At the river, they tied the horses to a tree. He'd planned to climb the same boulder as last time but thought better of it. "How about if you spread that blanket in the shade?"

She responded without comment. The area was protected on three sides by dense foliage. No one would be able to sneak up on them without being heard.

Kara laid face down, eyes closed while cradling her head in her arms. Jeff sat next to her staring at the river and keeping an eye out for trouble. He knew Kara too well by now to believe that everything was fine. Something was definitely bothering her, and it seemed to be more than a possible hit on her life. "You're quiet this morning."

"Nothing to say."

"That's a first."

"Very funny." She sighed. "Someone sent a message to me through Tad."

Jeff shifted. "What kind of message?"

"They know where I am."

"Who is they?"

"Wish I knew. But if I had to guess, I'd say Alvarado is messing with me. Trying to get under my skin. He likes to play mind games."

No wonder Kara had seemed distracted when she'd arrived at the ranch. "You okay?"

"Peachy." Sarcasm dripped from her voice.

He remembered the uneasy feeling he'd had outside Kara's apartment last night and frowned. "Trouble seems to follow you. Do you have the note? I'd like to see it."

Kara shook her head. "Wish I'd never heard the name Luis Alvarado." She rolled over and shielded her eyes with her hand.

Jeff looked around. He knew she was in danger but hadn't believed she'd been found. Things just changed. "You're an easy target out here. We should go."

"No," Kara said.

"But—"

"I said no."

"Fine but not for long." He frowned, lifted

binoculars to his eyes, and studied the land around them. It seemed they were alone, but it was hard to say for sure. "I don't understand something."

"What's that?"

"Why you're still alive. If Alvarado's hit man has found you, he wouldn't waste time. You'd be dead."

"What's your point?"

"What's there to gain by letting you know you've been found? I suspect there's more to this than we realize."

"You mean, maybe the note was more innocent than I thought?" Kara sounded hopeful.

"Could be. Or the weasel is toying with you like you said." He winced at the look of despair his words brought to her sea blue eyes. "You want to leave town?"

"No. I'm on a case, and I'm depending on you and Tad to keep your eyes and ears open."

"I don't like it, Kara. You're allowing yourself to be a target, and to what end?"

"We lock up several lowlifes. I figure I'm safer with you by my side than if I go off on my own."

Sooner or later Alvarado would tire of his game, and Jeff couldn't stop a sniper's bullet. But arguing seemed futile.

Kara rested her hand on top of his. "Let's talk about something more pleasant." She grinned. "Invite me to stay for dinner tonight?"

"Okay. Stay for dinner. What about lunch?"

"Thanks, lunch sounds great," Kara said. "And I'd love to stay for dinner too. But don't forget to let Veronica know you invited me."

Jeff chuckled and leaned across her torso, resting his palm on the blanket blocking the sun from her face. "You're rather conniving today. What else is going on in that head of yours?" He tapped her forehead with his finger.

"Nothing special. I hate cooking and a meal invite keeps me here for the day—where ironically, I feel safest. Since my investigation revolves around the ranch, it's a no-brainer."

Jeff looked down at her pixie-like face and saw vulnerability. This wasn't the same Kara he'd been keeping an eye on for the past year as she bamboozled Miami's most notorious drug lord. This Kara had looked death in the face one too many times. His gut clenched at the thought of losing her. When had he started to care so much? No matter what, he'd make sure she was safe. She flashed an unsteady grin. If only he could tell her that everything would be okay. His fingers itched to touch her long hair, but he held himself in check. "Do you want to head back now? You shouldn't be out in the open like this."

Kara sighed. "I suppose we should."

"You suppose so, huh? And I thought you had better things to do than sit out here with me."

Kara chuckled. "I never said that." She stood and folded the blanket.

A few minutes later, the horses clopped along the tree-lined dirt trail at a slow pace. "Do you have a map of this ranch?" Kara asked. "I'd like to see how far it spreads."

"I'm sure Eric has one. What are you thinking?"

"Thought I might map out our camping trip. You're still working on that?"

"Yeah, but it's not going to happen as soon as we'd hoped. Eric said we needed to wait a couple of weeks."

"Why?"

Jeff shrugged, hating to voice his real thoughts on the subject.

She turned toward him. "He doesn't want us to stumble onto something. A drug run must be planned sometime in the next two weeks. We have to be out there no matter what."

"I know. I know." How would he do it without Eric finding out? "Any ideas?"

"Let me work on it. I'll think of something."

"Fair enough." Jeff kept an extra watchful eye on their surroundings as the horses plodded through the wooded area.

Back at the ranch now, he followed Kara into the barn and saw the surprised look on her face when Veronica greeted them from the office as they went into the barn. Jeff went into the office and closed the door behind him. "I invited Kara to spend the day here and to stay for dinner."

"No problem, Jeff. Thanks for letting me know. Did the two of you have a nice ride?"

"We did, and thanks for being cool about Kara."

Veronica rose and made her way toward the door. "I like her, and it's nice to see you two together."

Jeff forced a smile. He liked Kara also—too much. He left the office and nearly bumped into the object of his thoughts as she rounded the corner of the stalls from the direction of the arena.

"Everything okay with Veronica?" Kara motioned with her head toward the office.

"Sure is. You, lady, are playing on the ranch today. I have a call to make. Blaze is taken care of?"

Kara nodded. "Just turned him out."

"Good. Would you mind taking care of Lulu for me?"

"Not at all. Jake helped me with Blaze, but I don't mind rubbing down Lulu."

"Thanks. I'll catch up with you in a bit. I have an errand to run. You going to be okay?"

"Of course. Go."

Jeff double-timed it to his SUV then headed down the driveway. He didn't want anyone to overhear this conversation. It was time he and Tad had a talk.

After Kara finished with Lulu, she slipped into the office. There had to be some reason Veronica kept coming in here other than to spy on Jake. She scanned the papers on the desk without touching anything. Nothing looked out of the ordinary.

Kara felt along the paneled walls for a trigger to open a secret compartment. She had one hand raised to feel the wall and the other at about waist level when she sensed a presence and looked over her shoulder. "Jake." She yanked her hands to her sides. "I uh…"

His eyes twinkled. "You dancin' with the wall?"

She crossed her arms and grinned. *Dancing?* Now

there was something she hadn't thought of. Was he serious? "I haven't had a better offer lately, and I didn't want to get out of practice."

Jake chuckled, flipped the switch on the radio to a country station, and opened his arms. Kara stared in disbelief.

"Don't leave a fella hangin'. You wanted to dance, didn't you?"

Kara moved into the circle of his arm and rested one hand on his shoulder. He took the other in his hand. "Now isn't that better?" Their bodies swayed to the music.

"You're a few steps up from the wall." Kara did a spin under his arm. "Tell me, how did you get so good at dancing while working a ranch?"

"I don't spend all my time here."

"Where do you spend your free time?" She nearly tripped as he spun her away from him. Nice move, but she was a lousy dancer.

He caught her waist. "Careful now. I can't have you gettin' hurt, or Jeff will be breathing down my neck."

"Sorry. I'm a little rusty. So how do you spend your free time?"

"There's a bar in town, and a couple of my buddies live nearby."

"Hello."

Kara turned startled eyes to the door then disengaged herself from Jake's grasp. Just when Jake had started to open up, Jeff had to show up. As usual, his timing couldn't have been worse.

Jeff stood in the doorway. A scowl covered his face, and he looked ready to punch Jake.

Kara's pulse quickened.

Jake chuckled "Don't go and git yourself in a dander. The lady wanted to dance." He flicked off the radio and motioned for them to leave the office. Jake followed them out then walked away and busied himself with one of the horses.

Jeff placed his arm across her shoulder and spoke under his breath. "What was that all about?"

"Calm down. It's not how it looked."

"Fine. I came to see if you're ready for lunch. Veronica has a table set out on the porch. Don't worry. It's secluded, so you won't be out in the open."

"Perfect. I'm starving. Let's eat." They left the barn with Jeff's hand resting on her back as though she belonged to him. Jeff deserved an Oscar for his acting abilities. If she didn't know better, she'd buy his jealous act.

Halfway to the house, he whispered. "What was that all about?"

Her explanation came out in a rush. The whole time she spoke, Jeff's frown seemed to deepen. "I'm just glad he didn't want to know what I was doing in the office." Kara chewed her bottom lip and looked up at Jeff. "Although I don't believe, for a minute, he didn't suspect something."

"You're probably right. Jake isn't a simpleton. I hope you didn't blow your cover. You took a big risk to find evidence that would have to be thrown out since you didn't have a search warrant."

Kara's shoulders sagged. She'd let her urgency to solve this case override her training and commonsense. Seemed her world was racing out of control, and she couldn't slow it down. Kara stopped at the bottom of the front porch stairs and took in the sight.

Veronica had covered a small round table with white linen and set it with simple ivory colored plates. In the center of the table, three glass cylinders of varying heights held lit candles. Cut flowers were tucked among their bases. "This is amazing," Kara said.

Jeff pulled out her chair with a flourish. "M' Lady, your feast awaits."

Kara giggled and sat. She relaxed into the seatback when she realized how private the setting was. Vines shaded them on two sides, and the house blocked another angle. Jeff was right. If there was a shooter out there, he'd have to work hard to get at her with such limited access. Finally, she could relax.

She licked her lips and nearly drooled at the delicate spread. Chocolate-covered strawberries rested beside a turkey, ham, and cheese croissant and a scoop of chicken salad. Tall glasses filled with lemonade sparkled in the dappled sunlight.

"Did Veronica do this just for us?"

"I think the plan was a romantic lunch for two." He unfolded a crisp white napkin and dropped it on his lap.

Kara bit into a large ripe strawberry and closed her eyes. "Mmm. She succeeded. Have you tried these? They're so sweet!"

She turned in her seat to see who Jeff was looking at. Veronica and Lauren watched from the kitchen window. He reached across the table to place his hand on Kara's. She ignored the tingle his touch created in her fingers and fed him a bite of her strawberry.

"Wow, you're right. They are sweet."

Kara reached across the table and wiped juice off his chin with her napkin. He caught her hand up in his and held it as their eyes locked. Kara's heart pounded. This felt too real. If she could believe the look in Jeff's eyes. No. She refused to go there. She gently pulled her hand from his grasp and cleared her throat, breaking the moment. "Your sister-in-law missed her calling."

"I don't know what calling you're referring to, but she sure knows how to serve a romantic lunch." He picked up another strawberry and guided it to her mouth.

Her eyes widened as the juice dribbled down her chin. He rose slightly from his chair and leaned forward to kiss the juice away.

She caught her breath as he placed a butterfly kiss on her cheek. "You better be careful. Your family will be pushing for a wedding invitation if you keep this up," Kara whispered.

He sat back in his seat, a silly grin covering his face. "What makes you think they aren't already?" He chuckled then stuffed a forkful of chicken salad into his mouth.

Twenty minutes later, Veronica returned with Lauren by her side as Kara and Jeff finished their meal. "How was everything?"

Kara placed her napkin on the table and sat back. "You should open your own bed and breakfast. You're a fantastic cook."

Veronica laughed. "Just last week, Eric said the same thing, but I don't think he realizes how much work's involved with operating a B and B. Between my work with the horses and keeping this house running,

I'd never survive."

Lauren grasped one plate in each hand. "Sure you would. I'd help out, Mom. It'd be fun to have people around. I could even provide the entertainment."

Veronica caressed her daughter's face. "I'm so blessed to have a daughter like you, but I think you'd change your mind as soon as the first inconsiderate person showed up. Not all guests are as kind as your uncle." Veronica nodded to Kara and Jeff.

"I was wondering," Kara said. "I've never been camping, and a few friends in town mentioned that they'd like to take me. Would it be possible to camp on your property near the river?"

"I don't see why not," Veronica said. "Go ahead and tell your friends they're more than welcome."

Kara grinned. "Wonderful. Thanks. The only thing is one of them will be leaving soon for California, so we'd have to go next week."

"Shouldn't be a problem. You two enjoy your afternoon." Veronica disappeared into the house with Lauren by her side.

Kara took a sip from her glass and winked at Jeff.

"You're amazing." He grasped her hand. "Come on. Let's sit in the swing."

Kara allowed Jeff to lead her to the other side of the porch where a swing hung from posts. "What's come over you?" Kara lifted her hair and sighed as the breeze blew over her warm skin.

He glanced toward the barn. "Nothing, I'm just trying to reclaim my territory."

She laughed. "Trust me. You have nothing to worry about." She scooted closer to him and whispered, "Put together a small team, and make sure there's at least one woman. Veronica would think it's strange if all my friends were men."

"No problem. Let's plan to leave Monday."

Later that day, long after Kara left, a commotion drifting through the open kitchen window grabbed Jeff's attention. Careful to avoid the creaky first step on the porch, he crept to the bench below the window and sat.

"I don't understand what the big deal is," Veronica snapped. "What difference does it make when Kara and her friends go camping?"

"I already told you, I have a big order to deliver on the other side of the pass," Eric said.

Jeff heard frustration in his brother's voice and felt guilty for being partly to blame for the confrontation.

"So what?" Veronica asked. "You'll be gone a couple days. Big deal."

"I don't like the idea of Kara and her friends being out there when I'm not home."

Veronica's voice faded, but he heard a door slam from somewhere inside the house.

The back door opened, and Jeff nearly jumped.

Eric did a double take when he spotted Jeff. "Did you hear all that?"

Jeff nodded. "I didn't mean to eavesdrop."

"I told you I had deliveries to make, and next week wouldn't work. Why'd you go behind my back and talk to Veronica?" His angry tone was nothing compared with the storm brewing on his face.

"I didn't. Kara did."

"Inform Kara there will be no camping trip next week." Eric strode down the steps and out to the barn.

Jeff winced. This was not the way to get on Eric's good side. Time for plan B. Pulling his phone from his pocket as he walked to his SUV, he called Kara. "Hi. Next week is off, and Eric is angry."

She sighed. "Now what?"

"I go on a recon road trip. Thought I'd check on what Eric's up to."

"Want company?" Kara asked.

"Yes, but you need to stay here. If you're never at your nail salon, people are going to start to wonder about you and start asking questions." He'd make arrangements with Tad to have extra security on Kara while he was away.

"It's not a big deal to close up shop for a couple days."

He heard desperation in her voice. Was she afraid to be alone? No way. Kara was one of the bravest people he knew. "Sorry. Not this time."

"It's fine. I have more than enough to keep me busy here."

"Good. I think he's planning to leave Monday."

"My client is here. Gotta go"

Jeff pulled the silent phone from his ear. He'd gotten to know Kara well enough to know something wasn't right. He wanted to help her, but for now, he had a job to do.

22

"Hi Marci," Kara laid a towel across her lap. "I'm all set up to do your pedicure."

Marci sat in the corner chair and cautiously dipped her toes into the water.

Kara noticed her flushed cheeks and tired looking eyes. "I can adjust the temperature if it's too hot or cold." Kara reached for a pitcher to fill with water.

Marci slid both feet into the tub and sighed. "It's just right." She pulled a bottle of coral polish from her purse. "I brought my own polish. It makes touch-ups so much more convenient."

"I agree, especially since I don't sell polish here." She lifted Marci's right foot, rested it on a towel, and got to work—it looked as though she'd had a pedicure recently. "How's your summer going? Are you and your son enjoying the park?"

"We were there yesterday, but you know how it is. Too much to do and not enough time. Making matters worse, I can't sleep. Nothing seems to help, and I'm so tired."

"Sounds familiar. I wish someone would make a magic energy pill."

Marci's foot tensed.

"I'm sorry. Am I hurting you?"

"No. You're fine."

Kara's gut was seldom wrong, and right now, it told her she was close to finding out something big. "If you're sure." She placed Marci's foot back in the tub of water and started on her left. "I used to work in Miami and—"

"Miami! It's such a great city. Everyone is so beautiful and tan and in such great shape."

"I'll take that as a compliment. But you're in great shape too." If she were honest, Marci was borderline too thin. "How do you stay so trim?"

"I'm a workaholic, and I don't have a big appetite."

"Lucky you. I love food. It's a constant battle with the bulge for me." Kara massaged Marci's feet, which finally began to relax. Looked like she still had the touch.

"You hide it well," Marci said.

Kara chuckled. She finished up the massage then wiped Marci's nails in prep for polish. "Clothes hide a multitude of sins. I should probably step up my workout routine. I like to run, but since I've been in town, I've been doing more horseback riding than anything."

Marci nodded, but a troubled look rested on her face.

Kara slipped flip-flops onto Marci's feet—a trick she'd learned way back in her early years as a nail technician. She applied the base coat to both feet then started on the color. She worked in silence letting their conversation sink in. Unless she was way off, Marci was an addict. She suspected cocaine. A user experienced a jolt of energy and reduced fatigue when they were high. But the side effects of the highly addictive drug were evident in Marci—dilated pupils, loss of appetite, as well as insomnia.

"Finished." Kara twisted the cap tight and handed the polish back to Marci. "What do you think?"

"Very nice."

"Thanks. Relax for a few minutes, and let your nails dry. I wouldn't want you to smudge them."

"I'll be careful. I need to go." She stood. "See you."

With practiced nonchalance, Kara followed her to the door and locked up. She wasn't ready to approach Marci about her suspected drug usage yet. But when the time was right, she'd use Marci to the DEA's advantage. If only she didn't have a child. Kara hated it when children's lives were messed up because of their parents' addiction. At least the woman appeared to be a good mom—though how she managed, Kara had no idea. She was definitely the exception and not the norm.

That was a problem for another day though. Right now, she had clients to cancel and a bag to pack. No way was she going to let Jeff follow his brother without backup.

Kara crept across the yard wearing all black to blend with the cover of darkness. The front door to the main house opened slowly and a lone figure quietly stepped down the stairs. Thankful there were no motion sensor lights, she pressed against the barn and held her breath. Her pulse pounded in her ears.

Two men came out of the shadows and met near Eric's truck. Their voices carried in the thin night air— Spanish. Apparently, the men wanted money and food. Eric handed a bag to the men, and in return, they stuffed a piece of paper into his hand.

Kara slid to the ground and squatted, hoping no one would notice her. Meanwhile, an army of crickets sang a song disrupting the quiet of the night. The men were distracted and didn't seem to expect trouble, but she wasn't fooled. These men were armed and dangerous. Outmanned and outgunned were not odds she liked. Best to stay put until the danger parted.

Eric lowered his voice and walked with the men toward the barn.

Kara's heart skipped a beat. She looked around for cover. Her gaze landed on the water trough. Perfect. She slid between the lower bars of the fence and crawled behind the trough. Her hand squished into something dry and chunky—*Disgusting.* She wasn't paid enough for this.

Eric closed the barn door. She chanced a peek over the top of the water trough and didn't see anyone. Crouching, she slipped back through the fence. Twenty or so feet away, Jeff's SUV mocked her. Could she make it that far without being spotted, or should she turn back? She'd come too far. The moon hinted that day was near. She had to move *now*.

The barn door remained closed. What were they doing in there? X-ray vision sure would be nice. The smell coming from her hand reminded her of a more pressing matter. Kara wiped it on a nearby bush then dashed for Jeff's vehicle. The back door was unlocked. She climbed inside, closed the door softly behind her, then squeezed down on the floor of the backseat. The dome light hadn't turned on. Jeff must have fixed it so it wouldn't. Good thing too, considering their line of work.

"What took you so long?" he asked softly.

Kara nearly yelped. "Scare a girl half to death, why don't you? I didn't see you in here."

He chuckled low.

"How'd you know I was coming?" She lifted her head just enough to see Jeff slumped low in the front seat. The tinted windows made it impossible to see him from the side. Good thing his vehicle was parked facing away from the men or they could've seen him through the windshield.

"I didn't. Just suspected."

"What are you doing out here anyway?" Kara hissed.

"I heard the floorboards creak outside my bedroom and decided to investigate. What's that smell?" Jeff whispered.

Her face heated. "Manure. You don't happen to have any wet wipes, do you?"

"Hold on."

The glove box clicked. Then she felt something drop on top of her stomach. "I always keep a tub around. You never know when you'll need them."

"Spoken like a true country boy."

"Ha. I learned that trick in Miami from all those hours fishing off the pier while keeping an eye on Alvarado and his operation."

"Strange. I don't remember seeing you."

"Thanks to an arsenal of disguises. My favorite was the bearded old man. I seemed to always get lucky whenever I wore that beard."

Kara wadded the soiled wipe into a ball and wrapped a clean one around it. "What do you think is taking Eric and his buddies so long? He's been in there for at least thirty minutes."

"I don't know, but the sun's almost up. If he doesn't hurry, I'm going to have to slip back inside. I can't have him find me out here."

"Did you get a look at the men he was talking to?"

"Yes, and I was able to take some pictures," Jeff said.

"Excellent."

"I'm going to check out the barn. Be right back." Jeff opened the driver's door and slipped into the darkness. The door barely registered a click in the pre-dawn air as he shut it.

Kara pressed the light on her watch—four thirty.

A few minutes later, the driver's door opened. "They're gone, probably out the back side."

"Now what?"

"We wait."

Kara's back and shoulders cramped, and she tried to shift her weight without jiggling the vehicle. Surveillance stunk.

"Hold on. The barn door's opening. Here we go," Jeff whispered.

Eric's diesel engine started up nearby. "We're going to lose him if we have to wait for him to get far enough ahead of us."

"Don't worry. It's all taken care of. Tad has a team in place, and we'll change vehicles a little ways outside of town."

Jeff started his vehicle and followed.

Kara scooted onto the backseat and strapped in. "Pretty morning."

"Mm-hmm."

She rolled her head side to side and rubbed her neck. "I'm getting too old for this kind of thing."

Jeff chortled. "If you're too old, then so am I. And I'm *not* too old." He caught her attention in the rearview mirror and winked.

"Fine. But next time, I want to drive." Kara watched out the side window as they drove through the deserted town. Porch lights lit a smattering of houses. Other than the sound of the tires on the road, complete silence surrounded them. It appeared everyone still snuggled in their beds—oh to be so lucky.

A non-descript car pulled forward from the cover of the woods as Jeff pulled off to the side of the road. "Grab your bag. This is our stop."

Kara scooted out of the cramped quarters and hopped into their new transportation. She didn't recognize the agent to whom Jeff handed his keys and missed the few words they exchanged, but she trusted Jeff to have this planned to the nth degree.

Jeff sat behind the wheel and started the engine.

"We have some time to make up, and if we don't hurry, he'll be too far ahead to track." He signaled and pulled out onto the highway.

Kara sat back and kept her eyes on the tracking beacon as Jeff sped forward.

Jeff followed the red blinking light on the map of his phone and pushed the gas pedal hard to make up for lost time. After a few miles, he eased off the gas satisfied with their position. It looked like they were at the perfect tracking distance. No way would Eric suspect he'd been followed.

He sank a little deeper into the seat. Experience said they could be playing this game for hours. "Can I ask you a personal question?"

"Sure. But I don't promise to answer."

He didn't expect she would. "Fair enough. You mentioned being angry with God."

"Yeah?"

"I was wondering how that's going." Getting personal was taking a risk, but a risk worth taking to his way of thinking.

"I'm still angry."

"You want to talk about it?"

"Not particularly."

"Well, we have to talk about something, or I might fall asleep." He wouldn't, but talking would make the time go faster.

"Fine," she huffed. "I don't understand why the

God who promised to never leave us or forsake us allowed my cover to be totaled and why I was nearly killed." She paused. "You sure you want to hear all of this?"

"Absolutely." His grip tightened on the steering wheel.

"Okay. You asked for it. I also don't get why when Gail, who happens to be an awesome Christian, prayed for me, those things still happened. I mean I know I'm not the best Christian in the world. I only make it to church a couple times a month, and I almost never read my Bible anymore." She paused again then spoke softly. "I guess I understand why He'd forget about me, but why didn't He listen to Gail?"

Jeff nearly stopped the car. Kara was hurting big time, more than he'd realized, and he wanted to set her straight, but stopping was not an option. "I'm sure God would be happy if you went to church more often and read His word on a regular basis, but He doesn't hold that against you, Kara. He loves you regardless of what you do or don't do. That's why it's called unconditional love."

"Then why did He let all that stuff happen? We could be back in Miami right now doing our jobs. Instead, we're stuck investigating your stepbrother."

"First off, I don't know why God does or doesn't do anything. But I do know that you're alive, and for me that's good enough. He never promised life would be easy. We both know it's not. It's filled with challenges that feel way too big, yet somehow, we manage. I like to think He helps us."

Kara sat silently staring out the window.

"As for Eric, I think I made it clear I didn't want this assignment, but I'm glad I'm here. No matter the outcome." He eased off the accelerator as he took a sharp bend in the road. "The bright side in all of this is we got to know each other and work together." He glanced over at Kara to see if anything he said sunk in. Her eyes met his, and he nearly forgot to look back at the road. The depth of emotion he saw on her face touched him in a way he had never experienced. *Lord, I could use a little help here.* "Think of it this way. God knew I'd need you on this assignment. He knew you're the perfect person for this job and that no one else would do. Yes, you got a little beat up, and you have a killer on your trail, but Kara," he looked over at her again to make sure she was listening, "you're alive. That bomb could have killed you. Don't give up on God. He hasn't given up on you."

Kara pointed to the tracking screen. "Eric's turning."

Jeff furrowed his brows. Did she hear anything he'd said? The blinking light on the screen stopped. He slowed.

"What's your plan?"

If only he knew. He always had a plan, but this time, he couldn't think past the chase. Should he confront Eric? Or should he simply observe from a distance? Jeff spotted Eric's truck in someone's driveway quite a ways off the main road. No way could he pull over without being noticed. After continuing down the road a little, he eased into a scenic pullout. "I'm going to park. We'll hoof it and watch from a distance. Looks like whoever he went to meet hasn't arrived yet, so if we hurry, we may see something."

"Okay." Kara checked her sidearm and grabbed the pack with recon equipment.

He parked then locked and loaded his Glock. "Let's do this." They ran across the road into a field covered with sagebrush and large junipers. At least the vegetation would provide shelter from detection. They jogged back about a quarter mile.

He raised his hand to warn Kara. They crept forward and stopped, taking cover in the middle of tall weeds, about twenty yards from where Eric sat in his pickup.

A cloud of dust trailed a Jeep as it drove toward Eric. Kara snapped several pictures from their prostrate position on the ground. The Jeep stopped and a white man, about five foot ten stepped out and walked toward Eric. The camera continued to click. Jeff strained to hear the conversation, but Eric and the man spoke too quietly.

"What do you want to do?" Kara asked in a hushed tone.

"Keep taking pictures." Jeff's gut clenched when Eric handed over a large package wrapped in brown paper. The other man tore open a small section of the package and handed another bag to Eric.

"Let's go. I want to be near the car before he leaves." Grim determination spurred Jeff on as his world seemed to fall apart around him. He'd been obligated to investigate Eric to the best of his abilities, never believing for an instant that Eric was a drug smuggler, but now? What else could've been in the package? *Eric, what are you thinking?*

23

Kara rode beside Jeff and glanced at him. He hadn't said a word since the hand off between Eric and their unidentified subject at the first stop. She frowned. This wasn't good. The silence in the car about drove her mad. She couldn't take it any longer. "You ready to head back to the ranch?"

Jeff's hands gripped the steering wheel and his biceps bulged. He looked ready to pulverize someone. "Yeah. I'd like to see those pictures you took."

"No problem." She clenched and unclenched her fingers. They'd followed Eric to six drops and watched as he exchanged packages every time. Eric reeked of guilt, and her heart ached for Jeff. Her friend and partner hurt big time, and she had no idea how to help.

He slammed his fist on the steering wheel. Kara jumped. "How could he do it? I just don't understand. This isn't Eric. He wasn't a troublemaker when we were kids. I was always the one in trouble." He glanced her way with tortured eyes.

Kara's throat burned. He'd been a pillar throughout

all of this, and it stunk to watch him fall apart now. "I'm so sorry, Jeff. We still need to analyze the photos. We don't know for certain that he was delivering drugs." Although what else could it have been?

He reached for her hand and squeezed it. "Thanks, but I think we both know what went down today. He sure wasn't delivering bagged lunches." He held her hand a bit longer than necessary and took a long slow breath. "Lord, please give us wisdom with this case and help my brother and me." He glanced her way with pleading eyes, prompting her to pray.

Kara's eyes widened. She couldn't do it. But she had to, for Jeff. She took a deep breath then let it out. "Jesus, please be with Jeff. He's hurting and he needs You. Amen."

"Thanks."

"You're welcome." Her heart pounded. Not only had she not prayed in awhile, but she never prayed out loud. It felt weird, but if her prayer comforted Jeff, then it was worth a little discomfort. She shifted in her seat to get a better look at him. "What's the plan?"

"We analyze the pictures. I'll report our findings to Tad and Gary and let them decide how to proceed."

An hour later, Jeff turned right onto Main Street in Sunridge.

"Will you drop me off at the end of the ranch driveway? I left my car in the woods across the street."

"Sure. After I shower, I'll meet up with you at your place."

Kara nodded. She'd love a shower herself. Grime caked under her fingernails, and she was certain a bug or two had crawled down her shirt. She shivered—yuck.

Jeff eased onto the shoulder of the road. "See you soon." He grasped her arm before she could get out. "Thanks for barging in on my sting."

"You're welcome."

Jeff turned the spigot to hot and waited for the steam to rise before stepping into the shower. He let the water sear his skin. Maybe the pain would shut out the war that waged inside him. When white-hot pain reached his senses, he adjusted the temperature. He wondered if this was what Christ felt like when He was betrayed? Except Eric hadn't really betrayed him, at least that wasn't his intention. Jeff was certain of that. Eric had no idea Jeff would be pulled into his illegal activities. But pulled in, he was, and now this became more personal than he'd ever imagined. Turning off the shower, he stepped out.

He needed to see those pictures. After slipping on a pair of jeans and shrugging into a button-up shirt he went downstairs.

Jeff walked into the kitchen where Veronica stood, washing dishes. "Sorry I missed dinner."

She looked over her shoulder. "That's okay. You look nice. Hot date?" She dried her hands on a towel. "You forgot to shave."

He rubbed the slight scruff on his face. "Oh well. Maybe I'll grow it out for a while. See what Kara thinks."

"Kara's a lucky girl." A shadow of sadness filled her eyes, and she turned back to the dishes. "Have fun."

Jeff hesitated. His brother's marriage was none of his business, but it was clear Veronica felt neglected. Too bad he couldn't tell her it wasn't another woman taking her husband away. Then again, maybe she already knew. But if her comments about Marci were any indication, she didn't. "You need anything while I'm out?"

"No, thanks."

Jeff opened the front door and jerked when Eric surprised him.

Eric pulled his hand back and grinned. "Hey, there. Everything go okay around here today?"

"Better ask Jake. I was out." He moved past Eric and went to his SUV without giving his brother a chance to question anymore about his day. It was best to keep a little distance until he could sort out things.

Jeff walked into the alley and knocked on Kara's apartment door. She should've had enough time to get the pictures uploaded onto her computer. The door swung open, and Kara stood before him wearing oversized gray sweats and a T-shirt, a size or two too big for her small frame—but cuddly. Where had that thought come from? *Focus, man.*

"Come on in. You're too fast. I haven't had a chance to do anything but shower. The camera is by my computer. Go ahead and get started." She walked into the small bathroom and closed the door.

The hum of a blow dryer filled the otherwise quiet room. Time to get back to work. He pulled out a chair from the table, powered up the computer, then connected the camera to the laptop. The pictures uploaded in a matter of minutes. He scrolled through each one looking for something he'd missed earlier.

The blow dryer turned off, and Kara padded over to the table. Jeff's senses heightened when she pulled up a chair beside him, crowding his space. "You smell nice." He'd been distracted by Kara before, but tonight, he craved the comfort of someone stable, reliable, and familiar. All day she'd been understanding and never rubbed his brother's crimes in his face.

"Good old-fashioned soap and water." She nudged him with her elbow. "Scoot. I'll do this."

He dragged the chair to the right, allowing her full access to the laptop. "What do you think?"

"I don't see anything helpful yet." Her hand curved over the mouse. Pictures spread across the screen in several rows. "Okay, here we go."

Adrenaline pumped through Jeff's veins. The telephoto lens Kara had used did the job well. With the eraser side of a pencil she pointed at the screen.

"Look there." She enhanced the photo, and a clear image of kilos containing white powder showed on the screen. "Cocaine is my best guess." She looked at Jeff, her face etched with concern. "You okay?"

Jeff scooted the chair back and stood. He walked to the other side of the tiny studio apartment. The walls felt like they were closing in. How did she stand to live in this hole? He strode back to where Kara sat, watching him. What was she thinking? That he couldn't finish the job? Well, he could, and he would.

"I'm disappointed and angry, but don't worry. I'll do my job."

"I never suggested otherwise." Kara looked over her shoulder. "But the team would understand if you stepped back on this one. Tad can set up a raid. You wouldn't have to be there."

Emotions he'd never experienced warred inside him. He wanted to hug and strangle Kara at the same time. Her compassion was almost too much to handle.

He shook his head. "No. I'll see this through. But I can't think here. I need air."

"Okay."

He moved to the door and turned. "You coming?"

"I can't. There's a bullseye on my back. I'd be the perfect target strolling around in the middle of the night with few civilians out and about."

How could he have forgotten? He knew how, but it wasn't an acceptable reason. Everyone had problems, and Kara's was life and death. He may not be able to fix Eric's bad choices, but he could at least refrain from putting Kara's life in danger. He sat on her sofa. "I'll stay here."

She squared her shoulders, and her gaze bore into him. "What do you mean you'll stay here?"

"To think."

"Good. Because there's no way you're spending the night. This place is too small."

He chuckled. "I agree. How about we get Tad over here to help us work this out?" A third body would crowd the space further, but the tension in the room would ease with Tad as a buffer.

Kara made the call. "He'll be right over."

Fifteen minutes later, Tad knocked and stepped inside. "What do you have?"

Kara went through the photos again, this time with Tad looking over her shoulder as Jeff watched from the couch. He'd seen enough pictures to know his brother was guilty.

After about a half hour, Kara gasped. "It can't be."

Jeff stood and walked over to the table. He rested his hands on the back of her chair. "What?"

Kara enhanced the picture and pointed to a face on the screen. His stomach dropped. This was bad. Why hadn't they recognized him this afternoon?

24

Kara pushed back in her chair and faced Jeff. "What am I going to do?"

Tad printed the picture. "What's going on?" He looked from Kara to Jeff then back at the photo.

"That's Victor." Jeff rubbed the back of his neck.

"Last name?" Tad asked.

Jeff shook his head. "Unknown. He just goes by Victor. He is, or was, employed by Luis Alvarado, Miami's biggest drug lord. I'm not sure what happened, but one day he was there, and the next he was gone."

"Until now," Kara said.

Jeff took out his phone and snapped a picture of the computer screen. "If Alvarado is involved in the drug ring here, we're going to make the biggest bust in history."

"Or he could be the man sent to take care of Kara," Tad said.

Kara paced the small space. She'd dated Victor while working for Alvarado—all part of the job. He'd dumped her when she wouldn't sleep with him, but that wasn't what concerned her. He did Luis's dirty work. As much as she didn't want to think about it, Victor very well could be the man sent to kill her. At least he hadn't seen her when they were surveilling Eric. "Do you remember where that picture was taken?"

Jeff appeared to be thinking. "Looks like Prineville."

"You covered a lot of territory today." Tad walked to the door. "Be sure to e-mail those pictures to the field office in Bend." He let himself out.

Kara locked the door then went back to the table where Jeff stood.

He stepped toward her. The passion in his eyes made her knees weak and her pulse accelerate. She nearly stopped breathing and reached for the nearby chair, holding on tight. When he looked at her like that, she wanted to forget he was her partner. Maybe this pretending to be romantically involved was going to their heads.

"Ready to call it a night?" Kara croaked.

"I was going to ask you the same thing." He stepped closer, invading her space. "I'll pick you up at nine and bring you to the ranch."

"I have a client at nine."

"Cancel. Your life is more important than polishing some woman's nails." He wove his fingers through her hair. "I've wanted to do that for a while now. It's as soft as I imagined."

Kara's eyes locked on his, and her breath stuck in her lungs. She was sure he could hear her heart pounding. She swallowed hard and continued to hold his gaze as he tipped his head and lowered his mouth nearly touching hers. She stepped back, breaking the moment before either of them did something they'd regret.

He stared as if dazed then shook his head. "Sorry. This day must have addled my brain. I'm stressed and not thinking clearly." He frowned. "I'll see you in the morning." He stepped into the night.

Kara sighed. Talk about stress! Another moment like that, and she might not have the strength to pull back. Jeff was everything she ever wanted in a man—strong, kind, dependable, honest, emotionally there, real, easy on the eyes, and a Christian. She furrowed her brow. At least being a Christian had been one of her criteria, but now? No matter. They were partners.

Kara slid the dead bolt into place and moved through the connecting doorway to check the storefront and make sure it was locked up. A shadow slipped away from the door as she approached. Kara plastered herself against the wall, reached for her side arm, and winced. She'd left it on her bed. She crept to the door and chanced a look out the window—no one.

25

The next day Kara sat in the passenger seat of Jeff's SUV. "Where're we going? I thought you were taking me to the ranch."

"We're detouring."

"Why?" Unease filled Kara.

"Because I need to be in the fresh open air without a bunch of people around. Do you have any idea how hard it is to think surrounded by people all the time?"

Kara chuckled. "You're kidding, right?"

"I guess you do understand. In Miami, I'd talk it out with one of the other guys, or I'd go sailing. Sometimes I'd find a long pier to fish off of, but here I'm surrounded by open land, and I can't escape because of my brother."

"I get it, Jeff." She understood the need to think. Their almost kiss last night and the shadow outside had cost her several hours of sleep. After the lights were out, she lay staring at the ceiling thinking about Jeff and how much she wished her feet had stayed planted and her brain would've listened to her heart instead of her head.

Jeff parked and walked around to open her door.

"Thanks. Why are you being such a gentleman?"

He kicked a rock with the toe of his cowboy boot. "Aw shucks, ma'am. I'm jest doing the gentlemanly thing." He had the twang down perfect.

Kara grinned and wrapped her hand in the crook of his arm. "Why, thank you kindly, sir."

He patted her hand and walked to a nearby wooden bench nestled between the woods and the lake. The water shone green from the reflection of the trees, and a slight breeze kept the summer air cool.

Jeff rested his arm on the back of the bench and gazed at the lake while Kara looked around for signs of trouble. Only one other car sat parked in the lot, and so far, she hadn't seen the occupant. Since it had been there before they'd arrived, she wasn't too worried about a killer lurking nearby. Not to mention, this was an unplanned stop, so there'd be no way a sniper or anyone else could be ready and waiting.

Kara turned and faced him. "Last night after you left, I went up front to double check the locks. Did you happen to go that way to your car?"

"No. Why?"

"It looked like someone may have been peering in. It's hard to say. I only saw the shadow as the person walked away."

"I'm glad you're being careful." He turned to her.

Oh no. He had that look again. "Jeff, about last night—"

"Shh," he whispered. His fingers entwined her hair. He lowered his face and kissed her softly.

193

This couldn't be happening, but it was. She closed her eyes, blocking out the world around them for just a moment. Then the warmth of his lips vanished, leaving her tingling from head to toe. She opened her eyes and stared straight into his.

"Kara you are so—"

"We need to talk."

His eyes widened, but he didn't say a word. He wasn't going to make this easy.

She grasped his hand. "I really like you, and you're a great kisser." She rubbed her chin and looked closely at his face. "But you and I can't be."

"Too late. We're already involved. Yesterday when we were doing surveillance, I realized I couldn't deny my feelings any longer."

"Try harder. This is a bad idea."

He sighed and seemed to think a moment. "You're right. I'm sorry. It won't happen again unless it's for the job."

"Thank you, but no more kissing me period until you shave that beard or it grows in better—it's scratchy." In truth the scratching was nothing compared to how his kiss addled her. She had to focus on her job and not her heart, and when he kissed her for pretend or not, she forgot she was wearing a Glock.

He frowned. "Come on. It's not that bad, is it?" He rubbed his fingers over his chin. "If I don't kiss you, how will anyone believe we're a couple?"

"Hold my hand. Give me googly eyes. Be creative. Flowers are always nice."

"I don't see what the big deal is." He jutted his

chin. "I like my shadow."

She rolled her eyes. "You've never been kissed by someone with a scratchy face."

He laughed. "Okay, but you're making romancing you difficult if I can't kiss you. What's everyone at the ranch going to think?"

"Tell them the truth. I won't let you kiss me until your beard grows in or you shave."

"Fine. Guess I could shave." He looked at his watch. "We need to head to the field office for a few hours. Tad will meet us there to go over some details, and then there's a team meeting. After that, we could go out for a late lunch if you want."

"Sounds good to me."

The meeting with the taskforce went longer than expected, and Kara's stomach rumbled. She shouldn't have skipped breakfast. Kara kept a watch for the restaurant on their way to their meeting.

They'd spent the better part of the day going over intel and comparing notes with the taskforce team. Operation Trail Ride had several topnotch agents. She was proud to be working with them. It was only a matter of time before they broke this case wide open.

She'd reported her suspicions about Marci, but they all agreed it was too soon to use Marci to their advantage. She still couldn't figure out why the woman seemed familiar. It wasn't like her to forget a face.

"Found it." Jeff swung into the parking lot of the restaurant. He parked and hustled around to her side. "If the food tastes as good as it smells, I'll be grateful. It's been a long day."

"Tell me about it." Kara's stomach rumbled again. She smacked her hand over her belly.

"Mine's been doing that for the past two hours." Jeff led her inside the restaurant.

A waiter approached and seated them at a table for two overlooking the Deschutes River. "Our special is halibut cheeks."

Kara tuned out the waiter and gawked at the decor. The place was hip but with an outdoorsy feel. The walls were painted deep orange and brown, and the high ceilings boasted modern metal fans.

Jeff touched her hand. "Something wrong?"

"No. Where'd the waiter go?"

"I told him we needed a few minutes to decide. Those halibut cheeks sounded delicious, didn't they?"

"Yes. Is that what you're ordering?"

"I think so, how about you?"

Too bad she hadn't been paying attention to the waiter. "Maybe. I'm not sure." She picked up the menu and studied the seafood fare. Her gaze stopped at seafood linguini. "I know what I want."

The waiter approached at that moment, and they each placed their order.

Jeff smiled at her from across the table. "This is a nice change of pace." He took a sip from his water glass, and his gaze wandered over the room.

Kara had already studied each patron. No one

seemed to show them any special interest. For now, it seemed she was safe. "Tell me about what your childhood was like with you and Eric." She fiddled with the napkin in her lap and watched the emotions play across his face.

"When we were kids and our parents first married, we didn't get along at all. Eric hated me. His dad was nice, though, and that made up for Eric's attitude. Over time we established a routine. He did his thing, and I did mine." He looked across the table with sad eyes and shrugged. "Two strangers living under the same roof."

"How awful. Didn't your parents notice?"

"One day, a couple months after our two families joined, I was playing up in the barn loft. Eric and his dad came into the barn. I overheard him lecturing Eric about being nice to me. Eric was pretty angry. He shouted at his dad that he loved me more than his own son. Dad denied it."

"So he treated you like his own son, and Eric was jealous?"

The waiter arrived with their food and conversation stopped.

Kara took her first bite and closed her eyes to enjoy the full impact of the flavor. "Delicious."

Jeff chuckled then forked a generous amount of fish into his mouth.

Kara swallowed. "Do you think Eric's still jealous of you? You're grown adults now and from what you've told me, it seems he's closer to your parents than you are." She set her fork on the plate and leaned forward a little. "You're sure he doesn't know what you do for a living?"

He nodded. "Positive. I asked my parents to keep it to themselves. I know they wouldn't say anything. They're aware of our rocky past. Yes, we're getting along right now, but in reality, Eric's almost never around the ranch yard, and when he is, he keeps to himself."

Kara shook her head. "That's so sad. You have to make it right with him while you're here."

Jeff muttered something under his breath, but Kara missed it. From the look on his face, she probably didn't want to hear it anyway.

Kara took her last bite of linguini and relaxed back against the dark grained wooden chair. She wished she'd worn pants with an elastic waist. Of course, it would help if she owned a pair. She rubbed her waistline. "I won't need to eat for days after that meal. Fabulous!"

"No kidding." Jeff stuffed one last bite of halibut into his mouth. "Do you want to head straight back to the ranch or go exploring?"

Kara glanced at her watch. "I'd love to relax awhile and admire the restaurant." A swordfish hung on a wall nearby. She sighed. "But we better not play tourist. It's getting late."

He pulled out his wallet, paid, left a generous tip on the table, and then guided her out of the restaurant to the well-lit parking lot.

"There's no reason to be so attentive. No one here needs to think we're an item."

"Everyone who comes in contact with us must believe we're a couple," Jeff spoke quietly. "It's a small world, and you never know who might see us. To anyone who notices, we're a normal couple out for an evening on the town."

"In that case," Kara playfully replied and rose up on tiptoe to plant a kiss on his cheek, "thanks for dinner."

"Is that the best you can do?"

"No, but it's the best you're gonna get, Mr. Whiskers."

Jeff chuckled and unlocked the door to the SUV to let her in.

Kara and Jeff drove in restful silence enroute to Sunridge. Her thoughts swirled. Jeff was a great partner, and she trusted him with her life, but now it seemed as if he wanted her to trust him with her heart as well. Could she?

Kara jerked to the side when the SUV swerved to the right and nearly ran off the road. She gripped the armrest and pulled her seatbelt tight. "What happened?"

Jeff fought the rig and pulled off to the shoulder. "I don't know. A blowout maybe." He opened the door, stepped out, walked around the front to the passenger side, and squatted.

The back window shattered, and a bullet lodged in the dashboard. Kara ducked and covered her head with her arms. Several more rounds hit the rig.

"Jeff!" She unbuckled and threw open the passenger door. "Get in." She climbed into the driver's seat, waited for Jeff, then floored the gas.

Jeff slammed the door as they peeled out. "We can't outrun him. The tire's flat."

"Watch me."

26

Kara veered off the road onto the dirt, making an immediate sharp left to avoid a huge tree. The Ford bounced, rattling her teeth. She checked her mirrors, but no one seemed to be following them. "Where's the gunman?"

Jeff looked over his shoulder. "I can't see anyone. I think you lost him."

Kara heard the surprise and admiration in his tone. "I've always enjoyed off-roading." She lifted her foot from the accelerator and coasted to a stop. "Well. That was fun." Sarcasm dripped from her voice. She looked over at Jeff. "You hit?"

"No. I was going to ask you the same thing."

"I'm fine, but we can't just sit here and wait for the shooter to find us," Kara said. "And that wheel is about destroyed. Any suggestions?"

"Besides praying? No."

Kara jerked her head toward him and grabbed her phone. Maybe a trooper was nearby. She called the local dispatch and gave their location the best she could.

Jeff opened his door. "Come on. I'm not sitting around here waiting for trouble." Glock in hand, he stepped out of the rig.

Kara followed. "Backup's coming." Looking around for a safe hiding place, she pointed to some rocks. "Over there. If we can get to the other side, we'll have a wall blocking us from view and still be able to see when help arrives."

Jeff nodded, and they ran.

Kara crouched low beside Jeff and whispered. "I don't see anyone."

"We're not far from the ranch. You want to hoof it out of here?"

"I suppose, but I'll need a ride into town," Kara said.

"I don't think so." Jeff turned to her. Concern showed clear in his eyes. "You're staying in one of the guest rooms tonight."

"But—"

"No arguments. How many times does someone have to try and kill you before you stop trying to do everything on your own? I know you don't want to give up your freedom, but someone tried to kill you this evening."

"Fine. I'll stay tonight. But only because I don't have a car. Tomorrow, I'll phone Gail to pick me up."

A low growl vibrated in Jeff's throat. This woman was

going to be the death of him. Never in all his years with the DEA had he encountered someone so stubborn. Didn't she get that Alvarado wanted her dead? He could protect her at the ranch. He couldn't do that at Gail's house.

Jeff glanced at Kara and caught the unguarded look of fear on her face before she realized he was watching.

An impassive look slid into place. "What?" she asked.

"It's okay to be afraid. I know my heart rate sure accelerated when we were being shot at."

She stared at him a moment before her face fell, and he pulled her into his arms. His shirt dampened as her quiet tears fell. If only holding her would make everything okay, but this was the real world, and a hug didn't make murderers disappear.

He brushed his fingers through her hair. "It's okay. No one expects you to be tough all the time."

Kara pulled back. Mascara ran down her cheeks. "Will you please shut up and stop being so nice?"

Jeff's eyes crinkled. He gently rubbed the tears away with his thumb. "Sorry."

She finished wiping her face and nodded toward the road. "Looks like Tad." She stepped forward.

Jeff grabbed her hand. "We don't know if someone's waiting for you to give him a clean shot. Just stay here while I go talk with Tad."

"What makes you think you're not a target?"

"I'd already be dead. He had the perfect shot when I got out earlier."

She crossed her arms. "Fine."

Jogging across dirt littered with lava rock, Jeff stayed alert for trouble. "Thanks for coming."

"No problem," Tad said. "When dispatch mentioned Kara, I said I'd handle it. Where's your rig?"

Jeff pointed toward the trees. "Think you can arrange for a tow and another vehicle?"

"Already done. There's an identical black Ford Escape waiting for you in Bend. We'll switch the plates and no one will be the wiser. Where's Kara?"

"Hiding. You see anyone on your way here?"

"Passed a few cars, but nothing suspicious caught my attention. I think the shooter's long gone."

"Good." Jeff motioned for Kara to come over but kept alert just in case Tad had missed something.

A flash of metal caught the last remaining rays of sunlight before the distinct ping of a silenced gun went off. "Kara! Down!" He yanked his Glock from his holster, turned and aimed at a lone figure standing about twenty feet to the north, then fired once—silence. Holding his gun with both hands, he approached the shooter. He lay on his back with a single shot to his head.

Jeff shuddered and his gut clenched—his first kill.

Tad and Kara ran toward him. Kara looked down at the face of a white male, approximately thirty. "I don't recognize him."

"Me neither," Tad said. "But we'll know who he is soon." He walked away and made a call.

Kara touched Jeff's shoulder. "You okay?"

"I've been better. You?"

"Alive. Thanks to your expert aim."

"No. Thanks to God. I don't know how I made that shot. It was divine intervention that helped me see him at all."

Kara bit down on her bottom lip, clearly taken aback by his answer. This exasperating and beautiful woman needed to realize that God was on her side, and regardless of what she thought, He was protecting her.

27

Jeff woke early the next morning. Last night seemed a distant memory. Sunlight glinted off the window and lit the room. He moaned and draped his arm over his eyes. He'd forgotten to close the blinds. Not surprising considering everything that'd happened.

Kara slept in the next room. Even with the hit man's death, Jeff had insisted she spend the night.

When he'd signed on to investigate Eric, he never dreamed their old assignment and this one would be connected. Now they needed to decide how to proceed. With the hit man out of the picture, it seemed Victor was their only remaining threat from Miami. He would get a tail for sure. No way would he let that sorry excuse for a man get near Kara again.

Back in Miami, he'd watched Victor and Kara sunning on the yacht. The man couldn't keep his hands off Kara, but she kept him in line. From what he'd heard through the grapevine, her lack of physical action was the reason he'd dumped her. She'd been forced to resort to other tactics to get information about

Alvarado.

He kicked the sheets off, grabbed his clothes, and crossed the hall to the bathroom. Flipping on the shower, he stepped in. Now to figure out how the Gonzaleses fit into this whole scheme. The files had indicated that the couple arrived shortly after the previous alleged drops. Jeff sensed that they'd show up at the ranch today, and he'd be waiting.

Jeff scuffed his hands up and down his face. Maybe he should shave—nah. Kara's warning not to kiss her had surprised him, but maybe it was for the best.

Who was he kidding? It wasn't for *his* best not to kiss Kara. The minty taste and softness of her lips made it hard to forget how much he'd enjoyed her kiss, but more than that, he cared about her and wanted to be near her. Which may be the biggest reason she was sound asleep in Eric's house. Had his partner been a guy, he wouldn't be sleeping here.

He shut the water off and dried quickly before he missed the Gonzaleses. Officially, he was on administrative leave due to the kill, but he could make contact with the Gonzaleses unofficially. There had to be some connection to their arrival so soon after Eric's drops. Jeff slid into his jeans and pulled a dark blue T-shirt over his head before heading to the barn on the pretense of cleaning the stalls.

Granted, the stalls needed mucking, but he hoped the Gonzaleses would arrive soon. Gravel crunched beneath the tires of an F350 pulling a horse trailer. He watched from the open barn door as a Hispanic couple stepped from the truck.

He walked toward the couple. "*Buenos dias, como estan?*"

"Buenos dias, *Senor*," Fernando Gonzales said. "You speak Spanish?"

"*Si,*" Jeff said. "I'm Jeff Clark. Eric's my stepbrother." He held out his hand.

Fernando grasped it in return. "Fernando and Andrea Gonzales. We're in the horse business. Your stepbrother runs a fine operation."

"Thanks. Anything I can help you with?"

"We have a horse to board." Fernando looked over Jeff's shoulder. "Is Eric around? I'd like to speak with him."

"Sure. He's in the house. You want me to get him?"

"No. I'll go to him. Andrea, darling, I'll be back soon."

Jeff furrowed his brows, forced a smile, and addressed the woman. "We're happy to board your horse."

"Of course, you are." She strode to the trailer. "Gayetta is temperamental. Watch and learn." Andrea opened the door and climbed in with the mare. She spoke in soft, soothing tones. A minute later, horse and owner stood by the side of the trailer. "That is how it is done." She handed the reins over to Jeff, brushed her hands off, and climbed back into the front seat of the truck.

What an odd woman. He clicked his tongue and guided Gayetta into the barn. Such a beauty. The white Arabian stood tall and proud with her tail high. It seemed owner and horse matched up well, at least in respect to pride.

Jeff glanced toward the house and saw the men talking on the front porch. Eric stood with balled fists. He had to get within hearing distance of that conversation. Maybe he'd be able to sneak in through the kitchen.

Checking to make sure Andrea was occupied, he slipped around the back of the property and ran to the kitchen door—locked. Time for plan B. He walked right up the porch stairs. "Hi, Eric. I see Fernando found you."

"Yeah. Thanks."

Jeff walked past the men and went inside, closing the door behind him. He stood still with his ear to the door—nothing. Blast. The door was solid. Several windows looked out onto the porch and one was slightly open. Veronica was nowhere to be seen, and Lauren was still asleep. He went down on all fours then belly crawled under the windows. Bingo.

"I understand," Eric said.

He heard the click of boots and then Eric softly cursing.

Jeff shimmied as fast as he could away from the window. He stood and bolted up the stairs. From his bedroom window, he'd have a clear view of the Gonzaleses. He sat on his knees and peered out. Eric had followed Fernando to their truck. Jake approached the group. Fernando nodded and climbed in then drove away. What had he missed?

A soft knock drew him from his thoughts. He stood and opened the door.

Wearing rumpled shorts and a T-shirt, Lauren looked up at him. "Hey, Uncle Jeff. Mom needs to know if you want breakfast. She's making waffles."

He grinned at his niece. "Sure. Waffles are my favorite. I'll be right there."

"Okay." Lauren turned and trotted down the stairs.

Jeff closed his bedroom door and followed. He entered the kitchen on his niece's heels. Eric sat at the table drinking coffee.

"Fernando leave already?"

Eric coughed, and coffee splashed on the table.

"You okay?" Jeff asked.

"Fine. Swallowed wrong." Eric wiped his mouth with a napkin. "Yes. They're gone."

"Good. I didn't care for their uppity attitude."

Veronica dropped a metal spoon, and Eric jumped. "Sorry," she said. "Guess I got a little too vigorous stirring the batter."

A second later, the waffle iron sizzled and the room smelled like breakfast on a Sunday morning. Except this was Wednesday. Jeff poured himself a mug of coffee and sat at the table with Eric and Lauren. "You two have anything exciting planned for today?"

"No," Eric said.

"Just practicing my violin." Lauren reached for her glass of orange juice.

He looked at his brother. "How about fishing? I haven't been since I arrived, and I've heard this is prime territory."

Eric shrugged. "Sure, I guess fishing would be okay."

Jeff's thoughts shot to Kara. "Oh no!"

"What?" Veronica turned with wide eyes.

"It was really late when we came in last night—"

"We?" Eric asked.

"Yeah. Kara's asleep in the guest room next to mine."

"No, she's not," Kara said as she entered the kitchen. "Good morning, everyone."

Jeff hid a smile behind his napkin. Though her hair was pulled into a bun, her clothes from yesterday were sufficiently rumpled. She must have slept in them. "Morning, beautiful."

Veronica raised the lid on the iron revealing a golden-brown waffle. "Welcome, Kara. I hope you're hungry."

"I could eat." She looked over at Jeff. "Can I get a ride back to my place after breakfast?"

Veronica placed a plate at one of the empty spots. "Enjoy."

"Thanks." Kara sat and poured warm maple syrup over the top. "This smells like Christmas. My mom used to make waffles on Christmas morning."

"Never any other time?" Lauren asked.

"No. Not that I remember. We were a cold cereal kind of family. Mom only cooked breakfast once in a while."

"My mom cooks almost every morning."

"You're a lucky girl." Kara looked over at Jeff and gave a sheepish grin.

Jeff swallowed the last of his breakfast and washed it down with coffee. "When you're finished, I'll run you home. How could he have forgotten she was still sleeping right next door to his room? Guess the whole thing with the Gonzaleses really captured his attention, as it should've. He grinned. It looked like he could be attracted to his partner and still do his job.

Kara stood and rinsed her plate.

"Ready?" Jeff took his dishes to the sink.

She nodded. "Yes. Thanks for breakfast." She gave Veronica a quick hug and followed Jeff out the door. Once in the identical Ford Escape the DEA had provided late last night, she sighed. "Your family's nice."

"Thanks. Sorry about not waking you. When the Gonzaleses drove in, I went into work mode."

"No problem. You learn anything new?"

"Only that Eric looked very uncomfortable around them and that he doesn't seem to like Fernando. I tried to eavesdrop but missed everything except Eric saying he understood." He shrugged. "Wish I knew what they were talking about." After turning onto the main road, he drove toward town. "Eric and I are going fishing later. Maybe I'll be able to weasel some information out of him."

"Be careful. You don't want to give away what you know."

Jeff scowled. "Understood. I have a feeling there's more to this than we're seeing."

"I'm sure there is. But I also don't think you should let Eric see your interest in Fernando. He might become suspicious."

"I know how to do my job." The edge in his voice

was justified. She should trust him by now. Hadn't he proven himself?

"I didn't mean to imply otherwise."

Jeff released his tight hold on the steering wheel and turned into the alley behind Kara's apartment. "Keep in touch."

"Count on it." She paused with her hand on the door. "You doing okay? I mean after last night and all."

"I'm fine." He didn't like killing the hit man, but under the circumstances, he'd had no choice. At least it'd been kept from the media since this was such a massive undercover operation. The shooting would still be investigated, but discreetly. He was on leave until the investigation was complete. But his superiors assured him it would only last a day or two at the most. His cell rang. "Jeff here."

"I have something."

Jeff mouthed that it was Tad. She didn't move.

"The shooter was Alex Zockman," Tad said. "His most recent employer was Luis Alvarado."

"Thanks. I'll let Kara know." He ended the call.

"What?"

"The shooter was on Alvarado's payroll."

"Figures."

He watched Kara walk inside her apartment without even a glance back. What was going through her mind? Was she happy, relieved, what? At least they knew for sure that Alvarado was behind the hit. That had to count for something. How long until Luis found out his man failed was anyone's guess, but he hoped it would be later rather than sooner.

Jeff opened the front door and hollered, "Eric you ready? We wait much longer, and it's gonna be too hot to fish."

Eric came around the corner from the kitchen. "Almost. Just getting ice for the cooler."

"Good thinking. I plan to catch the limit."

Eric gave a humorless chuckle. "Still aiming high I see."

"What's that supposed to mean?"

"Nothing," Eric said. "Come on. Let's go."

Jeff grabbed the poles and trudged after his brother, feeling less like fishing every second. This was going to be a long morning. Somehow, he had to pick Eric's brain about the Gonzaleses without making him suspicious.

"I thought we'd drive out to the edge of my property and hike to the river." He placed the cooler in the bed of his truck. "Be right back."

Jeff put the poles and some portable chairs in the truck bed.

Eric deposited the tackle box in back. "Okay. Let's go."

"So how about those Gonzaleses?" Jeff studied Eric's profile. "They're a real piece of work. I'm surprised you put up with them."

Eric worked his jaw. "They're not that bad."

"But still, I don't think I'd make my barn available if they were always so nasty."

"You're not me."

"True." Jeff stared out the side window. Maybe he should take Kara's advice after all.

Thirty minutes later, Jeff and Eric parked and hiked to Eric's fishing hole with the ice chest and chairs and set them on the bank of the slow-moving river and cast their lines. Before Jeff could sit, the line tugged, then nothing. Some lucky fish snagged his bait and got away. He reeled in the line, baited the hook, and cast again.

He glanced over at Eric who sat with a scowl on his face and a white-knuckle grip on his pole. "You know if there's something bugging you or if I've done anything to offend you, we can talk about it," Jeff said.

Eric shrugged.

"You don't still hate me, do you?"

"What?" Eric jerked his head toward him. "Where did that come from?"

"I just thought since you didn't like me when we were kids, it might be interfering with our relationship now."

"What makes you think I didn't like you?"

"I heard you say it to Dad once. Then there was that time I found itching powder in my sheets."

Eric chuckled dryly. "As I recall you wasted no time in ratting me out."

"True. I don't think things have been the same between us since."

Eric rubbed the back of his neck. "Funny, I haven't thought about that day in years."

"Seven years, perhaps?"

"Huh?"

"It's been almost seven years since we last saw one another. I just figured"

"Oh." Eric paused. "Good grief. You were what? Eight or nine when that happened? You must think I'm some kind of monster. Things weren't that bad between us, were they? I mean I grew to accept sharing my dad with you. And it was kind of nice to have a mom around again." He smirked. "And having a little brother to tease was all right too."

Eric's words could not have surprised him more. Had he misunderstood his brother all these years? They could've been friends, maybe even avoided this whole drug smuggling thing. They'd never been close, and he'd always assumed it was because of that one incident. Had he unconsciously held back from Eric? "I didn't think you were a monster."

"Thanks. How did we get on this topic anyway?"

"I can't remember." Shock reverberated to the soles of his tennis shoes. All these years wasted.

"How are things going between you and Kara?" Eric reached into the cooler and pulled out a bottle of water.

"What do you mean?"

"Don't play dumb with me, little brother."

Jeff chuckled. "Things are fine with us."

"Duh, but do you think she's the one?"

"The one?"

"Stop answering my questions with a question. You know what I'm asking. Is she the one you're going to marry? I haven't seen you interested in anyone since Beth."

Jeff's stomach clenched. He'd planned to propose to Beth shortly before he joined the DEA. When she'd dumped him, she'd said he'd be married to his job, and she'd be a widow by default. He sighed. Eric was right. He hadn't dated anyone seriously since Beth. The way he saw it, she'd probably been smart in breaking off with him. What kind of life would they have had together? He was married to his job. Jeff re-baited his hook and cast his line. "I don't know. We've only been seeing each other for a couple of weeks."

Eric cast him a sidelong glance. "I knew Veronica a week before I was certain we'd marry."

"You're a lucky man. We don't all have that kind of clarity." Could he and Kara have something more than friendship? He'd like a relationship with her, but they couldn't work together and be married.

Something tugged on his line. He set the hook and reeled it in.

Eric netted the trout, and laughed. "Looks like one for the record books," he teased.

Jeff frowned and removed the hook from the small trout then gently released it back into the river. "You shouldn't laugh. At least I caught something. I haven't seen you reel in a fish."

"I'm waiting for the big one. You wait and see. At just the right moment, he'll come along and chomp onto my hook."

Right now, Jeff wanted to catch the trout of all trout. He reeled in his line, checked the bait, and cast again. Just as the hook sank beneath the surface, he got a bite. His line spun out fast.

"Set the hook!" Eric exclaimed as he jumped up from the seat.

Jeff stood and jerked the pole up to set the hook. He reeled in the line and let the fish run with it. He pulled back on the pole and reeled in a little more line. The fish fought hard, but Jeff won. Eric netted the sizeable trout. Jeff felt his face split into a grin. Oh yeah, he'd caught the big one. Now he needed to catch the big one calling the shots in this drug-trafficking scheme, and Eric was going to help him whether he wanted to or not.

28

With the hit man dead, Kara felt more at ease and decided to take advantage of the reprieve. Surely, Alvarado wouldn't have had time to send anyone else after her yet. She hefted the saddle onto Blaze and ran her hand down his neck as she spoke softly into his ear. "You're such a beauty. How about you and I go for a ride?"

"Hey, Kara."

Kara jumped away from Blaze.

Jake walked toward her. "Why so jumpy?"

She shrugged and cinched the strap around Blaze's belly. "Want to ride with me? Jeff's out fishing with Eric, and I don't want to ride alone."

"Me? Well, I guess I could spare an hour."

Kara flashed him her best smile. "I really appreciate this."

"No problem. I'll saddle Henry."

"Sounds more like a name for a mule. Why'd you name him that?"

"He *is* a mule. The best mule you'll ever find too.

He thinks he's a horse and is more surefooted."

She laughed out loud. "Okay, where's this mule of yours?"

"He doesn't get along with a couple of the horses, so I built a lean-to for him behind the bunkhouse."

"I can't wait to meet him." She mounted. "I'll be at the end of the driveway when you're ready."

Twenty minutes later, Jake stopped next to her. "There's a nice trail through the woods up ahead. Want to try it out?"

"Sure. Lead the way." Kara stayed by his side as he moved forward. They took a winding path through BLM property. Sunlight filtered through the branches of tall ponderosa pines. Dry grass brushed the legs of her horse as she plodded along. Fifteen minutes into the ride, Kara broke the silence. "I heard you had an early morning."

"Yep. I don't like being woke from a good dream. 'Fraid I was a bit angry at those Gonzaleses. They think they can show up whenever they want. Makes me want to show them the business side of my fist."

Kara's brows rose. She'd never seen Jake this passionate about anything. "Guess I better never wake you."

Jake chucked. "You have nothing to worry about. If a pretty lady wakes me up, she certainly wouldn't be in any danger of my fist."

Kara cleared her throat. Time to change the subject. "How long have you worked for the Waters family?"

"About a year. I was at a ranch in Southern Oregon before here for fifteen years."

"That's a long time. Why'd you leave?"

"Owners sold to some out-of-towners. I got lucky when this position opened up—perfect timing."

Kara swatted at a fly. "I'd say so. How do you like working here?"

"It's mostly okay."

"Only mostly?"

Jake shrugged. "You had a long enough ride? Henry's gettin' tired."

Kara wanted to force Jake to talk, but he clearly wasn't going to offer any more information. "Sure, let's head back. Thanks for coming."

He winked. "I'm happy to oblige a pretty lady whenever I can."

Kara turned her horse around and stopped. A small ramshackle building sat hidden amongst the weeds and trees. If she hadn't turned at that exact spot, she never would've seen it. Averting her eyes, she encouraged her horse to keep moving. No sense in alerting Jake to her discovery. "Where are we? I don't remember ever coming this way with Jeff."

"Can't say exactly." He chuckled. "I got a bit turned around. All that jabbering we were doing."

Kara frowned. How does a cowboy lose his way? She noted the dense foliage and followed after Jake. Maybe she'd be able to make it back here on her own.

Jake made a sharp right and followed a deer path. Silence enveloped them. Not even the birds sang.

Kara tensed. Something wasn't right. Why was everything so quiet? The small hairs on the back of her neck stood on end. She encouraged her horse to move faster. "I'll race you."

"You crazy? Henry can't outrun your horse. Plus, it's not safe. They're liable to turn an ankle."

"Oh." She hadn't thought of that. She kept her gaze forward but scanned every square inch. A twisted and gnarled six-foot juniper blocked their path. Jake veered to the left.

A twig snapped off to the right. Someone or maybe something was watching them. "What kind of wild animals are there out here?"

"The usual. Deer, rabbits, squirrels. You aiming to see some wildlife?"

"Not really. Just curious." Maybe a deer had snapped the twig, and she was overreacting. But she couldn't shake the feeling of being watched. Did Alvarado send more than one hit man? They came into a clearing.

"Here's where I made a wrong turn." He eyed her closely. "You okay? You look worried."

"I'm fine now that you know where we are. Guess I'm not as much of a country girl as I'd like to think."

"City slicker or not, no one enjoys being lost. But you're safe with me and Henry. This ole boy's as good as a homing pigeon."

Just so long as they got back to the ranch in one piece. If they'd wandered into a drug trafficker's camp, they'd be in trouble. She followed Jake along a clearly marked trail and ten minutes later, they were back on the driveway heading to the ranch. "Thanks for taking me out." That was one experience she wouldn't soon forget.

"No problem. Henry needed to stretch his legs."

"I know the feeling." She longed to dismount and run. What had freaked her out? She'd investigate the area as soon as Jeff could go back with her. Hopefully, the landmarks she'd noticed on the way out would look the same on the way in.

29

A knock sounded on Kara's apartment door. She rose and felt for the .380 she'd strapped to her ankle. *Where's a peephole when you need one?* "Who is it?"

"Gail."

Kara's shoulders relaxed, and she opened the door.

Gail reached out and pulled her into a hug. "I've missed you. Where have you been?"

"Here and there." Her friend knew she was here on a case and shouldn't be asking about her whereabouts.

Gail frowned.

Kara reached out to her. "Sorry. I didn't mean to keep you standing at the doorway. Come in and have a seat. Can I get you something to drink?"

"Iced tea, if you have any." She lifted her hand. "This envelope was taped to your door."

Kara forced herself to act disinterested. "Thanks." She held it from the top corner and placed it on the table.

"Aren't you going to open it?"

"After we visit." Kara pulled a jug of tea she'd made

yesterday from the fridge and poured them each a glass. "Have a seat." She settled into an easy chair.

Gail sat across from her and looked around the space. "Where do you sleep?"

"The daybed." Kara pointed to the cluttered bed pushed up against the wall connected to her nail salon. "It's a mess right now, but it's comfy enough."

Gail gave her a skeptical look. "Uh-huh. I guess since it's only you, this small space works fine."

"True, and I pretty much only sleep here."

"Between whatever you're working on for the DEA and your nail studio you must stay busy, so I guess that's why I never see you anymore." Gail sipped her tea.

"Yes, I do. But, Gail, it's imperative that you don't mention my real reason for being here to anyone."

"Honestly, I don't even know why you're here except that it's work-related. Although, if you'd like to share, I'm all ears."

"No, I wouldn't." She reached out and squeezed Gail's hand. "For your own safety, please forget my employer."

Gail's eyes widened. "I didn't realize it was such a big deal. I promise I'll keep quiet."

"Thank you."

Kara rose to adjust the temperature of the air conditioner. She could slide open the window and let the cool evening breeze do its job, but she didn't want to invite trouble into her apartment.

Gail stood to leave. "I won't keep you." She gave Kara a once over. "You're looking a little thin. Are you eating okay? I know how you *love* to cook."

Kara chuckled. "I manage, and don't worry. I'm not starving." She patted her waistline. "I'll stop by and visit sometime soon."

"You better, or I may have to make a pest of myself every evening." She placed her glass in the sink, hugged Kara, and turned to leave.

"See you later." Kara walked her to the door then locked up after she left. Slipping on a pair of latex gloves, she slid a knife across the top of the envelope. Removing a folded piece of paper, she caught her breath and stared at a snapshot of her and Jeff sitting on the park bench.

"I'm everywhere," was written in black marker across the picture.

Kara dropped the note on the table and stared. It seemed no place was safe. Had Luis hired a team to take her out?

She should call Jeff. Then again, all he'd do was worry and lose sleep. At least one of them should rest well tonight. She'd tell him in the morning.

Too bad there wasn't a firing range in town. There was nothing like target practice to blow off a little steam. The picture stared up at her from the table. She grabbed her cell and phoned Tad.

The sun warmed Jeff's back as he jogged up beside Kara, who was striding up the sidewalk not far from her place. "Hey. I got a call from Tad early this morning."

"Tad has a big mouth."

Jeff gripped her forearm and pulled her across the street. "Let's go to the park."

Kara let him guide her without protest. Once at the park, they sat on a bench a short distance from the playground. "Tad said the picture was clean and that it was printed on a home printer."

"I know. Not much help. I should've known Alvarado would send more than one person after me. If anything, he's thorough." She lunged to her feet and walked back toward her apartment. "I can't sit here and do nothing. This isn't going to stop until that man is dead."

Jeff didn't like the sound of her voice. "What are you thinking?"

"That I need to lay low."

"Then what are you doing out here? You're making yourself an easy target."

"Someone needs to find Alvarado, and put a stop to this. I'm sick of being shot at."

Jeff placed his hand on her shoulder. "I won't let anything happen to you, Kara. You're forgetting about Victor. He might still be involved with Alvarado. All we need to do is find him."

Kara flung her apartment door open and walked inside. "And what?" Sarcasm dripped from her voice. "Walk up to him and say, 'Hey, we spotted you doing a deal. Talk to us or else?'"

"Works for me."

"Not gonna happen. If we talk to him, this entire case is blown. He'd never give up information, and we'd risk everything. No. We have to ride this out. For all anyone associated with the cartel knows, I left Miami to escape Alvarado. There's no reason for anyone to think I'm here for any other reason."

Jeff stared at the woman he believed he was falling in love with and something inside him snapped. "I'm putting an end to this once and for all." He turned on his heel and reached for the door.

"Stop!" Kara grabbed his arm and pushed him against the door.

His eyes widened. Rage filled her eyes.

"You will not jeopardize this operation." Her words came out in a rush.

Kara's coffee breath warmed the air between them. Her firm grip felt like a vice on his forearm. What was he doing? He knew better than to go rogue and ignore procedure. He dropped his head. "I don't want to lose you."

She relaxed her hold and took a step back. "You're not going to lose me."

"We need to take care of Victor." He saw the stubborn set of her jaw. Why wouldn't she listen?

"Jeff, you're allowing emotions to cloud your judgment. Think like a cop."

She sure knew how to strike a low blow. "Fine. I want you to stay at the ranch."

She shook her head. "No. I'm staying here. I have a job to do, and so do you."

"I hate this."

Kara giggled. "Welcome back. Thought maybe I'd lost you in the deep dark place of fear. Aren't you the one who said that God's watching out for me? Don't you think He still is?"

He pulled her into his arms and buried his face in her hair. "I'm sorry. Yes. God is watching out for you. But promise me you'll be careful."

"Promise." She pushed him away. "Now get out of here. I have a client soon, and I know you have work out on the ranch."

She had that right at least. Plus, he'd been cleared to resume his normal investigative duties an hour ago. His number one priority—breaking Eric.

Kara closed the door behind Jeff then headed into the salon. She pulled out her phone. "Gary, it's Kara. Any news on Alvarado?"

"We've tracked him to Peru. It's only a matter of time now."

"You plug the leak yet?"

"Not sure. I'll have to get back to you on that one."

"Victor's nearby. I think he might still be working for Alvarado. Any way you can do some checking around?"

"I'll see what I can find out. You okay?"

"Fine, for a person on a hit list."

"Point taken. Stay safe. I'll get back to you ASAP."

Kara wanted to throw her phone across the room, but the front door opened, stifling the impulse. "Marci. This is a surprise. How are you?"

"Desperate for a fill. Do you have time?" She held up her thumb. "I have to give a presentation this afternoon, and I want to look my best."

"I do have someone scheduled, but since she's not here yet, have a seat." She made quick work of fixing the damaged nail then sat back to admire her handiwork. "What do you think?"

Marci held out her thumb. "Perfect." She handed Kara a ten-dollar bill and stood. "If I land this job, you'll have to help me celebrate."

Kara grinned. "Absolutely." Marci was making her assignment of getting close to her easy. At least one thing was going her way.

Marci waved good-bye as she left the shop.

Kara checked her watch. Looked like her client was a no-show. She cleaned her station and locked up. No sense in waiting any longer. She had an investigation to do, hit man or not. First on her list was that shack she'd spotted. If only she could find her way back.

She grabbed her phone. "Jeff, you have time for a hike?" If someone was back in the woods, she didn't want to announce their arrival by riding horses.

"Sure. When?"

"Now."

"Anything I need to know?"

"I spotted a shack yesterday when I was riding with Jake. I want to check it out."

"Okay. I'll be waiting."

Kara filled a backpack with water, ammo, trail mix, and a camera and then strapped her backup weapon into the holster on her shin. She slipped a loose long-sleeve blouse over her tank to conceal her Glock then grabbed her keys and headed out.

30

Careful to avoid any twigs that could snap under her weight, Kara led the way toward the shack. At least she hoped she was going in the right direction. Jeff squeezed her shoulder and pointed. The ramshackle building stood a few hundred feet off to their left. They both dropped down onto hands and knees.

"What do you want to do?" Jeff asked.

"I was hoping to get a closer look and see if the place is being used."

"Okay. I'll circle around the back. You approach from the side." Kara nodded and crouched low. She watched Jeff run the few hundred yards to the building then followed from a side angle. The shack had no windows. She pushed down her frustration and listened. The only sound she heard was the blood rushing through her ears.

Jeff tapped her shoulder and whispered, "I'll go in high. You go low."

"Wait. Let's try knocking."

Jeff's eyes widened, and he looked at her like she'd

lost her mind. "Nothing like letting them know we're here."

"I know, but I have a feeling. Trust me."

"Okay." Jeff drew out the word as if to wrap his mind around what she was asking.

Kara reached for his hand and held tight as she knocked. No answer. "Hello! Anyone home?" Silence. She reached for the handle.

Jeff shot out his other hand and stopped her. "It could be booby-trapped."

Kara felt her heart pound harder. "Any suggestions?"

"Let's sit back and wait awhile. See if anyone shows up."

Great. A stakeout in the mosquito-infested woods.

Voices approached. They bolted behind a dense bush.

"The coke will be late."

Kara recognized the voice. She wanted to see who was talking to confirm her suspicion. But the bush obstructed her view. A door opened and closed then opened and closed again. Footsteps sounded nearby then faded away.

A minute later they followed after the men. They stayed on the path she and Jake had taken and seemed unafraid of detection.

If only she could get a decent look at them. They both wore jeans, a long-sleeve cotton shirt, and a cowboy hat. She knew one of the hats. It had to be Jake.

A twig snapped, and Jake swung around.

Kara and Jeff crouched low. "Who's there?" He

mumbled, "stay put" to his friend then headed their direction.

Kara looked at Jeff as panic rose within. They stayed low and ran for a large tree to hide behind, but if they were caught, it would look suspicious. Footsteps crunching through the dry grass and weeds approached.

Jeff pushed her against the tree, blocking her from view. His breath mingled with hers. "Shh. Follow my lead." His eyes pleaded with her to understand.

She nodded.

"I said who's there?" The staccato of Jake's words projected irritation.

Jeff captured her mouth with his. She could feel his heart pounding.

"What in the world? What are you two doing out here acting like a couple of teens hiding from their parents?"

Jeff stepped back from Kara. "Uh, hi, Jake."

Kara wiggled her fingers. Heat singed her face. This had to be one of the most embarrassing moments of her life, and they weren't even doing what Jake thought they were.

Jake swore and walked away.

Jeff jogged up alongside Jake before he met up with the other man who had been with Jake. "Hey. Can we keep this between us? I'd hate for Eric to hear about—"

"Save it, Jeff. Your dirty little secret's safe with me." He cast a sly grin at Kara. "And here I thought you were a nice girl."

Kara took a deep breath and balled her hands into a fist. She would not hit him. This was how the job worked. So what if her reputation was now tarnished.

Jeff slowed to a stop, allowing Jake to increase the distance between them and took Kara's arm. "You okay?"

She nodded.

"I'm really sorry about that, but I didn't know what else to do."

"I know. You did the right thing. I just wish it hadn't been Jake. He made me feel so dirty."

Jeff reached up and brushed something from her hair. "Yeah well, you're covered in a bit of dust and stuff. I'm so sorry, Kara."

"Forget it. You saved our hides—again. I should be thanking you."

Jeff chuckled.

"What?"

"When I'm with you I tend to get into the strangest situations."

"Hmm. Now that I think about it the same could be said of you." They continued the rest of the way back to the ranch at a slow pace. Kara grasped Jeff's hand as they came into a clearing. Jake was already busy at work training a horse, and the other man was nowhere in sight. "How long do you think it will take for him to realize we're onto him? It's not like he had a viable reason for being out in the woods."

"You mean like we did?" His eyebrows raised, and his mouth quirked up.

She playfully punched him in the arm. "Don't you dare repeat that part to anyone."

He laughed out loud. "I won't." Jake had a keen

eye, and Jeff knew good and well he watched their every move. He pulled Kara into a hug and rested his chin on her head. "Give Tad a call and have him meet us at your place. I'll be right behind you."

Kara made a quick call to Tad. It was time to tell Jeff the real reason she didn't want to get involved with him. Her stomach churned much like it had every year on the first day of school. Only this time, she didn't have friends and a smiling teacher waiting to greet her.

Kara opened the door to her apartment, allowing Jeff to enter.

"Where's Tad? I thought he'd beat me here." Jeff sat on a cushy chair and propped his ankle on his knee.

Kara squeezed her hands together and sat across from him. "He's coming in a little while. I need to tell you something."

Jeff seemed to understand the serious implication, and his face grew pensive. "Okay."

"When I was a rookie cop, I fell hard for my partner. I was young and inexperienced. He was older and very smart. At least that's what I thought."

"I don't understand why you're telling me this."

"Because it's important. Please just listen. This is hard enough without you interrupting. One night, we answered a domestic violence call. Tony took the lead and walked up to the front door. There was shouting, and we could hear glass breaking. It sounded pretty bad.

He told me to call for backup. I had only walked a few feet away when I heard a shot. I whirled around, and Tony lay on the ground bleeding from his gut." She blinked rapidly as if to block the image from her mind. She'd played that moment over in her head so many times. "Tony hated wearing his vest, and the night he needed it most, it hung in his closet at home."

"I still don't understand," Jeff said.

"Tony died a few hours later. The guy in the house was high on meth. He didn't even remember firing the gun that killed the man I loved."

Jeff stood and knelt in front of her. "Kara, I'm not Tony, and you're not a young rookie. We both know the stakes of what we do, and we prepare for the unexpected. On a personal level, I don't know where we're heading. But I do know that I care a lot about you, and I'd like to pursue a relationship with you. If you need to wait until this case is over and we aren't partners anymore, then I'm willing to wait. I don't want to lose what we have."

Kara's insides turned to mush. When had she fallen for him? She knew they'd grown close, but now she ached for him to hold her.

Jeff took her hands in his. "What do you say?"

She nodded, fighting back threatening tears. No way would she cry. A firm knock at the door startled them both. Jeff pulled away and answered, allowing Tad in.

Tad looked from one to the other. "Am I interrupting something?"

"No," they both said at once.

Tad narrowed his eyes, but let it drop.

The three sat around the kitchen table, and Tad listened while Kara and Jeff filled him in on what they knew. Tad's eyes gleamed. "This is exactly the break we've been waiting for." He turned to Jeff. "Do you think you can flip Eric? We could use an inside man."

"It's possible."

Kara wanted to hug Tad for the compassion he'd shown Jeff. If they were able to get Eric's cooperation, there was a chance he'd never serve a day in prison.

"Okay. Let me know how it goes, and we'll meet at the field office tonight." Tad stood and let himself out.

Kara grasped Jeff's arm as he was about to leave. "Do you want backup?"

"With Eric?"

"Yes."

"He's my brother. I don't think he'll hurt me."

"He better not, or I'll have to add him to my list," Kara said.

"What list?"

"Just a bad joke. Go."

31

Kara raced blindly through the woods on the back of Blaze. Her captors followed close behind shouting her name. Searing heat radiated from the tree trunks. Branches dropped around her, splintering as they struck the rock-hard earth. She urged Blaze forward, desperate to escape. The horse shied at a fallen burning branch and stumbled, throwing Kara from his back. She struck her head on a rock and lay motionless.

Kara's eyes shot open as she awoke with a jerk from her nightmare. Acrid smoke filled her lungs. Through watery eyes, she saw her apartment glowing a hazy orange. She sat up and bumped a heavy object with her shoulder and forehead. Bright orange flames covered one wall like a waterfall.

She kicked the covers off and slid from the bed and crawled on all fours toward the sound of pounding. Coughing racked her body as she struggled to catch her breath. She crept closer to the door. Several cinders landed on her bare arms, and she slapped them away. Tears streamed down her face. She had to escape. Her fingers bumped into the contoured wall. She slid her hand up, hoping she'd found the door. *Where is it?* She crawled a little further, her hand feeling for the knob. *Lord, help me!* She yanked her hand back as it brushed up against the hot doorknob—finally. Grasping the edge of her nightshirt to protect her hand, she rose and unlocked the door then yanked it open. She ran from the building, coughing and gasping, and fell into Tad's arms.

"Kara, thank God, I was about ready to break down the door."

"Glad I saved you the trouble." Coughing continued to rack her body.

Tad grasped her arm and guided her away from the building. "The fire department will be here any minute."

"Why don't I hear any sirens?"

Tad pointed across the street and down about a block to a fire truck turning the corner. "The station's only a block away. There's no need to wake the entire town."

Kara nodded as she went into a fit of coughing. The fire truck pulled up in front of the building, and the firefighters got to work.

Tad guided her to a bench across the street away from all the action. "Any idea how this happened?"

"No."

An ambulance pulled up along the curb. Tad waved the medics over. "This is Kara. She was in the building and got out under her own power." He turned back to Kara. "Peggy will take care of you. I have to go." He made his way to the small crowd that had gathered during the past several minutes.

The woman smiled and studied Kara's eyes. "Nice

to meet you, Kara, although I wish it were under better circumstances."

"Same here." She nodded to Peggy's partner, a twenty-something guy who was all business and pushing a gurney toward her along the sidewalk. "I suppose you want me to get on that thing."

Peggy chuckled. "That would be helpful."

Kara moved to the gurney situated outside the ambulance and slowly eased down onto it.

"That's right. Now just lay back and relax."

How was she supposed to relax when whoever was trying to kill her had nearly succeeded? And on top of that, everything she had left in the world, which wasn't much, was probably burned to a crisp?

Peggy slipped gloves onto her hand and applied pressure to Kara's forehead.

"Ouch."

"Sorry. You have a gash, and I need to stop the bleeding." What seemed like forever, but was probably only a couple of minutes later, Peggy finally released the pressure on her head. "Open your mouth, please." After inspecting Kara's throat, Peggy shone a light up her nose. "You are one lucky lady. There are no signs of burning. You must have escaped the fire right after it started." She strapped an oxygen mask around her face. "How's that feel?"

Kara gave the thumbs up sign. There were too many flames for that. Maybe, like Jeff had suggested, God really was watching out for her.

"Have you ever ridden in an ambulance?"

Kara slowly moved her head from side to side. If Peggy told the hospital of her recent trip to the ER in

Miami, and they requested Kara's records, her past could blow up in her face. It would look awfully suspicious to have a dead person in their ER.

"Then you're in for a treat. My partner is a great driver. He misses all the potholes. You'll think you're riding on air."

Kara pulled the mask away from her face. "I don't need to go to the hospital. I'm fine."

"That's your call, but I really think you should get checked out. The cut on your head looks like it might need stitches. They're going to want to take a few X-rays as well."

"Fine. I'll go."

She took Kara's wrist in her hand as she looked at her watch. "Once we get you into the ambulance, we'll hook you up to a couple machines so we can better monitor you."

Gail's and Kurt's familiar voices hovered nearby.

"Kara, are you okay? Tad called us." Gail stepped close to her and took her hand.

Her friend's panicked voice shot like a bullet to Kara's heart. She turned her head toward Gail's voice. Kurt stood beside his wife holding her other hand.

The medic spoke in a reassuring tone, "I think it's safe to say Kara's going to be okay. She kept her wits about her and got out fast. We're taking her to St. Charles in Bend. You can meet us there if you'd like."

Kara closed her eyes as a young woman wheeled her

into X-ray. These people sure did make a big deal about a little smoke inhalation and a cut on her forehead. You'd think she was a trauma case or something. "What are they going to X-ray?"

The attendant looked down at the papers in her hand. "Looks like they'll be taking pictures of your head, neck, and chest."

"Thanks." Kara took a deep breath and willed herself to relax. She hated hospitals and detested the fact that she needed to be in one. The female technician entered the room and got right down to business. About thirty minutes later, Kara settled back in her room and waited for the doctor.

The door opened as Gail and Kurt entered. "How're you doing?" Gail sat in the seat next to the bed. "I'm so thankful you're okay. You could've been killed. God was sure watching out for you."

It'd been a while since Kara had felt like God cared about what happened to her, but today she must have had her very own angel. The wall clock read five o'clock. That meant the fire started sometime between midnight and three or so this morning. She'd gotten home late after her meeting at the field office in Bend. She should call Jeff before he found out about the fire from someone else.

"I appreciate you both waiting around to see me, but I think I should make a couple calls."

"Are you going to phone your parents?"

"Why ruin their European tour? I sure wish I had my phone." She looked around the room for a landline and found none. They must not expect patients to make calls from the ER.

Gail reached into her purse and pulled out her phone. "Use mine. Any idea how long they're going to keep you?"

"No. I'm waiting to see the doctor."

Gail looked to Kurt. "Do you want to go home or wait? It could be hours before they release her."

Kara tugged at the neck of her hospital gown. "I hate to ask, but I'm going to need clothes to wear out of this place when they do let me go. The nightshirt I was wearing when they brought me in isn't going to cut it. If you go home, would you bring me back something?"

"That settles it." Gail said. "We'll be back in an hour or so. You're planning on staying with us when you're released, aren't you?"

"I'm afraid you're stuck with me at least until I find somewhere else to live."

Gail stood. "Good. We'll hurry and be back before you know it." They moved toward the door.

For the first time, Kara noticed Gail wore a coat over her PJs, and Kurt had on sweats and a loud T-shirt. Good thing they were going home. "Wait!"

Gail turned around.

"Thanks for coming here to be with me."

She came back and gave Kara a gentle hug. "We love you. We'll be back before you have time to miss us."

"One more thing. I was wondering how you know for certain that God was watching out for me?"

A gentle look crossed Gail's face. She reached into her purse then pulled out a New Testament. "Faith. I've sensed that you've been struggling with that lately. If you feel up to it, read Hebrews chapter eleven. The

Bible explains it so much better than I ever could."

"How'd you know I was struggling?"

"I've known you too long not to know." She folded Kara's hands around the tiny New Testament and walked out of the room with Kurt.

Kara watched her friends leave, took a deep breath, and tapped in Jeff's number on Gail's phone. She'd think about what Gail said after she called him. He answered after the third ring. "It's Kara."

"What's wrong?" His voice sounded groggy.

"There was a fire in my apartment, and I'm at St. Charles Hospital in Bend."

"I'm on my way."

The line went dead. Kara stared at the phone for a second before disconnecting.

Jeff's feet hit the floor with a thud. He yanked on his clothes, pocketed his phone, and ran out of the house nearly taking down Jake as he crossed his path at the bottom of the porch stairs.

"What's your hurry?" Jake asked.

His heart nearly stopped when Kara said she'd been in a fire. "Kara's in the hospital. There was a fire at her apartment this morning."

Jake frowned. "Is she okay?"

"Don't know. I hung up too fast. I need to get to the hospital." He turned and jogged to his rig and yelled over his shoulder. "When Eric gets up, will you let him know what happened?"

"Sure."

The SUV's tires kicked up gravel as Jeff roared down the driveway. He entered the hospital parking lot twenty minutes later, thankful for the early hour. The lot had plenty of parking spaces and traffic had been light.

After speaking with the woman at the front desk, Jeff hustled through the hall until he found Kara's room. He knocked then opened the door. Kara lay in the hospital bed, motionless with her eyes closed. He walked to her bedside. Her skin shone pink, apparently from the fire, and she had stitches in her forehead. But other than that, she looked fine. He took a deep breath and let it out in a whoosh, thankful to see she really was okay. Her eyes opened slightly.

He smiled and reached for her hand. "Hey there. How're you feeling?"

"Alive."

He chuckled. "You've always had a way with words. Do you hurt anywhere? Are you burned?"

"I'm fine. A little smoke inhalation, some minor burns, and this crack on my head. No biggie."

Relief coursed through him, and he sank into the chair near her bed. "I'm glad. Is your place a complete loss?"

Kara shrugged. "Don't know for sure, but based on what I saw before they brought me here, I'd say yes. I woke up and got out of there as fast as I could. The fire department was on site a few minutes later." She tried to sit up a bit more in the bed.

Jeff jumped up and adjusted her pillows. He gently

fingered her hair away from her face and studied her stitches. The cut would probably only make a small scar. He wanted to do something else for her, anything, but he felt helpless. She had the staff to take care of her. He sat on her bedside and sighed. "I shouldn't have hung up so fast when you called. I imagined you were lying half dead here in the hospital, especially after our conversation about your first partner."

Kara coughed and then winced. "You should have phoned me back."

"I didn't think of that." He leaned in a little closer, not minding the smoky smell. Oh, how he wanted to hold her in his arms and never let go. He'd come too close to losing her. When had she become so dear to him?

"What is it?"

He shook his head. "Nothing. I'm glad you're okay. You want me to go see what I can find out about the fire and your apartment?"

"Yes. That would be wonderful. I hate not knowing."

And I hate to leave you so soon after getting here. Me and my big mouth. "You going to be okay?"

"Aren't I always?"

His mouth spread into a wide grin.

Kara giggled and then coughed. "Go—and hurry. I want to know what happened."

He rose slowly, reluctant to leave her side. "I'll be back as soon as I can."

"You'd better call first. I'm using Gail's phone until I can get a new one. I hope to be released as soon as

Gail and Kurt get back."

"Okay."

The area surrounding Kara's burned-out apartment and office smelled like a campfire. A single fire engine still sat out in front of the building and several firefighters roamed around. He walked to the side and spotted her car in the alley unscathed.

One of the firemen explained that the exterior walls of the building were extra thick as a precaution since the businesses were connected to one another. The fire investigator was inside. With little else to do, Jeff walked to the diner for a cup of coffee.

Thirty minutes later, he returned to Kara's place. A short man holding a clipboard stood outside her apartment studying the utility box. "Excuse me."

The man turned his way. "Yes?"

"Did you determine a cause for the fire?"

"I did, and who are you?"

Jeff held out his hand. "Jeff Clark. My girlfriend lived here."

The man nodded. "Deputy Baker mentioned you might stop by and said to fill you in on my findings. It looks like the fire was caused by faulty wiring. It's not the first time this has happened. We had a similar incident a couple of years ago. All these buildings need to be rewired, but the law's on their side, not mine."

"You're sure it was faulty wiring?"

The man narrowed his eyes and crossed his arms. "Positive." He walked away.

Jeff called out a thank you to his back. He'd thought for sure it had been arson. He checked his watch—eight o'clock.

He nodded to a nearby fireman watching for hot spots. "You mind if I go inside? My girlfriend asked me to get a few things for her."

"The structure is sound, but I'll have to come with you."

"Works for me. Thanks." Careful to not disturb anything, he entered the burned-out building. It wasn't as bad as he'd imagined. One whole side was charred, and a smoke line covered the ceiling, but the other side of her apartment seemed intact for the most part. Too bad the dresser was on the charred side along with what looked to have once been a purse. Where was her Glock? He used a pen from his pocket to carefully lift what was left of her purse. Her Glock lay beneath the charred leather. He stuffed it into his waistband when the firefighter wasn't looking.

Jeff did a one-eighty. The place would need to be gutted for sure. The water damage looked extensive. What could he hope to find? Electrical wiring wasn't his area of expertise, but Gary might know someone who could confirm what the fire marshal said. He thanked the firefighter and walked outside to his SUV and slid in.

"Gary, Jeff here. Kara's place caught fire last night while she was asleep inside. The fire marshal declared it faulty wiring, but I was hoping you could get someone over here to confirm."

"I'll get right on that. Is she okay?" His concern came through the phone line.

"Yes. Smoke inhalation, a gash on her forehead, and some minor burns, but she'll be fine."

"That's a relief. I'll take care of this and get back to you when I have something."

"Thanks." He could depend on Gary to make sure this fire was, indeed, an accident.

He checked the Internet for the number of the hospital. The chances Kara would still be there were slim, but he called anyway. He frowned when the receptionist informed him that she hadn't checked out yet. He hoped she was okay. Head injuries and smoke inhalation could be tricky, but Kara had said everything was minor. His pulse quickened, and he pressed hard on the accelerator.

Kara sat up in her hospital bed and thumbed through a magazine while she waited to be released. The doctor had informed her that since she was breathing okay and her X-rays looked fine, he'd release her as soon as someone came to get her, but he made her promise to seek medical help if she started having breathing problems. He also told her to make an appointment to have the stitches removed. She'd phoned Gail's house but only got her answering machine. Gail must be on her way.

Tossing the magazine aside, Kara rested her head on the soft pillow. A lump rose in her throat. The comment Gail made about God protecting her stuck in her mind. The car bomb had set off her anger toward Him. Until that time, she loved and trusted Him to always take care of her. Had God been with her all along? How else could she have survived all the attacks? She frowned. But why couldn't He have stopped it all from happening in the first place if He truly cared?

Her hand brushed against the Bible Gail had left. She opened to Hebrews chapter eleven as her friend had suggested and began reading. The chapter was filled with references to familiar Bible stories she'd heard as a child. Yes. It did take faith for Noah to build an ark, and for Moses to lead the Israelites through the Red Sea. She'd never really thought about it that way before, because as a child it never occurred to her that a flood wouldn't come or that the Red Sea could have drowned them all. She'd never once questioned that the outcome of those incidents could have been different because God was God.

When had she lost her trust in Him? Or was it lying dormant waiting to be realized? *Lord, I'm sorry for cutting You out of my life. I want to have the same faith that I once had, only this time I want my faith to be unshakeable.*

Trust Me.

Peace settled over her. A lone tear slipped down her cheek, and she swiped at it. How could she not trust God? After all, He had a pretty decent track record. *Lord, I am choosing to trust You. I still don't understand everything, but I will trust You.*

A weight lifted from her, and tears streamed down her face. She wiped them away with the back of her hand then remembered something her mother had once told her when she'd been bullied at school. She said that God allows the bad stuff to happen to make us stronger and that He will never give us more than we can handle with His help. Mom had been right. How could she have forgotten that? She was definitely a stronger person and agent now.

It's me again. I guess bad things have to happen like my mom said. It's all part of growing. But if it's okay with You, I'd love to stop growing for a while, and thanks for saving me from that fire.

Kara dried her eyes and smiled. It felt nice to be on God's side again. A light tap sounded on her door, and Gail entered with Jeff in tow.

Gail stood at her bedside and grasped her hand. "What's wrong? You look like you've been crying."

Kara laughed softly. "Nothing. In fact, I'm the best I've been in quite a while." She looked past Gail and made eye contact with Jeff. Something about him made her pause for a moment. What was different? She tore her gaze away from him and focused on Gail.

"If that sparkle in your eyes means anything, I'd say you're better than okay." Gail spotted the Bible in Kara's hand, and a knowing smile crossed her face. "I'm glad you've worked things out, my friend."

Kara held up the small New Testament. "You mind if I hang on to this for awhile?" Kara glanced at Jeff. He seemed to understand what was left unsaid.

"Keep it. I have another one at home." Gail lifted a

small bag onto the bed. "Sorry I took so long getting back. The phone wouldn't stop ringing with friends calling to check on you."

"Who called?"

"A few members from the singles' group at church and a couple of your nail clients. I can't remember their names. I finally had to put the answering machine on." She pulled a dress from the bag. "I hope this fits."

Jeff cleared his throat. "I'll be outside the door when you're ready."

Kara changed into the sundress Gail had brought then laughed at herself when she looked down at her feet. The fabric reached to the ground and the top half draped way too low.

Gail frowned. "I forgot to take into consideration our height difference."

Hands on hips Kara looked toward Gail. "I don't suppose you brought a belt to tie this up with and a top to wear under it?"

She undid the belt she wore and handed it to Kara. "Take this one. I knew none of my pants would fit you, but I thought a dress would work. I suppose pants would have been better after all. At least then you could have rolled the legs up." Gail slipped off her button-up sweater. "Use this too."

"Thanks." Kara belted the dress so it wouldn't drag on the floor then put the sweater on over the dress. "Will you take me by my apartment on the way to your place? Maybe there's something useable."

"I'm not sure that's such a great idea," Gail said.

"At least let me see for myself." Kara handed back

the cell phone she'd borrowed. "Thanks."

Gail reached for her purse and tucked it inside. "You're welcome. We could run by a store on the way home."

"I don't have any money on me. Let's just see what can be salvaged." Kara moved toward the door.

"You never were much of a shopper."

"Guilty as charged." Kara and Gail walked out of the room and came face to face with Jeff.

His eyes glimmered. "Looks like you're playing dress up, Kara."

"Ha, Ha. We're going by my place to see if anything survived."

"I was there. You won't find anything useable. Besides, I've heard you should never disturb anything after a fire until your insurance company sees it. Let me take you shopping for a few new things."

Kara looked down at herself. "I can't go shopping dressed like this!" She touched his arm. "Wait a minute. How's my car?"

"Intact. Apparently, the walls of the building are thick and your car escaped unharmed."

"That's odd. If the fire stayed in the building, how did anyone know to call the fire department?"

"Beats me, but I'll find out. Now, how about shopping? I'll even loan you the money," Jeff said.

"Gail was planning to take me."

Gail cut in. "Don't worry about me. You two go and have fun. I needed to bring you a change of clothes, and I did that." She turned to Jeff. "You take good care of her."

Jeff sobered. "Yes, ma'am."

Kara hugged Gail. "Thanks." Then she turned back to Jeff and looped her arm through his. "Let's go." Kara spotted a nurse coming her way with a wheelchair and groaned. "Not a wheelchair too. The clothes are humiliating enough. Is that really necessary?"

"Sorry. Hospital rules," the nurse replied.

Kara sat and crossed her arms with her eyes cast down. "Someone get me out of here."

Jeff chuckled as he took over pushing her out to his rig.

"So what's the news on my apartment?" She buckled up and looked at Jeff who sat behind the wheel of his SUV.

"What do you mean?" He put the vehicle in gear and drove out of the parking lot.

"Arson?"

"The fire inspector said faulty wiring." He pulled her Glock from his waistband. "I salvaged this for you, but you'd better check it out before you try to use it."

Kara reached for the weapon. "Thanks." She stuffed it into the belt under Gail's sweater. Kara could tell by his tone that he had his doubts about the faulty wiring. She wouldn't put it past Alvarado to resort to arson, but it wasn't his normal MO.

Kara sat beside Jeff in his SUV. "I assume you've spoken with Tad about the fire. What did he say?"

"Not much. He saw the glow from the fire through your window, called it in, and proceeded to pound on your door." He glanced over at her. "I can't pretend I'm not worried. This fire reeks of arson. I think you should stay at the ranch."

"Gail's expecting me to stay with her."

"Do you think that's wise? I can't protect you when I'm not with you. And you could be putting your friends' lives in jeopardy."

"True. It's not your job to be my bodyguard, though. This is exactly why we shouldn't get involved. Once emotions are in the mix everything gets complicated."

"Everything became complicated the moment I saw you fly through the air when your car exploded. Forget that I love you."

"You what?"

"Did I say that out loud?" He groaned.

Kara nodded and grinned. If Jeff weren't a Christian, she suspected she'd be hearing a string of curses right about now. "You dropped the L-word, but don't worry. I won't hold it against you."

"You won't hold it against me?" His voice seemed to raise an octave as he pulled the SUV off to the side of the road.

She'd been teasing, trying to keep the mood light, but apparently, Jeff had other ideas. "Um." She bit her lip then tried to smile. "Why'd you pull over?" Traffic whizzed past causing their vehicle to shake in response to the current.

"I tell you that I love you and you say, 'I won't hold

it against you'? What kind of a response is that?"

"A funny one?" she asked in a small voice.

"I'm not laughing."

Kara swallowed hard. "Sorry. I'm not good at this kind of thing. Every time I love someone, they get ripped away from me—first my cousin Dee and then Tony. Growing up Dee and I were close. We were the same age and inseparable. Then one day that all changed when she decided to try crack. She had a reaction to the stuff. I called 9-1-1, but it was too late. She was already gone."

"I'm sorry. How old were you?"

"Fifteen. That was the day I decided I wanted to go into law enforcement. I wanted justice for what had happened to my best friend."

"Then how'd you end up in beauty school?"

"I loved doing nails, and my parents were against me going into law enforcement. They paid for beauty school then I used the money I made doing nails to get a degree in criminology." She shrugged. "It worked out in the end."

Jeff shook his head. "You're amazing. I pull over because I'm ticked with you, and now all I want to do is hold you."

"Love's like that."

He raised a brow. "You know this from experience I gather?"

"Mm-hmm. Now that you mention it, I have a confession to make." She looked over at him in time to see a car slow to a stop beside them. The window lowered and the barrel of a gun poked out. "Down!"

32

The window shattered above Jeff's head. He threw the SUV into gear and floored the gas. How had someone pulled up beside them without either of them noticing it coming? Clearly, they were both distracted. He looked in his rearview mirror to see if the car tailed them. It was gone. He looked at Kara. "You okay?"

"Fine. You?" Kara brushed glass shards off her arms with a tissue.

"Same. It looks like the shooter took off in the opposite direction." Jeff turned onto a side road, pulled over, then got out. He shook glass from his clothing.

Kara ran around to Jeff's side coughing the whole way. Seemed her lungs were giving her trouble. Guess the fire had more of an effect than she wanted to admit. "I called Tad."

Jeff nodded. "It looks clear." He shielded his eyes from the sun. "I made sure we weren't followed."

"Good but it seems they are always one step ahead of us."

Which made him think they were being trailed via

GPS. He lay on the ground at the rear bumper, shining his phone's flashlight—nothing. He repeated the process under the front bumper. "Let's get moving."

Kara scrambled into the rig. "Where are we going?"

"The Bend field office. You need a working service weapon and a vest. And I want my rig checked for a tracker. I didn't see anything, but maybe it's too well hidden. I also think the timeline needs to be moved up. I want you to stay in Bend at a hotel. Tad or myself will contact you when everything is set up."

"What about Eric? Did you ever talk with him?"

"No, but that will be the first thing I do when I get back. Even if I have to follow him into the restroom, he's not escaping me this time." Admiration and a hint of fear filled Kara's eyes. He reached out and squeezed her hand gently. "Don't worry. God's got this all in His control."

"Good point. I'll snag a T-shirt and sweats at the field office too and then you can drop me off at a hotel. One of my clients told me about a place outside of town the other day that sounds perfect."

"Okay. You sure you'll be safe there?"

"I'm not sure about anything anymore, but I looked it up online and it seemed like a good option." She pulled out her phone and a moment later rattled off the address.

Whatever it took to keep Kara safe he'd do. That girl had wrapped her fingers around his heart, and he didn't want to shake her loose.

An hour later, after a detour to the DEA field office for equipment, Jeff made his way back to the ranch. He parked, grabbed a duffel bag, which held a bug detector, and walked toward the house.

Veronica sat on the porch swing. "How's Kara?"

He leaned against the railing and crossed his arms. "She has six stitches in her forehead and minor smoke inhalation, but she'll be fine."

"What a relief. When Jake told us she was in the hospital, we imagined the worst." She rose from the swing and walked toward the entrance to the house. "I'm glad she's okay. I can't imagine how frightened she must've been."

Jeff frowned. "Yeah. Is Eric around?"

"He's in his office."

"Thanks." Jeff went inside and climbed the stairs. With every step, his legs seemed heavier, and his pace slackened. He paused outside Eric's door. Without knocking, he entered—time to get this over with.

Eric looked up from the papers strewn across his desk. "You're back. Is Kara okay?"

"She will be." His gut clenched. Eric had no idea what was about to come down.

"What happened?"

"Seems the wiring was old and caused an electrical fire. She escaped on her own and only suffered minor smoke inhalation and a small cut on her head."

"How are you doing?" Eric asked.

"Me? I've had better days."

"I can tell how much you care about her. If that'd been Veronica, I'd have been out of my mind."

"I'm fine." No one needed to know all the traffic laws he'd broken in his rush to be by Kara's side. Having her with him today had felt good and right. He pushed up from his seat. "We need to talk. But first..." He locked the office door then pulled a bug detector from his duffel bag. He held his finger to his lips as Eric watched with wide eyes. Surprisingly, the place was clean.

"What's going on?" Eric asked.

"Funny. I was going to ask you the same thing." He pulled his credentials from his pocket and showed Eric. "I'll tell you what I know, and then you can fill in the blanks." Jeff kept his voice low as he explained all the photos he had of Eric's deliveries and how the DEA, FBI, and local authorities were working together to put him out of business. "Before you say anything, I want you to know that no matter what, you're still my brother, and I want to help you." He pulled a small digital recorder from his bag, pressed record, and placed it on the desk between them.

Eric nodded. His face paled, and he looked a little sick.

"I've been authorized to offer you a chance to help us out. In return, you and your family will be put into the witness protection program. Should you decide not to help, I'll get a warrant for your arrest and you'll go to prison for a long time. What's it gonna be?"

"I'll help. All this time, I thought you were a banker." He shook his head. "I sure wish you'd been here a year ago when those blasted Gonzaleses showed up and demanded that I board their horses or else they'd spread lies about my ranch and destroy me. They even threatened to hurt my family if I didn't do what they said."

Jeff schooled his face to reveal no emotion. It took all his training to not lash out at Eric. Didn't Eric know he could've gone to the authorities or at the very least contacted family? "I need you to state your full name and then tell me why you let them get away with it."

He nodded. "Eric Nicolas Waters. I can't afford to lose business. I know I look successful, but the truth is Veronica's family's been helping us out. Without her family, I don't know how we would've made it."

"Veronica went along with this?"

"She has no idea what's going on, and let me tell you, it's been a big strain on our marriage. But I couldn't tell her."

"Okay then. What about the drugs?"

"Not long after the Gonzaleses showed up for the first time, they told me to contact Jake. They wanted me to hire him. I'd had a couple kids working part time. I let them go to be able to pay Jake's salary. Luckily, the guy knows his way around horses. Anyway, the demands kept coming, and the threats got progressively worse until one day I found myself delivering cocaine. I knew it was wrong, but they were going to hurt my family. I had no choice." Eric's tone rose revealing his desperation.

Jeff felt his shoulders tighten. As fantastic as Eric's story seemed, he believed every word. "Okay. I need to know how this operation works, who's involved, and what's the timeline."

For the next forty-five minutes, Eric explained in detail everything CODE needed to know. "I overheard Jake yesterday tell someone about a delay. What's going on with that?"

"Beats me. No one's told me anything."

"As soon as you hear something, call me. I won't be around much today. I have to go get the window replaced in my Escape."

"What happened?"

"Someone shot at me."

Jeff wouldn't think it possible, but Eric's face paled further.

"Do they know you're onto them?"

"I'm assuming you mean the Gonzaleses or Jake, and to be honest, I don't know. Jake might be suspicious. But I suspect this trouble followed us from Miami."

"Us?"

"My partner, who will remain anonymous for now, and me."

Eric stood, knocking over his chair. "I'm out. This is getting too dangerous. If you're being shot at, it's only a matter of time before they turn on me. I need to get my family out of here."

Too bad Eric didn't think of that a year ago. Jeff strode over to his brother and placed a hand on his shoulder. "Do not make me arrest you. Pick up the chair and sit. We'll figure this out."

"Don't you see? This isn't going to end well. We need to go."

Jeff leaned down and made eye contact. "If you do anything out of the ordinary, they'll know. They've been watching you and your family for a long time."

Eric nodded, wild-eyed. "What do I do?"

"Stop freaking out and get it together. Your family's lives depend on it. We have a plan, but we need your help."

Eric nodded and swallowed hard. "Anything. I'll do whatever you tell me to do."

"Okay. For now, about all you have to do is tell anyone who asks that I'm with Kara."

Eric nodded.

Jeff backed away never letting his focus stray from Eric. "You going to be okay?"

"I am now. Thanks, little brother."

"Don't thank me yet. Things may get worse before they get better. Just remember, business as usual."

A sound in the hall drew his attention. But they were supposed to be the only ones inside the house. He drew his Glock and hurried to the door. He yanked it open and spotted Jake darting around the corner. "Stay here," he said over his shoulder and chased after the man.

Jake tripped and caught himself on the stair railing.

Jeff clamped his hand down on the man's shoulder. "Don't move." He aimed his gun at Jake.

Jake raised his hands. "I don't want trouble."

"Yet you were not only trespassing but eavesdropping too."

Jake blew out a breath. "There's something you need to know."

Talk about a turn of events. He motioned Jake back to Eric's office. "Take a seat." He pulled out his phone and pressed record. "Do you mind if I record this?"

"It's fine." Jake said.

"State your name and then tell me what your role is here."

Jake did as ordered, and an hour later, Jeff's mind reeled at all he'd learned. Jake had come to work for the Gonzaleses after they'd killed his sister. He'd decided to take the law into his own hands and infiltrate their organization to destroy them from the inside out.

Eric paced to the window. "This is so surreal. What I don't understand, though is how they didn't know you and your sister were related."

"Different last names, and I didn't live near her. I learned from a friend about her death and their involvement."

Jeff shook his head. "Did it not occur to you to go to the authorities?"

"Yes, but I didn't think they'd believe me. I have a record—petty theft. It's taken me years to get where I am in their organization, and now you're going to ruin it."

"Seems to me we both want the same thing." Jeff looked at his brother who was nodding. "We all want to put the Gonzaleses out of business. If your story checks out, we might be able to use your help. In the meantime, the two of you need to stick together. I don't want any funny business. Understood?" He looked to both men.

"There's one more thing you need to know," Jake said. "Kara's in danger."

33

Kara watched the parking lot from the motel's bedroom window. A red Subaru Forester entered the lot. The driver parked and stepped out. She narrowed her eyes. *Marci?* What was she doing here? Then again, she had told her about this place once when they ran into one another while in line for coffee. Her stomach tightened—had she been set up?

The woman walked into the building that housed guest services.

Kara pulled her new phone from her pocket and pressed Jeff's number. Voicemail picked up. "Hey. I have a situation here. Call me." She checked her Glock and secured it at her waist. She'd figured Marci for a user, but little else. Had she been wrong?

Marci strode out of guest services and made a direct path to Kara's building. How'd she find her so fast? Sure, she'd recommended this place, but she had no way of knowing Kara was there. The only person who knew her location was Jeff, and his SUV was clean for tracking devices. So how were they being followed?

She'd think it was her phone except it was new.

A loud rap sounded on Kara's door. Kara unlocked the sliders and went out the back. She'd circle around and trap Marci. A firm grip came down on her shoulder.

"Where do you think you're going?"

Kara whirled around. "Luis? How?"

"Get inside, Kara. I've had enough trouble from you to last a lifetime." He pushed her roughly back inside. "Answer the front door, and don't say a word."

"Answer it yourself."

Luis displayed the business end of a 9mm. "Open the door."

Kara swung open the door, and Marci strutted in. "Hi, sweetie. Surprised?"

Kara ignored Marci and turned to Luis. "What's going on? Why are you here, and why am I still alive?"

Luis laughed. He seemed to think the situation was funny. Kara shot a silent prayer up to God for help. She remained focused on Luis but kept Marci in her peripheral.

"You never were one for small talk." He kept the pistol trained at her head. "It's kind of amazing how this all has worked out in my favor. Marci moved to town right after your car exploded. She's here to keep an eye on some mutual friends of ours. When you showed up, it was fortuitous. Imagine my surprise when she called to tell me she'd met you in the town park?"

The evil look in his eyes made her heart pound. She was alone with not one, but two guns, pointed at her. Marci held a small pistol in her hand. At least she didn't seem comfortable holding it. Time to change tactics.

Without altering her focus, she addressed Marci. "How'd you and Luis meet?"

"We go way back. Remember I told you my boyfriend was in Australia? Well that was a lie."

Kara stifled a groan as an image of a brunette woman on Alvarado's yacht in Miami flashed in her mind—now she knew why Marci looked familiar. They'd never met and she'd only seen her at a distance the day her car exploded. She should've dug deeper into Marci's background, but she'd pegged her for a simple drug addict. "Where's your wife and kids, Luis?"

"This isn't about them. Since you've proven to be so hard to get rid of, I've decided to use you. Either help or you die." He shrugged. "What's it to be?"

Good question. They hadn't taken her weapon, but could she grab it and fire before either of them did? And what about collateral damage? According to the front desk, she'd gotten the last available room, so the rooms around them could be occupied. But if she cooperated, she'd be endangering the lives of her coworkers and Jeff.

"I'm running out of patience." His finger twitched. "One, two—"

"Okay," she said.

Luis lowered his gun slightly and motioned for her to take a seat.

"Before I help, I have a few questions."

"Fair enough."

Maybe she could buy enough time. "How'd you know I was here?"

"I've had you followed since the moment you left

the hospital in Miami."

"How?"

"I have eyes and ears everywhere."

"Even in Bend, Oregon?" Duh. Marci proved that. "I don't understand why I'm so important. I was gone, seemingly dead. I posed no threat to you."

"I don't need to tell *you* that drug trafficking reaches to every corner of the world. Now is that all?"

"I still don't understand why I'm alive."

He shook his head. "Me neither. I sent a team after you, but so far, you've managed to thwart them. I've decided you're more use to me alive than dead—for now anyway. Enough talking. You're wasting my time."

"Just one more question. How are you involved with the drug smuggling going on here?"

His eyes shone. "I have an interest in what's coming up from Mexico. I need you. You'll still do your DEA job, but I want half of any drugs you seize."

Kara shook her head. "No way." If she got caught stealing drugs from the DEA, she'd not only get fired, she'd likely end up behind bars.

"Either help me or you die." He shrugged as if her decision was of no consequence. "I'll find someone else."

"You have a good thing going in Miami. Why are you here?"

"Thanks to you and the Miami DEA it's too hot there for my organization right now. I need action. I like to keep an eye on my competition." He shrugged.

"Kara made up her mind. She'd help him, but in her own way. "Okay. I'll help." If things went the way she wanted, she'd take down Alvarado and the Gonzaleses.

Luis grinned. "Smart choice. I always knew you were smart." He went on to explain exactly what she was to do then pulled a small box from his pocket. Inside the box rested a device. "You must wear this at all times. I'm not stupid enough to believe you'd willingly help me. If you remove it, slip up, or tell anyone what you're doing, you're dead." He snapped his fingers, and she jumped causing him to laugh uproariously. "The great DEA agent is human after all." He slammed his palm down on the coffee table and got in her face.

His breath smelled of tobacco and sickened her stomach. She held her head high, meeting his challenge.

He snickered and backed away. "Marci will take you to Sunridge. You will stay at her place."

"Bad idea. Everyone will expect me to stay with Jeff."

"Your DEA boyfriend? Are you two getting it on?"

If only she could take him down without risking the lives of her neighbors. "Jealous?"

He slapped her face hard. Blood trickled down the side of her face. "Now look what you've done. Your stitches are bleeding. Marci, go clean her up. Then take her back to Sunridge. Dump her off a mile from the ranch. She can walk from there."

Marci grabbed her arm with surprising strength. Must be from carrying her son around.

"Wait!" He held up his hand. "You need to wear this."

"What is it?"

"A fantastic invention that will not only allow me to hear everything you say, but will monitor your heart rate. Should I decide you betrayed me," he pulled a phone from his pocket, "a simple code will activate an explosion. Put it in your bra. We both know it'll be safe there." He snickered and pulled a strip of paper off the back of the device. "Stick it to your chest. It's heat activated. If it leaves your body for more than fifteen seconds an alarm will sound, and you'll die."

"How will I shower?"

"Figure it out." He walked out the slider door without a glance in her direction.

Marci looked at her with disgust. "You had to go and make him hit you. Clean yourself up and make it fast. I have to pick up my son from daycare by five thirty."

Kara slammed the car door and forced one foot in front of the other. Marci dropped her two miles from the ranch. Guess she didn't know how to figure distance. Kara needed water. The sun was beginning to lower in the summer sky, but heat still radiated off the asphalt. The smell of dried pine needles permeated the air.

Kara focused on moving forward. If only she had a little water. She refused to allow a dry mouth, burning lungs, and a pounding headache to get the best of her. She had to make it to the ranch.

Fifteen minutes later, a black SUV blew past her. Then the tires squealed and skidded to a stop in the middle of the road. About ready to drop, thanks to the smoke inhalation from her apartment's fire, she couldn't make her feet move any faster. Had it only been a few hours since she'd been released from the hospital? It seemed like a lifetime ago. She heard a door shut and saw someone running toward her. It had to be Jeff, but the sun glared in her eyes, and she couldn't be sure.

"Kara! What are you doing here?"

She fell into his arms and buried her face in his chest. "I missed you."

He gently pushed her away from him and looked down into her face. Alarm shown in his eyes. "What happened? The stitches are torn. You look awful. I'm taking you back to the hospital."

"Water?"

"Just as soon as I get you inside." He picked her up in his arms, carried her back to his SUV, then set her down to open the passenger door. He opened a metal water bottle and held it out. "Drink."

She didn't have to be told twice.

He got behind the wheel and did a U-turn. "How did this happen? You look like you were in a fight."

"I leaned down and hit my head on a chair. No biggie."

"How'd you get here? Did you walk all the way from Bend?"

"Marci gave me a ride."

"Marci?"

Kara nodded and looked around for a piece of

paper but saw nothing. Somehow, she had to let Jeff know what was going on without speaking or writing. Morse code? No. That would come through on the wire. *Think!* She closed her eyes and leaned her head back. If Jeff thought she was sleeping, maybe he wouldn't say anything about the case.

"Eric's cooperating."

Kara opened her eyes and glanced at Jeff. "Great. I'm kind of tired. Do you mind if we talk later?"

"Sure."

She saw the confused expression on his face and wanted more than anything to tell him that every word they said was compromised, but then they'd both die. She'd do as ordered, at least for now.

Jeff pulled into St. Charles. "Just drop me off. I know you're busy."

"I am, but I'll come in with you and wait."

"Honestly. Jeff." She swallowed hard. "I need you to back off. We're moving too fast." The shock in his eyes turned to hurt. *Come on, Jeff. You know this isn't me. Think!*

He worked his jaw. "Sorry. I didn't realize showing concern for my partner—"

"Fine. Just pull over." If he didn't hurry, she was liable to heave on the seat. She'd hurt him big time. Her own heart ached at what she saw on his face. "I'll call you."

He pulled over and stopped. His lips set in a straight line, and he stared ahead.

She got out and closed the door. He drove away without a word.

34

Jeff tossed his cell phone onto the passenger seat after listening to his voicemail from Kara, saying she had a situation. He should've known something was up when she told him to back off. That wasn't the way she rolled. He made a U-turn at the next light and did his best not to speed.

He drove into the parking lot and parked. He'd find Kara and get to the bottom of things. "Excuse me. I dropped Kara Nelson off here a few minutes ago. Has she already been admitted?"

The woman looked down at a log of names and shook her head. "I'm sorry, sir. No one by that name has checked in with me. Are you sure she came to the ER?"

"No. I guess not. Where else would she go?"

The woman held up a finger and spoke into a headset. He rubbed the back of his neck and looked around the room. No sign of Kara.

Turning around, he made his way to the spot where he'd dropped her off. A lone form sat on the curb. He sprinted toward her. He'd missed seeing her since he'd parked and walked in from the other direction. Her shoulders slumped, and she looked bad, really bad.

He knelt beside her. "Kara?"

She looked up at him with glossy eyes. "You shouldn't have come back."

"You need help. That's why I'm here."

Her attempt at a smile looked more like a grimace. "I'm just really wiped out. All I need is water and an aspirin."

"Fine. I'll get you both." He wrapped an arm around her waist and helped her stand. "I parked over there. Can you make it?"

She nodded but leaned heavily into him. "Do you remember the first time you came to my apartment?"

Her voice was soft, and he strained to hear. "Wait 'til we get inside. It's too hard to hear you with all the cars."

She shook her head, reached up, and brought his face down to hers. "Remember what you did the first time you came to my apartment?" She gave him a hopeful look then released his face and resumed walking.

He thought back to the first time he'd visited her, but nothing came to mind. Frustration gripped him. What was she trying to tell him, and why wouldn't she just say it?

She jumped away from him and shouted. "You have a bug on your arm."

He shook his arm. "Is it gone?"

She narrowed her eyes and pursed her lips, while

making an almost imperceptible motion toward her own chest. "No. It's hanging on tight. Look. Right there."

He peered closer at her. Then like a speeding bullet smacking him in the forehead, he knew what she was saying. He'd mimed squishing a bug to make sure her place was clean from prying ears the first time he'd been inside her apartment. He flicked an invisible bug from his sleeve. "Got it. That thing didn't want to let go."

"No kidding. Reminds me of Sky."

They were at his SUV now, and he made sure she was secure before getting in himself. Sky was a guy they worked with in Miami. One day while Sky was sleeping in his desk chair after an all-nighter, someone had placed a cockroach on his chest as a practical joke. When he woke, he nearly wet his pants it scared him so bad. If he'd deciphered her motion and her clue right, she had a bug on her about chest level.

Now that he knew the what, he needed the why. Why didn't she remove it? "I'll take you back to the ranch where you can rest. I know Veronica has plenty of aspirin so you should be set." He yawned. "This has been a never-ending day."

"Sure has. I didn't know a day could feel this long. I guess that's what happens when you wake to find your apartment burning and filled with smoke."

"How about if you close your eyes and rest? I'll wake you when we get there."

He needed to piece things together fast. Kara said she had a situation, that Marci dropped her off, and she'd gone out of her way to get him to leave her alone when he'd brought up Eric. Anxiety seized him. Had he said something to endanger his family? He needed to talk with Kara soon.

Jeff led Kara into his bedroom, locked the door, and closed the blinds. He turned on the radio to a jazz station, then handed her a piece of paper and pen. He watched as she wrote, and it was worse than he'd guessed. He wrote back. *Let me see the device.*

She shook her head, and her cheeks flamed.

He scribbled fast. *This is not the time for modesty!*

No! Luis insinuated that it's a bomb, and it's activated by temperature. If it gets too cold it will blow. It also monitors my heart rate. If he thinks I'm up to something, he can activate the bomb remotely.

He'd never heard of such a thing. Kara had gotten herself into quite a mess. He needed to talk with Tad. They could replicate her body temperature, and even her heart rate with the right equipment. But what if Luis hadn't told her everything? What if something else would trigger an explosion?

Is there a tracking device on the bomb?

She shrugged.

From what she'd told him they'd have fifteen seconds to remove the device and plant it on someone, or something else. But that would only solve half the problem. Luis would expect to hear conversations. *Maybe we should keep the wire on you and feed Luis information.*

She shrugged again.

He studied her face. The fatigue and hopelessness he saw concerned him. *I'll figure something out. Go rest in the guest room and try to sleep.*

She rolled her eyes as if to say, yeah, right.

After a quick call to Tad, Jeff drove to Tad's place to meet up with him.

Tad opened the door when Jeff turned off the engine.

"What do you have?" Tad asked.

"Let's go inside." Jeff carried the bug sweeper inside his duffel and intended to use it before talking. He swept the room, and it came up clean. "Luis Alvarado accosted Kara. She has a heat activated wire on her chest that she believes will explode if separated from her body for more than fifteen seconds."

"What kind of wire are we talking about?"

"It's a heart monitor of sorts, heat sensitive, and she's wired for sound. I don't know what else. It may have a tracking device for all I know. Anyway, Luis is demanding she give him half the drugs from the bust when it goes down."

"He's got to know she can't get away with that."

"I don't think he cares. He wants her dead, and he wants the drugs. If she follows through, he gets both."

"I agree. We need to get the bomb squad over there."

"Not so fast. He also seems to know where she is at all times. My family is there."

"I see your point. Take her into the field office. I'll have the bomb squad waiting. I want to know what we're dealing with."

"That should work. Luis knows she goes there, so it won't look suspicious."

"Right. Our sources tell us the drugs will be here the day after tomorrow. The team is ready to go. We'll make it appear that Kara's going to give Luis the drugs then take him into custody."

"That may be easier said than done. He didn't tell her how she was supposed to get the drugs to him."

Tad rubbed his chin. "Hmm. I guess we'll deal with the details later."

"I don't like surprises," Jeff said.

"I hear you. But what other option do we have? Until Luis makes a move, we can only react."

Jeff hated to admit it, but Tad was right. No amount of planning on their part would help unless Luis played into their hands. "What about Eric? Did the information he and Jake provided help?"

"Yes. We were able to corroborate the info with what we already knew and went from there. This is huge. Teams in seventeen states will coordinate a takedown of several drug cartels." Tad grinned. "In less than thirty-six hours, it will all be over. And best of all, I think we can use the situation with Kara to our advantage and pick up Alvarado at the same time."

"I'm listening," Jeff said, though his brain was still stuck on the size of this operation. What did this mean for Eric and his family?

"We'll keep Kara out of the loop except for what relates directly to her. She doesn't need to know how big this is. You and I take a team in at the designated time and raid the shack you spotted. According to Eric, that's where the drugs are stored. Expect three heavily armed guards. Let Kara sign out what she needs. Then I'll have another team in place to apprehend Alvarado when it goes down."

"Assuming you can find him. The man has a way of blending in."

"So I've heard." A small frown creased his brows. "There's a taskforce meeting in the morning at eight. Make sure Kara understands what's going on. We'll have a dummy meeting with her at eight thirty to feed Alvarado information."

"Okay. What about the wire?"

"The bomb squad can check it out in the morning when we're in our meeting."

"Seems like a long time to wait to find out if she's wearing a bomb."

"If you go in this late, you're sure to tip off Luis. She's safer if everything appears normal. He needs her. If he thinks she's cooperating he's not going to kill her."

"Good point." Even for him, 10:00 p.m. was late. "We'll see you in the morning."

35

Kara watched Jeff pace his bedroom while talking on the phone. She wished he could put it on speaker, but then Alvarado would hear every word.

Jeff stilled.

"What?" she whispered. Something about Jeff's expression made her stomach knot.

Jeff held up one finger. "Okay, thanks." He stuffed his phone into his pocket and placed his hand on Kara's back. "That was Gary with some unsettling news. He sent a fire expert to your apartment. The expert found a small amount of wheat chaff in a light switch box."

"What does that have to do with anything?"

"Wheat chaff is highly flammable, and it can't get into the light switch box by itself."

"Arson? Why didn't the fire inspector see it?"

"It's easy to miss something like that. Especially if you're not looking for it." He glanced at his watch. "We have an appointment at eight."

She raised her eyebrows. Didn't he understand that everything she heard, Luis heard as well?

He grinned and patted her shoulder.

She nodded as understanding dawned. He had a plan, and she was the pawn. For once, she didn't mind. She grabbed a pad of paper. *What's going on?*

The bomb squad is meeting you at eight. Then at eight thirty there's a meeting.

Didn't anyone around here understand how Luis operated? If he suspected for one second that she'd told anyone about the wire, she was as good as dead.

Jeff mouthed, "Trust me," then said, "Let's go. We don't want to be late."

Kara left the field office with an extra spring in her step. The bomb squad assured her the device on her chest was not a bomb or tracking device—it couldn't even monitor her heartbeat. Alvarado was a lying, ruthless man, but at least he was only listening to her conversations—talk about a relief. Luis must really think she was gullible. She frowned. Okay, she'd been a little too easy to fool.

She looked down at the report Tad had handed to her at the meeting. It would feel so fantastic to arrest Luis. She'd play his little game, but in the end, she'd win. Finally, justice would be served, not only for herself, but for her cousin and her former partner. Justice for all those lives destroyed by drugs.

It seemed her life had been culminating to this one moment in time when she could destroy the life of someone who'd left nothing but destruction in his path.

Her gut squeezed a little, but she ignored the feeling of guilt eating away at her insides.

A minute later she sped down the highway toward the ranch. Why should she feel guilty for wanting to destroy Alvarado? He had destroyed countless lives. He deserved what was coming to him.

She turned into the driveway and spotted Jeff working on the pasture fence. Rather than drive up to the house, she pulled over and climbed the fence.

Jeff waved and hollered, "Watch your step. It can be a bit messy out here."

Kara narrowly missed a pile of manure and continued toward him keeping her vision trained on the ground. She didn't want to ruin her shoes, cheap sneakers or not. "You missed the meeting."

"Tad filled me in."

Kara nodded. "What happened to the fence?"

"Looks like someone got a bit too close with their vehicle and knocked a board loose."

"Why are you fixing it? I thought this was more Jake's purview."

"Eric and Jake are running an errand in town."

"Oh. No one said anything about hitting the fence?"

"Nope."

Kara watched as he finished up the repair. "Want a ride up to the house?"

"I'm covered in dirt and dust. You sure you want me in your car?"

Kara waved her hand in front of her face. "Whew, now that you mention it."

Jeff's face broke into a grin. He dropped his tools

and reached for Kara, crushing her to him.

Kara squealed. "Let me go. Gross!" She wiggled out of his arms and made for the fence, but not before he could catch her again in the circle of his arms. One thing about wearing Luis's wire made her happy. She no longer had to be nervous about a sniper attack. Luis wanted drugs and until she delivered or broke the rules of his game, she'd be safe.

Jeff looked down at her. "Lady, you can't get away from me." Without warning his lips met hers.

Kara forgot about Alvarado and tomorrow's bust as Jeff deepened the kiss. A horn beeped, and they pulled apart. Kara turned toward the driveway to see Lauren in the passenger seat of a red car.

"Way to go, Uncle Jeff."

Jeff waved. "Kara your car's blocking the driveway."

Kara felt her face heat. "Shoot." She climbed over the fence and looked back toward Jeff. "You coming?"

"No. Go ahead. I'll meet you on the porch in a little bit."

"Okay." The girls honked again and Kara jogged to her car. Too bad the driveway wasn't a bit wider. "Have patience. I'm coming." She got into her car and drove ahead.

In the ranch yard, she walked over to the porch swing and sank into the deep cushion. Lauren waved good-bye to her friend and followed after Kara.

Lauren perched on the porch railing. "I'd say my uncle loves you."

"You think so?" He'd said as much himself. But it surprised her that his fifteen-year-old niece had figured it out.

Lauren nodded. "Do you love him?"

She sucked in a breath and let it out slowly. She did not want to feed Alvarado any more ammunition to use against her. "I like him a lot, but love? I don't know." She gave a weak smile.

Lauren hopped off the railing. "I'm sure you'll figure it out." She walked into the house, leaving Kara staring with her mouth hanging open.

Jeff climbed the stairs of the porch, one hand in his jeans pocket. "Mind if I join you?"

Kara patted the spot next to her and decided to have a little fun. With a serious face, she addressed Jeff. "We need to talk." She had his attention. "I distinctly remember asking you not to kiss me until your beard grew in all the way, or you shaved. That display in the pasture clearly broke our agreement."

He rubbed his beard with his fingers. "Seems soft enough to me. I don't know what you're complaining about."

A giggle bubbled from her mouth. He pulled her to him and rubbed his chin along the side of her face.

"Yeow. Watch the stitches."

"Oh. Sorry." He slowly rubbed his beard against the side of her face.

She chuckled. "I need that skin you're trying to remove."

He released her and sat back with a satisfied grin on his face.

She could get used to this, but their job didn't allow for many light moments. She'd treasure this one.

36

After phoning Gail to explain that she'd be staying out at the ranch for a few days, Kara went to the barn in search of Jeff. Thankfully, Gail hadn't been put out by her change of plans. Her friend was smart and surely figured out having Kara at her house put everyone there in danger.

The bust would go down in the morning, and then it'd be time to go home. Kara couldn't wipe the grin off her face. Tomorrow, she'd arrest Luis Alvarado.

"What's the smile about?" Jeff asked.

Where was he? Kara swiveled from side to side.

"Up here."

She looked up and spotted Jeff peering at her from the loft. "I'm smiling because I'm happy."

He climbed down the ladder and sidled up to her. "I'm glad. It's about time."

"I know." She heard a large vehicle pull to a stop outside the barn. The Gonzaleses most likely—right on time. The textbook bust was imminent, and now all that they had to do was sit back and wait for Tad to give the order to move in.

Jeff nodded toward the house. "You thirsty? I could use a glass of lemonade."

"I won't pass that up." She took his hand, and they walked out of the barn together. "Something's not right." Jeff's hand tightened around hers. "Look, Fernando's on the porch with Veronica, and she doesn't look pleased. Where's Andrea?"

"In their truck, which is minus the trailer." They walked toward the house.

Fernando grabbed Veronica's arms and shook her.

"Not on my watch," Jeff muttered. He released Kara's hand, ran forward, and leaped up the porch steps. "What's going on here?"

Kara stood within listening distance—her senses piqued ready to react at a moment's notice.

Fernando's eyes narrowed. "The lady and I are having a conversation."

Jeff shook his head. "That's not the way we treat ladies around here. Get lost and cool off."

Kara's pulse increased. Fernando looked angry, and Jeff wasn't helping.

Fernando balled his fingers into fists and looked like he might take a swing at Jeff. Kara adjusted her stance, ready to assist her partner if necessary.

Fernando hissed. "No one talks to me like that."

Jeff shrugged and stepped back.

Kara kept her gaze focused on Fernando, who didn't budge. The snake had a murderous look on his face. The front door swung open, and Lauren sauntered out. Fernando quick-stepped toward Lauren, wrapped one arm around her neck, then whipped a switchblade from his pocket and held it against her cheek.

Veronica screamed.

"What are you doing? Let her go." Jeff raised his hands palms out. "I'm sure this is all a misunderstanding."

Kara reached for her Glock but held back. If she waited until Fernando passed by, she could get a clean shot. Better to keep her weapon hidden for now.

Tears slid down Lauren's cheeks. Veronica held her hand to her mouth, but a sob escaped. Kara glanced over her shoulder.

Andrea had moved behind the driver's wheel of their rig.

Fernando smirked. "I warned your husband not to double cross me."

"No!" Veronica wailed. "You said if we cooperated you wouldn't harm our children!"

Veronica knew? She'd understood Eric had kept his wife in the dark.

"Eric's done everything you've asked." Tears streamed down Veronica's face, and she clung to the porch railing for support.

"Blame him." Fernando motioned to Jeff.

"Jeff?" Veronica turned to face her brother-in-law. "What did you do?"

Kara read turmoil on her partner's face. Her heart ached for him, but what could he say? This was not supposed to happen.

Jeff's gaze pierced Fernando. "Come on. We can make a deal. Let her go, and I'll make sure no charges are pressed for attempted kidnapping."

Fernando's hold seemed to loosen. Jeff took a small step forward.

"Stop! Don't come any closer."

Veronica crumpled to the ground. "No, please." She reached her hand out to her daughter as Fernando dragged Lauren down the porch steps to the waiting truck. She stumbled, but he held tight.

Lauren's eyes were wide with fear. "Mom, help! Don't let him take me."

Kara kept her focus trained on Fernando, counting the seconds until she could reach for her Glock. She moved her hand. Automatic fire smacked the ground around Kara.

Andrea stood next to their truck. She held an AK-47. "That was a warning. Do not move, and keep your hands where I can see them."

Kara froze as Fernando passed her with Lauren in his grip.

Jeff stood helpless. Kara understood his dilemma. If he saved one of them, the other would die. If he did nothing, they might both live.

Fernando got behind the wheel and rammed into Kara's Civic, putting it out of commission. Andrea fired off a few more rounds at the ground around them as they drove past.

Jeff drew his Glock and aimed at the back tires.

Veronica lunged at him, grabbing his arm. "No! Lauren's in there." She sobbed into her hands and rocked back and forth.

He released his hold on the trigger, his target gone, and ran toward his SUV. "Come on, Kara."

"What about Veronica?"

"She'll be fine when we get Lauren back."

Kara glanced at Veronica and ignored the urge to comfort her. Jeff was right. They needed to move. She ran after Jeff and hopped into his SUV. After belting herself in, she called Tad.

"Tad, it's Kara."

Jeff gripped the steering wheel. "He should be able to get us some local help."

Kara spoke into her phone, gave their coordinates, and explained the situation.

"Okay," Tad said. "A few detectives are in the area. They're driving a dark green sedan and should be able to intercept the truck and discretely follow them until they stop or until the FBI sends someone to assist."

"Thanks." Kara ended the call and turned to Jeff. "Keep an eye out for a dark green sedan. They'll take over tailing them."

A grim look settled on his face as he raced after his niece and her captors.

"I know what you're thinking, but don't blame yourself. You had no idea Lauren would walk out at that moment."

"I don't understand what happened. How'd he find out that Eric told me everything?"

"Sounds like there's either a leak, or Eric has a big mouth," Kara said.

"Fernando will kill Lauren if we don't stop him. You know as well as I do, he's not going to let her live any longer than it takes him to shake us."

"She might be worth more to him alive than dead. We have a topnotch team working with us, and the

Gonzaleses are probably headed for the border. We'll get her back."

"You're right."

"There's no way they'll escape. There's an APB out for them, and border patrol won't let them leave the country. They made a big mistake when they took Lauren. Even if we never get them on drug charges, they'll go down for kidnapping."

Kara saw the struggle on Jeff's face as he reluctantly eased off the gas allowing the dark green sedan carrying two undercover cops to take over the tail. Investigating his stepbrother was one thing, but policy wouldn't allow him to rescue his niece. That was a job for the FBI. They were trained to handle kidnappings. Fernando and Andrea were no longer their responsibility.

Jeff waited until the truck was out of view and made a U-turn.

Kara leaned her head back and closed her eyes. *Dear Lord, we need a miracle. Please be with Lauren.*

The ranch driveway loomed ahead blocked by a police car with flashing lights. Jeff showed his badge, and he and Kara were allowed to pass. He parked near the barn next to a sheriff's vehicle. "It looks like Tad's inside. You ready?"

Kara took a deep breath and let it out slowly. "Ready."

They entered the house together. Veronica sat silent in a brown leather chair near the entrance. Tad stood at the mantel looking at family photos. He turned when Jeff cleared his throat. Jeff motioned for him to follow them into another room.

Tad followed close on their heels. "I heard the transfer went smooth, and they moved into place undetected."

"We wouldn't be here if they hadn't," Jeff snapped. He ran his hand through his hair. "Sorry, but you don't know what it took to let someone else follow them. They'd better be exceptional at their job. If anything happens to Lauren…"

"Calm down, Jeff. These guys will get her back. Your niece will be home soon."

Jeff nodded then rubbed the back of his neck. "What's Veronica told you?"

Tad took out a small notepad and consulted it. "She said Fernando was angry that Eric told you about the drugs."

"How'd he find out?"

"She doesn't know."

"Where's Eric?" He couldn't take much more of this. He needed a long vacation.

"Unknown. He didn't respond to Veronica's calls."

"Weird. He and Jake are running an errand in town. They should've been back by now." He pulled out his phone and made the hardest call of his life. "Eric, you need to come home. Fernando took Lauren."

He held the phone away from his ear and still heard Eric clearly calling him every name in the book. When the line went silent, Jeff slipped his phone into his pocket. Maybe by the time Eric got home, they'd have Lauren back.

Tad frowned. "That didn't sound good."

Jeff grimaced. "Nope."

Veronica entered the room and glared at Jeff. "This is all your fault! If Eric hadn't told you about the drugs, then he wouldn't have felt free to tell me, and I wouldn't have accidentally let it slip to Fernando about the DEA investigation when he questioned me about Eric. That man makes me so nervous."

"*You* told Fernando?" Eric claimed she hadn't known about the drugs, and it never occurred to Jeff that his brother would come clean with her now. "When?"

"On the porch, right before you cut in."

"Of all the—" Jeff pressed his lips together to keep from saying something he'd regret.

Tad stepped in front of Jeff. "Everyone, calm down. We will get your daughter back. There's no reason to be pointing fingers."

Kara gently guided Veronica to the sofa then handed her a glass of ice water. "They'll get your daughter back."

Veronica held the glass between her hands. "It's not fair." Her voice barely rose above a whisper. "Lauren didn't do anything wrong. She didn't even know about," she waved her hands in the air, "all of this—this madness. Why did he take her?"

Kara nodded to Jeff as he slipped out the front door with Tad. At a loss for how to comfort Veronica,

Kara sat silent. She had a million reasons for this mess, but none of them would help Veronica. She finally spoke. "I don't know why this happened, but I do know that we can pray for Lauren."

"I hadn't thought of that." Veronica frowned.

"He is right by her side. I guarantee you that." Kara reached her hand out slowly and placed it on Veronica's shoulder. "Let's pray."

Veronica shrunk away from Kara. "I can't."

Kara took over. "Dear Lord, we ask that You'd be with Lauren. Comfort and protect her from harm. Please guide all the men and women who are following them waiting for the perfect moment to rescue Lauren. Help them do their jobs well, Lord. Amen." Kara rose and grabbed a few tissues. "Here you go."

Veronica dabbed her eyes and attempted to smile. "Thanks. I didn't realize so many people were working to get my daughter back."

Kara chose her words carefully. She needed Veronica to understand what was going on, but at the same time didn't want to give away her own involvement in the investigation. "I overheard Tad and Jeff talking. The FBI is on the case as well as local undercover cops. Everyone is working together to bring Lauren home safely." She paused. "Jeff didn't mean for any of this to happen. If he could, he'd be the one out there right now working to rescue Lauren. Kidnapping is the FBI's jurisdiction."

"Thanks for telling me. I didn't know."

Kara squeezed her shoulder. "I'm going to go find Deputy Baker and Jeff. Will you be okay?"

"I won't be okay until Lauren walks through that

door unharmed."

"I understand. I'll be back in a while." Kara left in search of Tad and Jeff. She finally found them out in the barn.

The men turned when she entered the building. "How's she doing?" Jeff asked.

"Under the circumstances, remarkably well. What's the plan?"

"We figure they'll have to stop for gas at some point, and that's when a team will move in," Jeff said. "We've come up with a close guess as to where they'll have to stop based on the make and model of their truck and road conditions, assuming they left with a full tank of gas." They had maps of Oregon and California tacked to the wall. "We believe they'll need to stop somewhere around here." He circled the location on the map. "Of course, they could stop sooner. If we're lucky, they'll drive until they have to stop. It's a small town, and there are only two gas stations. The bureau has agents enroute to intercept right now, and they have multiple tails. The Gonzaleses are also being monitored through a tracking device that's been in place for some time. We're confident they can be apprehended with little or no collateral damage."

"Lauren should be okay at least until they stop somewhere," Tad added. "How about the two of you head back inside and keep Veronica company. She shouldn't be alone right now."

Kara slipped her hand into Jeff's. "Your sister-in-law needs us. We can't do anything productive out here."

He nodded.

37

Eric stormed into the house and swung straight at Jeff with a right hook.

Jeff leaned back barely avoiding the fist. "Calm down!" He raised his arms and adjusted his stance ready for anything Eric wanted to dish out. "Fighting with me won't solve anything."

"No. But it would feel good."

"I understand, but hitting me isn't going to bring your daughter home." Jeff watched his brother warily.

Eric backed off and then began pacing the room like an angry bull, clenching and flexing his fingers. His shoulders slumped and guilt covered his face. "I can't believe my worst nightmare is happening."

Jeff relaxed his stance a bit. "I get it, Eric." He was angry himself, and Lauren wasn't even his daughter. Too bad there wasn't a punching bag nearby. It seemed they could both use one.

Tad cleared his throat, and Eric seemed to notice him for the first time. "The FBI and local law enforcement are on the case. It's only a matter of time before they get Lauren back."

Eric sank into the nearest seat and focused on the floor. "But it won't be soon enough. Even one minute in the hands of Fernando is too long." He looked up at Jeff with pain-filled eyes. "You said everything would be okay. Instead, you've only made things worse."

Jeff blinked. "*I* made things worse? Why did you tell Veronica?"

"She's my wife. I figured since the DEA was on the case, it'd be okay. I thought you'd come in and arrest them, not get my daughter kidnapped!" His glare could've melted ice.

Jeff spoke in a low, hard voice. "I'm sorry about Lauren, but don't blame me. If you had gone to the authorities a year ago, this could've all been avoided. Instead, I had to figure everything out on my own, and Lauren got caught in the middle."

"Jeff probably saved your daughter's life," Tad added. "And from what I've been told, I'd say if he'd done anything other than what he did, there'd be a pool of blood on the porch right now. The Gonzaleses are being tailed, and our team says they can see Lauren in the vehicle. They were even able to get close enough to see that she's alive. Rest assured, no one will do anything that will endanger Lauren's life."

Eric rose from the chair. "I'll be with my wife."

Jeff nodded at Tad. "Thanks." He'd kept running through those moments leading up to Lauren's kidnapping and wondered if there'd been anything he could have said or done to prevent it.

"I believe every word I said. Lauren is going to

come home alive." Tad checked his watch then glanced out the front window. "Jake went into the barn. Let's follow."

"Sounds like a better idea than sitting in here."

They headed out together. Jake sat on a stool with his back against the wall of the barn staring at an empty stall. Jeff left Tad at the door and walked over to the man then leaned against the wall with his arms crossed. "I suppose you know about what happened today."

"It's a bit tough not to. When I heard Fernando grabbed Lauren, I wanted to rip his arms right off his body." He turned his angry gaze on Jeff. "What's being done to get the girl back? That man has ruined enough lives. I thought for sure I'd be able to stop him from hurting anyone else."

"Don't worry. We'll get her back and the Gonzaleses will pay for what they did." He had to believe Lauren would be okay.

A few hours later, Kara sat on the chair across from Veronica. She racked her brain for something to say, but no words would come. Lauren had been gone for five hours, and Eric had only hugged Veronica and said he'd be in the barn when he'd passed through an hour or so ago. Kara kept up her silent vigil, unsure how to console this distraught mother.

Veronica bowed her head, and her lips moved silently.

Kara watched in wonder as Veronica's face relaxed, and she straightened her shoulders as if a weight had been lifted. "You okay?"

Veronica nodded. "I gave my baby to Jesus. Whatever happens is in His hands."

Kara cleared her throat. "I have a personal question if you don't mind."

"Sure."

"Why aren't you angry with God? I know from recent experience if I were in your shoes, I would be."

Veronica looked taken aback. "I never thought to be angry at Him. Eric should've gone to the police a long time ago." Veronica threw her hands in the air. "How can I be angry with God when we brought this on ourselves?"

Eric burst into the hallway. "Come quick." He ran back out the door.

Kara hopped up. She called after him. "What's going on?"

He yelled over his shoulder. "Come to the barn. Hurry!"

Kara looked at Veronica who was now standing as well. "Guess we better move." The women ran out to the barn and stopped just inside the entrance.

"Veronica, over here." Eric patted the vacant spot next to him on a bale of hay.

Veronica rushed to her husband and sat close.

Kara stood in disbelief. A large white sheet lined one wall, and bales of hay had been placed nearby. A laptop sat on a table near the screen. Tad and another deputy occupied two stools. Jeff sat on a bale of hay with Jake on another one nearby. "What's going on?"

Jeff stood, sidled up to Kara, and spoke quietly into her ear. "An FBI helicopter is following the Gonzaleses and taping everything live. They're going to send the feed to Tad's computer, which he'll then project onto the sheet on the wall. We get to watch as the team moves in to retrieve Lauren." His face practically glowed with excitement.

Kara grabbed his arm and pulled him away from everyone in the barn. "That's great, but what if something goes wrong? You don't want them to see their daughter get killed."

"Nothing's going to go wrong. Have a little faith. These guys are the best." He squeezed her hand. "Besides, I've been praying."

"There's been a lot of that going on." She moved past him then glanced over her shoulder. "Aren't you going to watch?"

"Of course. I'm right behind you."

A hush blanketed the barn as the makeshift screen came to life. They had an aerial view of the Gonzaleses' truck as it moved down a two-lane road. Kara leaned into Jeff. "Where's all the traffic?"

"It's a pretty isolated stretch. They pulled off the highway and onto a county road. Looks like they're finally taking a pit stop."

"Are they going to take them at the gas station?"

"No. Too much collateral risk. The plan is to stop them before they get to the town."

Kara jumped when the truck tires burst.

Veronica cried out and grasped Eric's arm. "What

happened?"

"Spike strips were placed on the road," Tad explained.

The truck seemed to go out of control for only a second then drove off to the shoulder and stopped. The helicopter swooped in and landed in the middle of the road in front of the Gonzaleses' pickup. Several officers jumped out and trained their weapons on the pickup. The driver and passenger doors opened and the Gonzaleses stepped out with hands raised.

A second later, Fernando yanked a semi-automatic pistol from his waist and fired several times. The team returned fire. He turned and ran a couple steps before a darkly clad officer tackled him to the ground, yanked his arms behind his back, and cuffed him. Blood oozed from Fernando's torso.

Andrea lay face down on the ground without resistance, and another officer handcuffed her.

Kara glanced at Veronica and Eric. Veronica had a death grip on his hand, but Eric seemed oblivious. She looked back to the screen. The hard part was over. Now where was Lauren?

The Gonzaleses were put into the back of an unmarked police car. Lauren stepped down out of the pickup, arms raised.

"There's Lauren," Veronica shouted. Happy tears streamed down her face.

Eric buried his face in his wife's neck with tears of his own.

Cheers resounded in the barn. Tad and Jeff and the other deputy gave each other high fives. Kara tuned out the celebration around her and focused on the screen. Lauren looked unharmed, just shaken up a bit. She swiped at her face, her shoulders raised and lowered. Was she crying or breathing hard? Too bad they couldn't get a close up of her face. A female officer approached Lauren, and she lowered her arms. The officer escorted her to the helicopter and climbed up after her. At that moment the feed stopped.

Tad closed his laptop. "Show's over. I've arranged to have Lauren flown here. Let's give her a nice welcome."

Veronica wiped her eyes and stood. "I'll go bake her favorite cookies."

Kara breathed easy for the first time since Lauren had been taken. Only a couple of hurdles remained— Luis Alvarado and tomorrow's raid. Hopefully, nothing else would go wrong.

38

Not long after the barn was back to looking like a barn instead of a conference room, the *thwap-thwap* of helicopter blades urged everyone outside as it touched down. Dust kicked up and filled the air. A female FBI agent wearing a ballistics vest opened the door. She shielded her face with her arm, hopped out, then reached back and Lauren followed. Warned to not storm the helicopter when it landed, they all hung back and waited for Lauren to come to them.

Kara understood the look of pain and longing on Veronica's face. She wanted to run to the chopper and grab Lauren herself. This waiting business was not fun.

The agent nudged Lauren toward her family. She shuffled her feet at first then picked up momentum. Her face stretched into a smile as she launched herself into her parents' waiting arms.

Eric nodded to the agent who then turned and climbed back into the chopper. The helicopter took off, leaving dust in its wake.

Kara fanned her hand in front of her face and

coughed. The dust aggravated her smoke-damaged lungs. "Let's get inside."

Jeff and Kara followed the reunited family.

Eric turned to them. "You two are planning to join our celebration tonight, aren't you?"

Jeff shook his head. "I'd like nothing better, but we need to pass. I have some business to take care of, and Kara has a commitment." He winked at his niece. "You guys enjoy your family time, and Lauren, we're glad you made it home safely."

Lauren pulled away from her parents, walked up to Jeff, and wrapped her arms around his waist. "Thanks, Uncle Jeff."

Wide-eyed, he looked down and patted her on the back. "I didn't do anything."

She backed away. "I may be fifteen, but I'm not stupid. Besides, I watch TV. I know when Fernando put that knife to my throat, you wanted to shoot him, but you didn't because I could've been hurt."

Jeff swallowed. "You figured that out all on your own?"

"Well, sort of. I listened to the agents on the helicopter talking about you. They think a lot of how you handled yourself. So thanks."

He tweaked her nose. "You're welcome." He looked up at Eric. "Can I talk to you alone for a minute?"

Eric moved down the steps as his family went inside. "What's up?"

"I need you all to stay in the house until tomorrow afternoon. Jake and I will see to the horses."

"What's going on?"

"I can't say."

"Okay. Consider us under house arrest."

Jeff grimaced at Eric's attempted humor.

"Another thing. No company."

"Got it." Eric turned and took the stairs two at a time.

Kara walked with Jeff out to her damaged Civic.

He ran his hand over the severely dented front end. "What a mess. It doesn't look drivable."

"No kidding." She leaned against the door. "You didn't walk out here with me to talk about my car though. What's up?"

"Nothing. We need to head into Bend to meet up with our team."

True enough. They would be meeting with everyone to go over the final plan for the early morning raid. Then she'd take a short nap somewhere in the field office. She hid a yawn behind her hand. "Can I hitch a ride with you to the field office?"

"Of course."

"And I placed an order at the bakery for cookies. But the bakery is in Sunridge. Do you mind?"

"Nope. I forgot about your tradition of bringing cookies to everyone before a raid."

She shrugged. It was her thing. She always pigged out on cookies before a raid and, out of habit, bought enough to share with the team. No one here would expect it, but she didn't care.

Twenty minutes later, they strolled along the sidewalk in Sunridge. Kara held open the box of cookies. "Take whichever one you'd like."

"Thanks." Jeff grabbed a monster cookie and bit into it. "Good thing we don't eat like this all the time. Our arteries would be so clogged we'd drop dead of a heart attack."

Kara pulled a butter cookie from the box and took a bite. It melted in her mouth. No way would he ruin her ritual with his talk of clogged arteries. She looked around without seeming to. Luis had to be somewhere nearby. Then again, maybe one of his cronies was tailing her instead right now. She spotted a city slicker on the park bench across the street. He read a newspaper. Could be her tail, but it was impossible to say for sure.

"Kara!" Marci ran up from behind her breathless. "Didn't you hear me calling you?" She glanced at Jeff but other than that ignored him.

"No. What do you want?"

"Here." Marci stuffed an envelope into her hand then turned and walked away in the direction she'd come.

Kara's instincts told her the envelope contained instructions from Alvarado. It was about time, too.

"What was that all about?" Jeff asked.

"Beats me." She could tell Jeff knew as well as she did that Luis had sent his instructions.

Back at Jeff's SUV now, Kara laid the box of cookies on the backseat, put on her seatbelt, and opened the envelope.

Leave the package in the alley behind your building, tomorrow morning 10:00 a.m. sharp.

Jeff started the engine and pulled forward onto the main road. "How are you feeling?"

"Fine. I'm tired, but considering the events of the past two days, I'm doing well. How about you?"

"I'm ready for this to be over." They rode the rest of the way in silence. The transaction would take place in the alley. Good choice on Luis's part since her place was roped off. Thanks to the fire, no one would be around.

Her stomach churned. If she didn't learn to control her nerves, she'd get an ulcer. But didn't ulcers and busting the bad guys go hand in hand? She chuckled.

"What?"

"I was just thinking about how before every bust my stomach turns into a raging fire of acid."

Jeff nodded, clearly understanding. He finally turned into the field office parking lot. She assumed everyone there knew she wore a bug and would behave accordingly. But to be safe, she slipped a thick vest on and zipped it up to her chin. That ought to at least make it harder for listening ears.

Once inside, Tad swept Kara away into a conference room. "The team will be here shortly. Are you feeling up to tomorrow's raid? I know you still have stitches, and the doctor said you needed to rest. From what I can tell, you haven't done much resting."

"I'll be fine." She nodded to a blue couch pushed up against the wall. "I might crash on that for a few hours when we're done."

"Good idea."

The conference room door opened and a couple of agents filtered in along with local police. Jeff parked himself next to Kara while Tad sat at the head of the table. Kara listened intently as Tad outlined the solid plan. She itched to move out. As the meeting broke up, a couple of team members nodded to her, but no one spoke directly to her. They must know about the bug. One less thing she needed to worry about.

Jeff spoke softly in her ear. "Rest well. I'll make sure you're left alone." He stood and closed the door behind him.

Switching off the lights Kara conked out on the couch a few seconds later.

Jeff opened his eyes to find Tad glowering down at him. "What?"

"You slept in that chair all night?"

Jeff glanced at his watch—2:00 a.m. "Only half, apparently. It didn't make sense to drive home. This way I'm near Kara if there's a problem." After their meeting, the office had emptied out as the team went home to catch a few hours of sleep. No way would he leave her alone in here with Alvarado lurking nearby.

Tad chuckled and shook his head. "You've got it bad."

Jeff sat up ignoring his comment. "You're back

early."

"Habit. I like to make sure everything's in order before the masses arrive."

The conference room door opened, and Kara shuffled out. Dark circles rimmed her eyes. "What's going on?"

"Nothing," Jeff said. "Go back to sleep."

"I'm awake now." She pulled up a chair and parked herself beside Jeff. "Anything new going on that I need to know about?"

Tad shook his head. "No. Excuse me." He walked into another part of the building.

"You sleep well?" Jeff asked.

"Like a rock. Although the few hours of sleep I've had here and there over the past couple of days are beginning to catch up with me."

"I hear you. I've slept more than you, and I'm ready to crash for a week."

The front door opened, and two agents entered followed by a couple of police officers.

"Looks like it's time to move," Jeff said. The team had arrived. Seemed Tad wasn't the only one that liked to arrive early. The tension in the room could spark a fire.

Tad had organized a solid group, and they had a sound plan, but anything could go wrong, especially if Alvarado double-crossed Kara. But she seemed certain Alvarado would let them do their job since he wanted the drugs.

Tad walked back into the room. "Looks like everyone's here. Get your gear packed up and be ready to move out in fifteen minutes."

Kara huddled between a large ponderosa pine and a mass of weeds near the shack in the woods. Her heart pounded in the seemingly calm early morning. Crickets chirped and cool air chilled her. She pulled a ski mask down over her face.

"Go," Tad shouted.

Kara jumped up from her spot and ran with the team toward the cabin. All seven of them approached the only entrance. With one hard blow to the door it opened. They swarmed inside the small space. Voices around her shouted DEA, and another shouted police.

Three men scrambled off their cots, with raised arms. Flashlight in one hand and her Glock in the other, Kara shined the light on the men and trained her gun on them. Another agent shouted at them in Spanish to get face down on the floor. Kara approached cautiously and helped cuff the men. An officer led the smugglers outside, freeing up a little real estate to move around the warm room.

With a lantern, Tad illuminated the small one room shack, which held three cots, an arsenal of weapons, and several wood crates stacked in a corner. It shouldn't be too hard to find the drugs in this tiny space. Unless she missed her guess, the drugs would be in the crates.

She walked to Jeff's side and watched as he pried the top off one of the crates then moved on to the next.

Several hundred kilos of cocaine sat neatly in the crate. No way would she tip off Alvarado. "There must be thirty kilos."

Jeff raised a brow then nodded. "I agree."

Thankful for the cover of darkness, Kara, along with several agents, helped carry the crates out of the shack to several ATVs that had pulled up after the raid. It'd take more than a few trips on the ATVs to get all the cocaine back to their vehicles.

Satisfaction mixed with adrenaline pushed her forward in spite of a nagging headache. In a few hours, this would finally be over. Luis and his cronies would be in custody, and she'd have her life back.

Jeff walked up beside her. "How you doing?"

"Fine. We've got quite a load here. I'm taking the ATV. I'll catch up with you later," Kara said for Alvarado's sake. He knew she had the drugs and would be on the way to meet him soon. The trap was set. Now all Luis had to do was step into it.

39

Kara looked around the deserted alley. A lone cat meowed near a small dumpster where Jeff hid. From the backside, her apartment looked unharmed. It was hard to believe that inside, a charred mess still awaited attention. The charred mess of her apartment mirrored her heart of late. At least she was making progress on that front.

The hair on the back of her neck rose. Alvarado must be nearby. She placed the backpack near the stoop of her apartment door and waited. Two minutes later, a man wearing a red baseball cap, jeans, and a T-shirt walked around the corner. "You Kara?"

"Who wants to know?"

"Some guy gave me a hundred bucks to come back here and see if a chick had a package for him. I'm thinking you're Kara." He looked around the small alley. "Where's the package?"

She grabbed the backpack and held it up. "Tell the guy to come get the package himself."

He chuckled. "That's funny. He said you'd say

something like that."

"What else did he say?"

The man pulled a 9mm from his waist. "Don't take no for an answer. Now hand over the bag." The gun shook in the man's hand.

She raised her hands. "There's no need for that." She glanced toward where a sniper sat in wait to protect her. "I'll give you two hundred dollars to take me to him."

"He said if you offered me money, he'd double my pay, so thanks."

Kara studied the man's face. Strung out brown eyes stared back at her. Dark shaggy hair hung close to his face from under his baseball cap. "This must be your lucky day. I'm in a generous mood. I'll give you five hundred dollars now for taking me to him, and then after I see him, I'll let you live." She kicked the gun from his hand, grabbed his arm, and twisted it behind his back while slamming him against the building.

Clapping erupted from behind her. "Very nice, Kara." Luis walked up to her with his gun drawn. "I knew you were good, but really, that was impressive. You sure you don't want to work for me? I pay better than the DEA, and I could use someone like you on my payroll." He snapped his fingers. "Oh wait. You *were* on my payroll and double crossed me."

Kara shoved the guy she'd pinned against the wall aside and faced Alvarado. Her mind barely registered footsteps running from the alley. The 9mm lay on the ground between her and Alvarado. Why hadn't Jeff moved in?

Alvarado took another step toward her and motioned toward the backpack. "Is that for me?"

She nodded. Somehow, she'd dropped the pack when she attacked the other guy. Why wasn't anyone moving in? She forced her eyes to stay focused on Alvarado. If he had an inkling this was a setup, she was a dead woman.

He bent to pick up the backpack, never taking his gaze or the business end of his gun off of her.

"Before you go..." Her pulse thrummed in her ears. This was the moment she'd been waiting for. She whipped her arm forward and knocked the gun from his hand. He dove for it at the same time as her. They landed prone on the ground facing one another.

His eyes narrowed. "Give it up, Kara. You'll never beat me." Somehow, he still held his gun trained on her.

"Oh yeah. Think again." This was her chance to finish the man so he couldn't harm anyone else ever again. But could she move faster than he could pull the trigger?

Jeff bolted from his hiding spot and kicked the gun from Alvarado. He pointed his Glock at the man. "Don't move."

Kara stood, retrieved the drugs, then handed them off to a CODE agent who joined them in the alley.

Two uniformed officers flanked the drug lord and brought him to standing. One cuffed him and the other read him his rights and hauled him off to a waiting police vehicle.

"What was that about?" Kara asked. "Why didn't you let me take him and finish him off?"

"Excuse me? That's not how we operate."

Adrenaline turned to rage. "Give me a break. He tried to kill me, not once but multiple times. He's destroyed countless lives and would happily continue to do so," Kara hissed. "When do the good guys matter, huh? When do *we* get a little justice? What about all the kids that died thanks to the drugs he provided?"

Jeff's gaze softened for a second then hardened. "We are not God, Kara. Justice is *His* department. Besides, I think it's safe to say Luis Alvarado will never taste freedom again."

A uniformed officer rounded the corner and spoke with Jeff. Kara walked away. The truth of Jeff's words hurt like a knife ripping through her flesh.

She didn't care whether Luis Alvarado lived or died. She'd wanted him to pay for her cousin's death and for her prior partner's death. But Luis wasn't to blame. He had nothing to do with either incident. Yet, somehow, he had come to symbolize everything that was wrong in the world.

In reality, sin was to blame. And Christ had paid the price for sin. She was no better than Luis. No, she didn't deal drugs, but in her heart, she was filled with hate and unforgiveness for the crimes against her family and friends. She leaned against the side of the building and took several deep breaths. *Lord, I'm so sorry. I forgive Luis and all the others. Please forgive me and help me to remember to give You control, and that it's best when I let You do Your job and I do mine.*

"Hey," Jeff approached. "How are you doing?"

She leaned her forehead into his chest. "I'm sorry."

Jeff wrapped his arms around her. "Me too. I shouldn't have been so hard on you."

She leaned away and looked into his eyes. "No. You were right. I didn't realize it going into this, and it wasn't my intent, but I would've had no problem killing him. The man is evil and deserves to die. But that's not my call."

Kara only saw compassion in his eyes, no judgment or scorn. She reached down inside her shirt and pulled out the wire. "I'm so glad to be rid of that thing."

Jeff dropped the wire into an evidence bag and sealed it up. "Me too."

"Guess what?" Kara asked.

"Hmm?"

She stood on tiptoe, wrapped her arm around his neck, and almost laughed when his eyes widened. "I love you."

He grinned. "I like hearing you say that." He kissed her gently. "I love you too. I wish I didn't have to leave right this minute, but I need to go say good-bye to my family," Jeff said.

Kara saw sadness in his eyes. Eric, Veronica, and Lauren were all being placed into the witness protection program according to the deal Eric had made with the district attorney. Even though the major players were in custody, there'd be nothing stopping the cartel from hiring someone to kill Jeff's family before the trial to keep him from testifying. Eric would serve no time for his part in the drug smuggling operation in exchange for his testimony. "You want me to come?"

"No. I need to do this alone, but thanks for the

offer."

"Of course. I'm here if you need someone to talk to." Kara watched him walk away. The slump of his shoulders spoke a story of its own.

She checked her watch. Right about now two police officers and a DHS social worker would be at Marci's arresting her and taking her young son to foster care. Hopefully, Marci could be rehabilitated and reunite with her son someday.

Tad walked toward her. "I thought you'd want to know Jake was taken into protective custody. He agreed to testify against the Gonzaleses and give us detailed information about their organization." He grinned. "We did it."

Joy shot through her. "We did." The past hour would go down as one of the biggest busts in the history of the DEA, and she couldn't be happier to have been a part of it.

Jeff walked through the front door of Eric's place and found his family gathered around the kitchen table. "It's time. Are you all packed?"

Eric nodded and stood, extending his hand to Jeff. "Thanks for everything."

"You're welcome." He addressed his niece. "Are you ready for a new adventure?"

She nodded, but her eyes clouded with fear and uncertainty.

"Look at this as a chance to reinvent yourself. It could be fun."

Lauren nodded. "So this is good-bye?"

He nodded then faced his brother. "I'll see you at the trial. But," he turned toward Veronica and Lauren, "it would be too dangerous for them to be there."

"What about testifying against the Gonzaleses?" Lauren asked.

Jeff shook his head. "I'm not sure about that. We have enough on those two to put them away for the rest of their lives without your testimony. Plus, Jake has agreed to testify." He opened his arms. "How about a hug?" His family joined together in one big embrace.

40

Kara scooted up alongside Jeff on the tarmac in Redmond, with the newspaper in one hand and her suitcase in the other. "Did you see today's headlines?" She had been surprised to read a quote from the DEA spokesperson that the drugs had been smuggled inside the horses. From what she understood Jake had supplied that bit of information. As it turned out, he had been a huge asset and provided them with enough details to shut down, at least for now, a major drug thoroughfare.

"No. What are they?"

Holding the paper up so that he could see over her shoulder, she read out loud. "One Hundred Arrested in Multi-state Drug Bust." She pointed to the headline at the bottom of the first page. "Local authorities seize four hundred kilos of cocaine." She flipped to the second page. "This one's my favorite. Miami drug lord and local mistress arrested." She folded the paper and tucked it under her arm.

"Mistress?"

"Marci. I don't know where they heard she was his mistress, but it makes a good headline."

"Yeah, but the truth is much different, and a lot more painful for our side."

Kara folded the paper. Gary had informed them that Marci had been on Alvarado's payroll only because she'd been involved with Denver. The DEA's traitor had found it too dangerous to relay the department's movements to Alvarado and had used Marci to feed the drug lord his traitorous information. From what Kara could recall she'd only seen her on Alvarado's yacht that one time, but clearly the woman had been in contact with him or her cover wouldn't have been blown.

Jeff draped his arm across her shoulder. "Enough about work. How about this headline? Undercover and In Love."

"It has a nice ring to it."

"Maybe I should've become a journalist."

She laughed. "And miss out on the fun we've had?"

He took her suitcase and placed it on the ground beside them then pulled her into his arms. "Working with you has been quite the adventure."

"Back at you. What do you think's next?"

"No clue other than this." He lowered his head and captured her mouth with his.

Now this was her kind of adventure.

Author Notes

Dear reader, I hope you enjoyed *Edge Of Truth*. As a baby writer my passion was romantic suspense. Although this book caught the attention of a few publishing houses it was never picked up by one. After going on to publish 21 books both traditionally and independently, I decided it was time to dig out this story, bring it up to date, incorporate all the things I've learned as a writer over the past decade, and publish my first romantic suspense. I feel like my career has come full circle.

If you enjoyed reading *Edge of Truth*, I hope you will review it on Amazon or anywhere you find it listed for sale. I realize writing a review can be intimidating but all that is needed is a sentence about what you liked about the story. There is no need to summarize the story.

I am active on Facebook and would love to connect with you there. If social media isn't your thing, or if you simply prefer hearing from me once a month I invite you to sign up for my newsletter.

My goal is to publish one book a year in this series. In the meantime I have a couple more books releasing in 2019. The next installment to my Librarian Sleuth Mystery series releases from Mountain Brook Ink in November. If you enjoy romantic mystery I hope you'll check it out. I also have a Christmas novella releasing in

October. It is part of a story world in a series with six other authors. My book is titled *Sara's Gift*.

Blessings,
Kimberly Rose Johnson

Subscribe to my newsletter at kimberlyrjohnson.com
Amazon follow: http://amzn.to/2jpZj1C
Facebook: www.facebook.com/KimberlyRoseJohnson

More Books by Kimberly Rose Johnson

Brides of Seattle
Until I Met You
The Reluctant Groom
Simply Smitten

Melodies of Love
A Love Song for Kayla
An Encore for Estelle
A Waltz for Amber

Sunriver Dreams
A Love to Treasure
A Christmas Homecoming
Designing Love

Wildflower B&B Romance Series
Island Refuge
Island Dreams
Island Christmas
Island Hope

Contemporary Inspirational Romance Collection
In Love and War

Contemporary Novellas
Brewed with Love
Sara's Gift (Coming soon)

Made in the USA
Middletown, DE
19 November 2019